The Byzantine Cross

by

Dena Weigel

Dedication

Thank you to my husband and sounding board, Mac Bell, and my daughter, Tatum, for their love and support, my parents, Kathryn and Bob Weigel, my editor, Dave Pasquantino, and all the friends and family who have encouraged me along this journey.

Chapter One

The Battle of Montecassino, Italy, February 15, 1944

"Get off that mountain and return to base—now!" Lieutenant John Campbell's voice crackled through the field radio. "The general will not back you up on this."

"I'll be in and out," Sarah Kraft pleaded. She jammed the receiver deeper into the crook of her neck and rotated the jeep's steering wheel left. The tires caught the dusty road, and the jeep crept up the final switchback on Montecassino's south side.

Come on! Come on! Come on! I only need twenty minutes!

Back at headquarters, Campbell shouted again through the radio, but Sarah's attention shifted to the increasingly loud chorus of over a hundred B-17s warming up on the tarmac. Their engines droned menacingly, drowning out Campbell's voice. Loaded with bombs, they awaited the order to grind St. Benedict's mountaintop sanctuary to dust.

The road leveled off as the jeep entered a courtyard at the top of the mountain. Sarah slammed on the brake, cranked the wheel right, and skidded to a stop next to an open iron gate in the monastery's outermost wall.

Sarah scanned the empty courtyard but there were no signs of life anywhere. Only thousands of pink leaflets littering the ground, stirred up by the jeep's arrival. The Allies dropped them on the monastery two days ago to warn the monks of the planned raid.

It's now or never.

Sarah stepped on the gas. The jeep raced headlong through the arch and stopped in the center of a smaller courtyard. "I'm inside the first courtyard!" She shouted into the receiver loud enough to cut through the noise on the other end of the radio.

"Do you see anyone?" Campbell bellowed back.

"Not a soul. I don't think you need to do this."

Campbell continued yelling into the radio as the bombers' engines droned on, but as each plane took to the runway behind him, his words were overwhelmed by the noise. "…Nazi-occupied…court-martialed… supposed to have you in Rome in a week…" His desperation grew more intense with each word he spoke until at last he roared, "You're blowing your entire mission for a damned book!"

Not just a book. Sarah grimaced. *A record of every Christian relic in existence. The only record!* She backed the jeep up and aimed the bumper at a second archway. "If we lose this book, we'll never find the relics. The Nazis will have them all, and I won't let that happen!"

"They'll court-martial you for disobeying orders if you don't turn your ass around and get back here right now!"

Too late for that.

Sarah already knew the trouble that awaited her at headquarters. She'd stolen a jeep, lied to her military escort, and disobeyed the direct orders of the Fifth Army's highest-ranking officer. The only thing she could expect now—if her luck held—would be a discharge from the Office of Strategic Services and a free ride back to the States.

Sarah revved the engine, and the jeep lurched forward, racing through the second arch with mere inches to spare on either side. She braked in front of a third gate. It was locked tight and blocked the entrance into the innermost courtyard.

The gates narrowed the further Sarah went into the monastery, and this time, she doubted the jeep could squeeze through. Sarah swiped a strand of blonde hair from her face as she calculated her chances.

Well, you got yourself into this mess. You can't stop now.

Sarah threw the jeep into gear and stomped on the gas. The tires gripped the cobblestones as the jeep raced across the courtyard. The bumper smashed into the gate and broke the padlock. A resounding crash rang out when the gate swung backward and slammed against the stone wall. Sparks flew, and a terrible screech of metal on stone reverberated around Sarah as the jeep squeezed through the narrow opening.

Once inside, Sarah cranked the wheel hard to the right, spinning the jeep in a circle and stopping at the feet of a marble saint that stared across the courtyard with blank eyes.

Sarah had arrived in the inner sanctum.

"I'll be back at the base in twenty minutes," she promised Campbell.

"In twenty minutes, you'll be toast," he snapped in her ear. "Those bombers are carrying incendiaries. They're going to light that church up like a funeral pyre. Your funeral pyre!" He waited for a response, but Sarah stopped paying attention long ago.

Nothing stirred in the empty square. All the monks

and refugees left yesterday, and contrary to military intelligence, Sarah detected no evidence of a German presence anywhere. No soldiers, no vehicles, not even one Nazi flag fluttered overhead.

"I'm inside." She checked her watch. Ten minutes left before the bombers arrived. "I've got to go."

"Dammit, Sarah! You're always pushing the limit—"

Sarah threw the receiver onto the passenger seat and pulled the monk's map from her jacket pocket. She bypassed his scribbled writing to examine the drawing at the bottom of the page. Marble colonnades ringed the courtyard on three sides, and a grand staircase leading up to a long terrace completed the square. From there, an arrow on the map pointed to a rectangle representing the library left of the stairs.

Sarah stuffed the paper back into her jacket and patted the brass key hanging from a chain around her neck. If everything went as planned, she stood just one locked door away from her goal.

Sarah left the jeep running as she raced up the staircase two steps at a time. She reached the terrace in seconds and gazed out across the valley. Tiny black dots in triangle formation marred the pink early morning sky above the eastern horizon.

The first bombers! They'll be over the monastery in a matter of minutes.

Sarah counted doors as she ran, stopping at the seventh and removing the key from inside her shirt. She jammed it into the lock. A few turns of the rusty tumblers, a click, and the door opened. Shadows crisscrossed the interior of the library. Thousands of dust-covered books filled dozens of bookshelves under an interlacing web of arches. Scant light entered the room from windows set at intervals along the base of the domed ceiling.

This is a fool's errand. I'll never find the Byzantine record in all these books.

Sarah studied the map again. An *X* marked the spot where the monk said she would find the Byzantine record of holy relics. She jogged in that direction, turning down the fifth row of shelves and counting each bookcase as she went. When she got to the ninth, she stopped and gazed up to the third shelf from the top.

Sarah backed up a few steps, then took a running leap onto a table and thrust herself at the top shelves. Her body hit the bookcase hard and a sharp pain exploded in her hip. She toppled backward, her upper body landing on an iron chandelier hanging from the ceiling. She held onto the spokes of the chandelier with both hands as it swung around in a wide circle. As she neared the bookcase, Sarah extended her legs and grabbed a shelf between her feet. She pulled her body toward it, releasing the chandelier to clasp the topmost shelf with both hands and stand against the upper shelves.

The windows above her vibrated to the roar of powerful engines growing louder outside.

The B-17s! They'd arrive any minute.

Sarah scoured the books on the third shelf. Hanging onto the bookshelf with one hand, she pulled out each volume and quickly scanned the cover, dropping each one to the floor in her rush until she saw a double-headed eagle embossed on a leather cover.

The royal seal of the Byzantine Empire! Just like the monk promised.

The hum of the bombers' engines took on a more

ominous roar as they closed in on the abbey. Sarah twisted her upper body around and pushed off the shelves, landing on her feet on the marble floor. She stuffed the book into her jacket's inside pocket as she sprinted back through the library and out onto the terrace.

Sarah glanced at the bombers as she raced down the stairs to the still-running jeep. No longer tiny black dots in the sky, the angry swarm of B-17s were only a few miles away from the monastery. She reached the courtyard and jumped into the driver's seat and shifted into drive. She spun the jeep around and raced back through the three gates.

Out on the only road down the mountain, Sarah glanced upward and saw the bombers closing in on the monastery. She downshifted into first to take the first switchback and sand spun out from under the tires as the jeep struggled to grip the dusty road.

The first explosion struck the monastery's north wall, and debris rained down on the jeep, bouncing off the hood and over the cliff. Sarah wrapped her arm over her head as the jeep bucked and bounced across the rubble.

At the next corner, the jeep's back end slid sideways, sending the left front tire spinning out over the cliff.

No, no, no! Sarah gripped the wheel tightly and held the brake as she tried to steer away from the cliff. The jeep stopped, rocking back and forth over the edge with one tire suspended over the side. Sarah saw nothing but empty space below her. Holding her breath, she slowly moved the stick shift into reverse and pressed down on the gas. The engine roared, and the tires spun wildly, stirring up a cloud of dust before catching the earth and throwing the jeep backward and onto the road. She backed away from the edge, then shifted into first and continued the descent.

A second cache of bombs bombarded the abbey, and Sarah gripped the wheel with white-knuckle determination as the jeep pushed on through the debris.

"Come on! Come on! Come on!" she yelled.

Bombs came two, three, and even four at a time, but Sarah kept her attention on the cliffside ahead where a boulder larger than the jeep was peeling away from the mountain. If it landed on the road, the rock would block her only escape route.

Sarah shifted into high gear and pressed the gas pedal to the floor. The jeep raced the boulder to the point of no return, passing under its shadow seconds before the massive rock crashed on the road behind her. The impact sent a tremor through the road that lifted the back tires and threw Sarah into the steering wheel, bloodying her nose. Still, she held the wheel and turned down another switchback. She glanced into the rearview mirror and saw the rock settling on the road. Her blue eyes narrowed in the mirror's reflection as her determination to get off the mountain alive increased.

Another squadron of bombers advanced on the monastery and dropped their payload. Sarah glanced up, but a tower of smoke obscured her view as fire from the incendiary bombs caught hold of the beautiful eleventh-century monastery.

As Sarah turned onto the last switchback, she glanced once more at the monastery. A great sadness gripped her heart.

I may not have stopped the bombing, but at least the Byzantine record is safe.

She removed the book from her jacket, stuffed it into her backpack, then picked up the field radio. Campbell didn't answer, but she could hear others shouting orders on the other end of the line.

She tossed the receiver back on the seat and sighed.

Sarah didn't know what awaited her back at headquarters, but it didn't matter. To her, the mission was already a complete success.

Chapter Two

New York, September 1950

Sarah turned the knob on the microscope's lens until flecks of red paint came into focus. Faded and chipped, the artist's signature revealed two indications of accelerated aging that shouldn't develop after only twenty-five years.

But the streak of pink paint behind the signature...

Sarah squinted into the lens.

It's the exact color of the early morning sky during the raid at Montecassino six years ago.

Sarah sighed as she remembered the moment a boulder nearly ended her life. *It was such an exciting time, but those days are over.* She shook her head and chased the thought away. *No use mourning the past.*

The door to the laboratory slammed shut with a bang behind her. She jumped and smacked her eye against the microscope's eyepiece.

"You're sure about this?" John Campbell's deep voice echoed through the Elite Art Brokerage's laboratory. He crossed the sterile laboratory with long strides and passed Sarah's desk to the painting laying on the examination table. Worry lines creased his brow, but his impeccable appearance—suit, tie, and a close-cropped haircut—was perfect as usual.

"One hundred percent," Sarah said, rubbing her eye as she stepped away from the table to let her boss and friend have a turn at the scope. "See how the paint is lifting and breaking off around the edges of his signature? It's a cheap, low-quality paint that didn't adhere properly to the canvas. A museum-quality piece wouldn't show this kind of wear after only two decades."

"But he *is* the artist, right?" Campbell leaned over the lens. "That's what your message said."

"The painting is definitely a Torres, but this isn't the original artwork the client expects from us." Sarah sat down and massaged the back of her neck where a headache threatened to take hold. "Giorgio Torres was a notorious cheat," she explained. "Late in his career, he made copies of his earlier, more important work and sold those as the originals at double the price of their actual worth." Her research today matched the claims of a dozen disappointed art collectors.

Campbell's fist hit the table. "Dammit!" He crossed the room to Sarah's messy desk and pressed a button on the intercom. "Sharon, would you ask Waltz to meet me in the lab?"

"Right away, sir," his secretary's voice crackled back through the speaker. "Could I tell him why?"

"It's about the Tribbiani account."

"I'll let him know."

Campbell pushed a pile of books to the side and sat on the corner of the desk, then he folded his arms across his chest and asked, "Any more discrepancies?"

"The paint has faded and discolored in some areas, and the canvas is a loose, subpar weave. I've listed everything in the report."

The door swung open and Jacob Waltz, CEO of the company, hurried into the room. Worry was clear in his eyes when he glanced at Sarah and then to Campbell.

"What's going on here? Sharon mentioned a problem with the Tribbiani account."

"It appears we've purchased a fake," Campbell announced. "Sarah found evidence the Torres we picked up at auction last month isn't an original."

We? Sarah mused. *This is Waltz's mistake.*

"Impossible," he pushed back as he marched across the room to the worktable. "We got the painting from a reputable source." He stepped up to the microscope and twisted the knobs, pressing the thick lens of his spectacles against the eyepiece and squinting. "I see nothing unusual. His signature matches all the others. You can tell by the way he makes the circles in his *g*." He leaned back and pointed to the signature in the bottom left corner. "The seller's agent pointed this out to me at the auction house. See how they're shaped like squares?"

"This is his signature," Sarah said. "Torres is the artist, but this piece is a copy he created years after he'd sold the original artwork."

"How can you tell?"

Sarah gestured to the edge of the painting. "Look around the edges of his signature. The paint is lifting and cracking."

Waltz shrugged. "So what? What difference does that make?"

"The materials weren't made to last," Sarah explained. "They will deteriorate faster than better quality paints and prove this painting is not worth the amount Tribbiani paid. Not to mention, the value in art doesn't only originate from the final result. Capturing the original inspiration on canvas is also a large part of the value. Not even the artist himself can duplicate that."

"Ridiculous!" Waltz waved her analysis away with

a flick of his hand. "The value is the same."

"Maybe to an uneducated buyer." The cutting remark slipped out before Sarah could stop herself, and Waltz stopped to glare at her before turning his back to her to address Campbell.

"I don't think Tribbiani is too concerned about technicalities," he said. "We have the receipt from the sale. We can prove the painting is a Torres original."

"But we'll cheat him out of thousands of dollars."

"He's a millionaire. He won't care about a few thousand dollars."

"But this could ruin the company's reputation," Sarah pushed back. "We won't be credible if we allow this to slip through."

Waltz lowered his chin to glance at her over the rim of his glasses. "Let us handle the clients, Sarah. Your place is here in the lab."

Sarah bristled. She opened her mouth to speak, but Campbell stepped in between them before she had a chance to say anything more.

"I'll need you to update the file over the weekend." Campbell tapped a stack of folders on the desk with his index finger. "And don't add any of this new information. I'll handle it. Just stick to the basics."

"But the value of the art is the 'basics.' I have to include my findings."

Campbell shot her a dark look. "Just sign the report and have it on my desk first thing Monday morning." His tone left no room for debate.

"I can't do that," she said flatly.

Waltz's head whipped back around. "What did you say?"

"I can't sign off on a report that I can't back up with

evidence." She shook her head. "I won't do it."

"I'm afraid you'll have to, or you might just lose your job," Waltz threatened. Again, he gazed over his thick, black glasses at Sarah. "And I know you don't want that to happen."

"Of course not." She lifted her chin in defiance. "But I will not sign something I—"

Campbell handed her the folder and turned back to Waltz. "I'll work on the report with Sarah and have it ready for you first thing Monday morning."

"Good." Waltz said. The corners of his mouth crinkled into a smirk. "Now, Miss Kraft, you just keep looking through that little lens of yours and let professionals like Campbell here handle the client."

"We'll take care of the report." Campbell gestured to the door and let Waltz take the lead.

The discussion was over.

Always the money, never the art.

Sarah laid a white cloth over the painting, then walked to her desk. *The art doesn't matter. The client doesn't matter. Not even the company's reputation matters to him.* She traded her lab coat for her blue blazer, then picked up her purse and the folder and left the laboratory.

Sharon glanced up from her desk when Sarah got to Campbell's office. "Everything okay?" the secretary asked.

"Campbell wants to review the Tribbiani account. He'll be here in a minute."

Concern creased the space between the secretary's brows. "You look like you want to murder someone."

"Don't worry," said Sarah. "I promise not to murder your boss."

13

Sharon grinned. "Go right in then."

Sarah tossed her purse on the leather sofa and then crossed the room to stare out the window. Outside, a haze enveloped the city, turning the blue sky an ugly rust color. The perfect shade to match her mood.

Her hand tightened around the folder.

"Still as stubborn as the day I met you, I see," Campbell said, closing the door behind him.

Sarah turned around and shrugged. "You know me—Miss Congeniality."

"That attitude is going to get you into big trouble someday."

"It wouldn't be the first time."

He sighed. "This isn't funny, Sarah."

"Covering someone else's mistake is not part of my job description."

"That's not what I'm asking you to do." He sat down at his desk and rubbed his temples. "Ever since the day I met you, you've pushed the limit without regard for consequences."

"But Waltz doesn't care at all about the value of the art—or his clients."

"Maybe so. But you won't change his mind by arguing."

Sarah set the folder on the desk between them and sat down. "I could write an honest report," Sarah offered, giving Campbell a slight smile.

"I wouldn't expect anything else from you," Campbell said. He opened a drawer and took out a bottle of aspirin. "But that reckless honesty of yours will get you fired someday." He popped two pills in his mouth and swallowed them. "You just need a little finesse."

"How do you suppose I do that when Waltz wants

me to leave out the most important information?" Sarah challenged. "I won't lie for that sniveling little—"

Campbell pounded his fist into a pile of folders on his left, and a few papers drifted onto the floor. "Dammit, Sarah, there'll come a day when I won't be here to keep you from a disaster of your own making." He paused. "I know you're right about him, but you can't let him get to you."

"He doesn't bother me," Sarah lied. "It's what he's willing to do that's the problem. And it should be for you too. He's lying to the client and taking the chance of ruining the reputation of this company." She sat back in the chair and folded her arms across her chest. "I will not let him ruin my reputation along with it."

"Listen, I know how passionate you are about your work, and I will always try to protect you, but you are on his shit list now." Campbell sighed before he continued. "Look, you and I both know what a difficult time I had getting you a job here. Your military record is a big obstacle. You'll have to play the game and earn Waltz's trust if you want to keep this job. No matter how you feel about him."

That stung, even though she knew what he said was true.

"I'm trying to turn this place around," he went on. "But I need time."

"I know," Sarah relented. "But I can't sign off on this report." She slid the folder across the desk. "If he wants to lie to the client, it will be his signature on the report. Not mine. I won't let Waltz ruin my reputation, John. You can't ask that of me."

Campbell's expression softened when she used his given name, and Sarah felt a sharp pain deep inside her heart. *Pity. That's what he feels when he looks at me.*

"I would never do that," he promised. "But this Waltz situation could easily get out of my control." He waited for her to say more, to counter him with another argument, but she remained silent. "Now, about the report—"

Sarah only pretended to listen. She already knew what he wanted—a glowing report that would turn Torres's cheap painting into a masterpiece.

Instead, her thoughts drifted to a quiet little table in the back of her favorite diner where she would sip a coffee and forget about her day.

Chapter Three

Stockholm, Sweden, September 1950

Steam billowed out from around the sauna door as Yuri Feodorov entered the locker room. Nude but for a towel wrapped around his head, the boxer's muscular frame and deep-set eyes completed the picture of dark intimidation.

The roar of the crowd echoing down the hall from the stadium told him the last fight of the night had begun. The Russian used to be the main event, but years in the ring had taken their toll. He couldn't perform like he used to, but his strength and ruthlessness kept him in the ring far longer than other boxers.

Yuri stopped at the sink to swipe a hand across the condensation on the mirror. Another night of fighting, and his face was a bloody mess. He touched his swollen left eye and then stuck a finger in his mouth to touch the tooth that had been knocked loose in the fourth round. It would take days to fully reattach.

The other fighter fared much worse. Yuri had him on the ropes for four rounds until one blow—the "death blow," the crowd yelled—came close to breaking his neck. They would have loved him for that. Death in the ring. That's what the crowd wanted. But the referee ended the fight and declared him the winner before he could deliver the legendary uppercut and end the younger man's life.

Yuri turned sideways and rotated his arm around in a half circle. A searing bolt of pain shot through his shoulder as the joint jerked into an awkward position. He winced. The throbbing ache always reminded him his days in the ring were numbered.

Fluid trapped deep inside his lungs rose up to become a low, rumbling cough. A souvenir acquired long ago from his time spent inside a Soviet gulag. He snorted loudly and spit the offending phlegm into a corner of the room as he trudged toward a row of rusted white lockers. He went to his and opened the door. Inside, a manila envelope with no address or postage lay on top of his clothes. Opening it, he found a letter inside. It read:

Our plan is moving forward. The agency agrees and will provide assistance. It is crucial we meet as soon as possible. You'll find more information in the locker at the train station when you arrive in Rome. Call me at the number provided but be aware our conversations may be monitored.

He flipped the envelope over. No signature or identifying marks of any kind. He reached in again and found a black-and-white photo of an attractive blonde woman, her dossier, keys to a locker, and a one-way train ticket to Rome for tomorrow.

Yuri's mouth warped into a crooked smile as he studied the photo. In it, a woman stared at something off to her right as she crossed the street. Petite but athletic, she had curves subtly accentuated under a sweater and skirt. His pulse quickened as he sat down on a bench to read her profile.

Sarah Kraft
Age: 42

Educated in art history. Extensive high-level diplomatic experience. Speaks fluent German, proficient in Russian and Slavic languages.

1943-1946 - Served in the Office of Strategic Services in Europe. Worked with the French Resistance, monitored involvement between Hitler and the Vatican, and groomed exiled Romanovs for undercover work.

January 1945 - Traveled to Moscow as a U.S. representative returning Russian art stolen by the Nazis.

August 1945 - Terminated by OSS command under suspicion of theft.

Currently resides in New York, employed as an art insurance appraiser.

Few acquaintances, family in Colorado, no romantic interests.

His groin tightened as he gazed at the photo. *Interesting. Maybe she finds women more to her liking.* Yuri smiled at the thought.

She appeared young for her age, but a confidence in the way she carried herself told him she was used to taking on challenges.

Yuri smiled. He liked it when a woman challenged him, and this Sarah Kraft seemed like she would put up a hell of a fight. He shifted in his seat as his interest grew. *This assignment may offer more than just money.*

A door to his right opened, and a woman stepped inside. She wore a thin, white cotton robe tied loosely around the waist.

"Comrade Feodorov?" the Swede purred.

Yuri stuffed the papers inside and tossed the envelope into the locker.

"Are you ready for your massage?" She dropped her robe.

Younger than he typically liked, she lacked the curves that made her feel like a woman, but she'd do fine.

Her hips swayed provocatively as she led him into an adjoining room and closed the door behind them. She gestured to a padded table. "Please, lie down."

The woman's breasts brushed against his bare chest as she leaned across his body. "I assume you'd like a full-body massage?" she whispered into his ear.

Yuri grunted his answer as the image of Sarah Kraft filled his thoughts. He closed his eyes as he pulled the towel off his hairless head. He knew the sight of his blackened, misshapen right ear and the missing left one might startle the prostitute, but she'd get over it.

After all, just like him, she was a professional.

Chapter Four

New York City, September 1950

The feeling came on in a rush. An unmistakable energy sizzling up Sarah's spine, making her muscles twitch and her pulse race. She hadn't experienced the rush in five years, but she knew immediately what the sensation meant.

She was being watched.

Nothing obvious seemed out of place when Sarah took a seat in the back of the restaurant an hour ago. People talked in low voices, waitresses bustled around the dining room, and the banging of pots and pans coming from the kitchen echoed through the café.

The same people doing the same things they do every day.

Only the cherry pie had changed. So delicious only moments before, it now tasted like sawdust in her mouth. She pushed the plate away and picked up her coffee cup, exhaling slowly to rid herself of the strange feeling before taking a sip.

Ignore it. It's just another flashback from the war.

The last episode occurred over a year ago, and just like now, the flashback came on suddenly and without warning. Dark visions of bloody, broken bodies and bombed-out cities blending with the present until she couldn't tell where her memories ended, and her current life began.

But this time, something was different. This time, she didn't see horrifying images from the war. Everything around her was real and crystal clear. The people, the plates of food, the front door with a tiny bell that rang every time someone entered the restaurant. Even the people out on the sidewalk. Sarah could see and hear them all in real time.

Beads of sweat popped out on her brow.

A waitress stopped at her table holding a pot of coffee. "Can I get you anything else?" she asked as she filled Sarah's cup.

"No, thank you."

The woman nodded, left the check on the table, and walked away as Sarah stole another glance around the room. The other diners, both at the counter and around tables, focused on their plates, and the waitresses and the chefs in the kitchen hurried to fill orders. Nothing stood out as unusual, so Sarah turned her attention back to the newspaper she'd been reading.

The reports out of Eastern Europe today did little to make her feel better. The Soviets cut East Berlin completely off from the West. Their military rounded up opposition groups and was confiscating newspaper presses to crush communist resisters as they worked to stop the flow of East Germans escaping their sector.

Sarah flipped a few pages, following a headline about nuclear testing in Siberia, but the black letters faded to gray when another wave of anxiety washed over her. This time, the feeling grew too big to ignore.

The edges of the paper crumpled inside her fists, and her breathing increased to shallow, truncated gasps. Her muscles twitched in anticipation, and she fought the urge to jump up and run. She breathed slowly to calm her nerves, then she stood, dropped a few coins on the table, and strolled toward the door. She had to get out of there.

The air outside was thick with humidity. Sarah glanced up at the darkening clouds in the sky as she joined the people hurrying to the subway entrance at the end of the block.

Another blazing hot rush sent pinpricks of perspiration crawling up the back of her neck. She glanced back and forth at the people surrounding her. Everyone appeared suspicious now. Every shadow felt like a trap. She searched the faces of strangers for something, anything that would tell her she wasn't crazy. That someone was, in fact, following her.

The crowd thinned out after they passed the subway. At the next corner, Sarah made an abrupt right turn and glanced at the people behind her.

One man stood out from the rest. He carried no briefcase and wore a camel-hair coat and dark brown fedora pulled down low over his eyes. When she spotted him, he rotated away to face the street. His ramrod-straight posture and broad shoulders set in a perfect horizontal line betrayed the fact he was a military man.

He took a drag off his cigarette, hiding the ember inside his cupped hand. Something about that action struck a familiar chord.

Is he someone from OSS? The Kremlin? Neither made sense after all these years.

Sarah turned away and rejoined the other pedestrians walking to the next corner. As she passed a bakery window, she tried to get another glimpse at the man behind her, but the reflection moved too quickly, and she couldn't spot him in the crowd, so she continued on.

BOOM!

Sarah flinched when a clap of thunder rumbled through the streets. Everyone rushed to the next corner as the first few drops of rain spattered down on the sidewalk.

But where can I go? Not home. The police? But with what? I can't even prove to myself I'm being followed.

Across the street, a park caught her attention. There were few trees, and a large fountain in the center of the park. A sidewalk crossed the broad expanse and connected with the street on the opposite side.

The perfect place to draw him out.

Sarah crossed the street and walked through the park's open gate. As she rounded the fountain, she glanced behind her, but the man in the camel-hair coat had disappeared.

A bus pulled up to the curb on the other side of the park, and Sarah hurried to catch it. She climbed on board and found a seat in the back. As she settled in, she kept her eye on the door and waited.

If the man in the camel-hair coat really is following me, he'll have to find me right here on bus number 17.

Chapter Five

"Watch your step, lady!" the driver yelled as Sarah exited the bus. He slammed the door shut behind her and drove on, leaving Sarah alone on the curb.

The man in the camel-hair coat had disappeared as abruptly and mysteriously as he had materialized, along with the odd feeling she'd first felt in the diner.

Sarah sighed. *Maybe it's just my imagination.*

After riding around the city for three hours anxiously scrutinizing every passenger, Sarah was tense and tired. Her thoughts shifted to the bottle of scotch waiting for her at home. One glass would soothe her frazzled nerves.

Maybe two.

Maybe three.

The rainstorm had picked up strength and Sarah yanked the collar of her coat up to her chin as she hurried down the empty street toward her apartment. One lonely lamppost outside her building cast a triangle of light through the rain, the only sign of life she noticed as she climbed the steps and went inside.

Wet footprints led Sarah down the hall, each pair disappearing under the closed doors of her neighbors' apartments, until only one set of footprints remained. Men's shoes. Sarah's apprehension grew. Her anxiety roiled in her stomach as she followed them all the way to the end of the hall to the door of her apartment.

An orange glow seeped out from under the door, setting off an alarm inside Sarah much too pronounced to ignore.

She tested the knob. It rolled freely in her hand, and the door clicked open.

The smell of smoke caught her attention first. She peeked inside and glimpsed shadows dancing around the walls of the living room, cast there from the orange glow of a fire.

That's bold, starting a fire in my hearth.

Sarah slipped out of her shoes and opened the door another few inches, then she stepped silently inside. She stopped in the kitchen. Silent as an assassin, she slid two knives from the block on the counter and continued down the hall to the living room.

The camel-hair coat was draped over a dining chair. The brown fedora lay on the table beside it.

He's here!

The crunch of leather drew her attention to a chair facing the fireplace where the light outlined a bald head and broad shoulders.

"Welcome home, Sarah," a deep voice said.

Her hand tightened around the knife's handle. "Stay where you are."

"You don't recognize me?" The stranger moved to stand up. "Surely, it hasn't been so long since we've seen each other that you've forgotten your old—" He stopped midsentence as the first knife flew past his left temple and sank with a thud into the mantel behind him.

The man raised his hands above his head. "Whew! I forgot about your Wild West skills. Those might come in handy."

Wild West? Two words, and a flash of recognition.

"Albert?"

As he turned to face Sarah, light from the fire illuminated his face. He opened his arms wide and said, "In the flesh."

Sarah lowered her hand still holding the second knife. "What are you doing here?"

"Being thankful you aren't carrying a gun." Albert gestured with his thumb over his shoulder to the quivering knife sticking out of the mantel behind him. "Is it safe yet?"

"Yes. Yes, of course." She gave her old friend and mentor a hug. "You scared me!"

Albert held out his hand to block the embrace and grasped her hand still clutching the knife. "I can say the same about you."

"Sorry." She set the knife on the table and removed her blazer, shaking off the rain before draping the jacket on the chair next to his coat. "Next time, maybe you should call me before you break into my home." She gave Albert a quick hug and asked, "Would you like a drink? Or did you already help yourself to a glass?"

"Have you got any of that scotch you like so much?"

Sarah smiled. "Ice?"

"Yes, please." He sat back down in the chair. "I hope you don't mind me starting a fire. It was a wet walk over here."

"Not at all. I might even enjoy it once my heart starts beating again." Her hands trembled as she poured their drinks, leaving amber puddles on the credenza around their glasses. "How long have you been following me?"

"Just this afternoon."

She handed him a glass, then plopped down in the chair opposite him. "You had me thinking I was crazy."

"You should trust your instincts more."

"I haven't found them too useful lately." She held her glass up to point a finger at him. "As you saw for yourself today."

He chuckled. "You knew what you were doing. You spotted me within the first few blocks." He lifted his glass in a mock toast. "And good idea getting on that bus, by the way."

Sarah scrutinized Albert from head to toe. Four years hadn't changed him much. A little less hair and a few more pounds, but he still carried the same commanding presence and stoic expression she remembered. A military man through and through.

"What are you doing in New York? Something going on at the UN?"

"No," he said. "I'm here to see you."

"Me? What about?" She waved her empty hand around in a circle. "Why all the theatrics?"

"I just wanted to put my own instincts to the test."

"You're losing your touch," Sarah chided. "I can tell you're lying."

Albert's voice took a lower tone, and his expression grew grim as he studied her closely. "I think you can help us with some information."

"Oh?"

"Do you remember much from your visit to the Kremlin?"

"Some. The whole trip only lasted five days." She paused as she thought about her time in Moscow. "It was a diplomatic mission, so our escorts watched us pretty closely. Why?"

He cleared his throat before speaking. "There's been a new development, and I think you'll find it very interesting."

"Is Stalin up to something?"

"It looks that way. There are rumors about some experiments his scientists are conducting using a special kind of energy."

She laughed. "I'm afraid I can't help you. You need a scientist."

His grave expression never wavered. "We think you are exactly the person who can help us."

"Why?"

Albert leaned forward, cupping his glass in both hands as he met her questioning gaze.

"It's about the Byzantine Cross, Sarah. We think they have it."

Chapter Six

"The Byzantine Cross?" Sarah sputtered the name. "Are you sure?"

"You're surprised?" Albert asked.

"Of course! The cross hasn't been seen in public in over thirty years. After the tsar abdicated the throne, no one—not even the Romanov family—knew what happened to it. The cross is more legend than real at this point."

"Our sources told us the Soviets discovered the cross inside the tsar's museum at the Kremlin a few months ago."

"A little black cross about six inches long? No jewels or carvings?"

"Yes," Albert said. "They said it stood out because it was so plain."

Sarah smacked her palm down on the arm of her chair. "I knew it! It's the cross in the tsar's coronation portrait. Those Romanovs never would have worn such a plain ornament unless it was important."

She smiled as she remembered the painting. In it, hundreds of people surrounded the coronation ceremony depicted in the center of the canvas. Light streamed down from above, landing on the tsar who was dressed in an ornate gold robe trimmed with fur. Several rows of medals were pinned on his right chest and a single black cross was pinned to his left. "Have you seen any photographs of the cross?"

"No."

"I'm not surprised. The duchess said the cross is revered in Russia and only worn on special occasions."

"The duchess?"

"Grand Duchess Militza, the tsar's cousin. She took refuge at the Vatican during the war and helped me identify the Russian art we'd confiscated from the Nazis."

"You didn't see the cross when you toured the Kremlin?" Albert asked.

"I'm afraid not. We only spent one afternoon at the museum." Sarah closed her eyes to picture the dozens of glass cases she'd seen during the tour. "All the religious items are kept together, so I could point you to the right room if that helps."

He ignored her offer. "What did this duchess have to say?"

"She told me the cross is a holy relic and highly regarded by the Russian people."

"Did she say why?"

"No. The cross wasn't part of my work, so I didn't press her for information."

Albert sipped his drink while Sarah searched her memory.

"The Byzantine Cross," she mused. "Does anyone know how it's connected to the Byzantine Empire?"

"Not yet. We'd hoped you would."

"Sorry. No one I spoke to knew of its origins, only that it appeared during Ivan the Great's reign. He married a Byzantine princess—Sophia Palaiologos, the niece of the last emperor. The cross must have come to court with her."

Sarah walked to a bookcase and ran a finger along a shelf. She stopped at an oversized book with the Romanov double-headed eagle on its cover. "I did hear something interesting, but I couldn't confirm the information, so I left it out of my final report." She carried the book back to her chair and flipped through a few pages. "You've heard of Rasputin, haven't you?" She handed Albert the book.

"Of course." He laid the open book on the coffee table and leaned in to examine the images.

Sarah pointed to a black-and-white photo of the man the Russians called the Mad Monk. "This is a picture taken five years after he began his relationship with the royal family."

In the image, the Orthodox monk sat in the middle of a group of six older priests. He'd parted his greasy, black hair down the middle, following the line of his bulbous, crooked nose, and an unkempt beard spread out across his black robe. A caption under the photo read, "Rasputin, 1910."

"Look at those eyes," Albert said. Even in a reproduced black-and-white photograph, Rasputin's light eyes with their intense glare appeared mesmerizing.

Sarah sat back in her chair and took a sip of scotch, savoring the effects of the liquor as it calmed her nerves. "Some say he had the power to hypnotize people just by staring at them, but the duchess never confirmed the rumor."

"What does Rasputin have to do with the cross?"

"He had the cross in his possession when he died. Something the rest of the royal family hated him for. They believed giving the cross to Rasputin was a sacrilege."

"Interesting." Albert glanced up from the book. "But that doesn't explain Stalin's fixation with it."

"Look at this." Sarah scooted to the edge of her seat and leafed through several pages, pointing to photos as she went. In every image, Rasputin's expression remained the same. Always glaring straight at the camera, always the same stoic face.

"All these photos are dated prior to 1905, the year he met the tsarina."

"Now look at this." She flipped back to the first picture of Rasputin and ran her finger down a long chain that crossed his chest and disappeared inside the folds of his black tunic. "You won't see this chain in any photos taken before he met the tsarina."

She flipped a few pages to a collection of images of Rasputin, his family, and the theological school in St. Petersburg where he'd studied. No gold chain appeared in any of the photos.

"But after 1905, you see the chain in every picture." She moved on through the book, stopping at a few pages to show Albert the same gold chain. "I haven't seen a photo of the cross on Rasputin, only this chain."

"You're right," Albert said mostly to himself as he flipped back and forth through the book. "Is there a picture of the cross?"

"Unfortunately, no. Militza told me no photos were ever taken of the cross."

Sarah took the book from Albert and turned a few pages to a photo of Rasputin surrounded by a group of women dressed in formal gowns. She pointed to a woman seated on his right who gazed up at Rasputin's inscrutable face with a slight smile. "This woman is the grand duchess." Rasputin stared straight ahead. "She once told me the Byzantine Cross hung from the end of that chain," Sarah said quietly as she traced a finger along the image of the chain. "According to her, he kept it inside his robes next to his heart at all times."

"They just gave him a holy relic? He carried this cross around in public?"

"That's what she told me."

Sarah sat back in her chair and waited while Albert thumbed through the book. "You knew the tsar's son was a hemophiliac, didn't you?"

"I'd heard that, yes."

"According to the duchess, the tsarina gave the cross to Rasputin believing its supernatural powers would enhance his ability to heal."

"Did it?"

"That's a matter of opinion, really. But of all the doctors who tried to help the boy, only Rasputin could stop his bleeding in a matter of minutes. Even from miles away. That power, whatever it is, gave him a lot of influence over the tsarina."

"What happened to the cross after his murder?"

Sarah shrugged. "The duchess told me Rasputin's assassin took the cross from his corpse and returned it to the tsar, but no one really knows for sure since the details of the crime weren't widely reported." She paused, trying to remember the conversation. "This all happened just a couple of years before the communists took power, and nobody's shown any interest in finding out more since the royals have left Russia—until now, of course," she added.

Albert leaned back in his chair. "Did anyone else have anything to say about the cross?"

Sarah thought back to the many conversations she'd

had with the exiled Russian elite. "Some of the Romanovs believed Rasputin's powers became demonic in the last years of his life."

"Demonic? Why would they believe such a thing?"

Sarah stood and pointed to Albert's empty glass. "Want another one?" Albert handed her his glass to her, and she walked to the credenza and picked up the bottle. "You ready for this?" she asked as she filled both their glasses.

"Go ahead."

"Along with Russian Orthodox, Rasputin followed another, shall we say, less 'traditional' religion called Khlyst."

"Never heard of it," Albert said.

She handed him his glass. "You'd remember if you had. The religion combines Christian beliefs with local pagan traditions." He gave Sarah a curious glance, prompting her to continue. "Khlyst followers believe your soul is drawn closer to God through the act of penance, so they created a sinning ritual."

"A sinning ritual? What's that?"

"It could involve anything. The goal of the ritual isn't focused on the sinning, but rather the prayers for forgiveness that come later."

Albert shot Sarah a confused look.

She continued. "Each time a Khlyst follower participated in the ritual, they ended the service by confessing their sins and performing penance."

"Isn't that what's done in every religion?"

"Yes, but in Rasputin's case, the sinning was required." She tapped a finger on the photo of Rasputin and his followers. "They performed the sinning ritual over and over again, believing they could draw the Holy

Spirit into their souls every time they prayed for forgiveness."

"What sin did they commit?" Albert asked.

Sarah smirked. "Group sex."

Albert's eyebrows shot up. "Orgies?"

She tapped the photo again. "He doesn't seem like much of a ladies' man, but Rasputin had a lot of lovers. Many from St. Petersburg's highest social class."

"Really?" Albert examined the photo of Rasputin surrounded by his followers. "How big was this Khlyst religion?"

"Just a few followers. Mostly people from the city's elite circles, like the duchess. In fact, she introduced Rasputin to the tsarina."

"And the Romanovs believed in his special powers?"

"Not everyone, but the tsarina sure did. To her, he was the next best thing to God."

"So that's how he ended up with the cross." Albert leaned back in his chair and clasped his hands behind his head in what Sarah called his thinking pose. She searched a few more pages and landed on a photo of Rasputin with the tsarina and her children. "The duchess believed the power of the cross kept Rasputin alive during the first two assassination attempts."

"There was more than one?"

"There were three," she said. "First, they poisoned him, then they shot him several times. When that didn't work, Rasputin ran outside to escape, but his assassins caught up to him at the Neva River and threw him in."

Sarah turned to another photo. This time, the image showed Rasputin's frozen corpse lying on the ice after being dragged from the water. "See how his arms are frozen above his head, and his fingers are curled as if clawing his way through the ice?" She met Albert's gaze. "He didn't die because he was shot. He drowned."

A soft hiss came from the fireplace as a burning log settled into the fire.

"Whew!" Albert exhaled loudly. "That's a damn good argument for divine power, I'd say."

Sarah eased back into her chair and took another sip from her glass. "Do your sources think the cross has some sort of power?"

Albert picked up his own glass and studied it a moment before speaking. "The evidence our European intelligence community collected mentions experiments conducted by Stalin's top scientists. Real top secret stuff."

"What are they looking for?"

"We don't know for sure. Maybe nuclear power, maybe something psychological."

"Psychological weapons?" Sarah considered the idea.

"Unconventional weapons used to affect the mind of the enemy." Albert gestured to the photo of Rasputin. "Hypnosis is one example."

Sarah considered the legend of the Byzantine Cross. "The duchess only spoke of Rasputin's ability to heal. She never said he could control one's own mind."

Albert waved a hand in the air dismissively. "I'm only speculating, of course, but we do know their scientists have been sequestered in Siberia for months working on several top secret projects."

"But communists are atheists," Sarah said. "They don't believe in spiritual powers. Scientists, too, for that matter."

Albert shrugged. "Who knows? Maybe they believe there's a scientific explanation somewhere in there."

Sarah straightened up and walked to the fireplace. "The Byzantine Cross," she murmured as she stared into the flames. "I thought we'd lost it forever."

"Sarah." Albert's soft tone caused her to glance up. "We want you to go after it."

Chapter Seven

"Me?" Sarah asked. "Why?"

"You know more about this Byzantine Cross than anyone," Albert said. "And you've been to the Kremlin."

"But I've been out of the service for years."

"Just four."

She shot him a dirty look. "Five."

"Right, five." Albert stood up and joined her at the mantel. "Regardless, we need someone who has your knowledge and skills. Besides, you only left us a few years ago."

"I didn't leave the service, Albert. I was terminated." Bitterness tinged her words. "And on trumped-up charges, I might add."

Albert brushed off her accusation. "You still know what you're doing. You proved that today when I followed you. Your instincts are as sharp as ever."

She hesitated as she searched for something in his expression that would tell her this was all a joke. That he wouldn't ask her to go back to the very people who had thrown her to the side so callously. She studied him for any hint of deception, but his expression remained intense and serious, as always.

"No, Albert, I can't." She shook her head and stared at the fire. "Not after what they did to me."

He paused a moment before clearing his throat, then said, "After more facts came to light, we realized we'd made a mistake. We never should have let you go."

"Is that official?" she asked.

"That—and personal."

As she stared into the fire, Sarah wrapped her fingers around the handle of the knife still stuck in the mantel. "It's too late to do anything about that now, isn't it?"

The question went unanswered, and silence hung in the air like a wall separating her from Albert.

"I risked my life," Sarah murmured. "For years, I ran from the Nazis and hid in the shadows so your other agents could get the information they needed." Her hand tightened around the knife's handle until her knuckles turned white. "Then, they set me up so they could let their personal favorites carry on after the war." Anger spilled out between her words. "I would have given my life for the service, and they just cut me loose." Her voice shook with rage. "I was left with nothing. Nothing!"

"I'm sorry, Sarah."

"Sorry?" She spun around to face him. "It's too late for sorry, Albert. Because of those lies, I'll never find another job in intelligence."

"Here's your chance to get right back in where you left off," he said.

"It's not that easy. You're asking me to sneak into the Kremlin, for God's sake!"

Albert laid a hand on her shoulder, prompting her to look him in the eye. "Listen, no other agent at the CIA has been inside the museum except you, and you know what to look for. No other agent is more qualified than you."

"So, it's called the CIA now, not OSS? Are they trying to clean up their reputation through a simple name change?" She brushed his hand off her shoulder. "I'm not buying it."

She crossed the room to pick up her glass and took a drink before facing him. "Look, it has been a long time since I've gone undercover. Surely, you have some embedded agent in Russia who can do it."

"You still know what you're doing."

"Because of today?" She laughed. "That stunt you pulled means nothing."

"Okay, then tell me this. Why didn't you call the police when you came home and found someone here? Didn't even think of it, did you?" He wagged a finger back and forth between them. "You and I both know you can do this."

"What about my record?" Sarah asked. "They can't just fire an agent on suspicion of being an informant, then invite her back."

"Your record has been expunged. It's clean."

"Just like that?" She snapped her fingers. "And it's over?"

"Yes, just like that. We know you didn't have anything to do with the theft."

"Who, then?" she pressed. "Who stole those maps?"

"That's confidential. Just know we are fully aware you had nothing to do with it."

"Confidential?" She laughed. "Someone framed me, got me fired, destroyed my reputation, and you expect me to come back without knowing who is responsible?"

"When I can tell you, I will."

Sarah threw her hands up in frustration. "It's too late, Albert. I've moved on. I have a new life now."

"Oh?" he countered. "It's Friday night in New York. You had coffee, took an extra-long bus ride around the city, and came home. Doesn't seem like much of a life to me."

Sarah glared at him. "Maybe that's what I want right now."

"That's the biggest lie I've heard yet." Albert said. "You love the work. You thrive on it. I knew it back in the war, and I know it now."

"You think I'm so easy to read? You don't know me anymore."

"Oh?" He walked over to stand behind her. "I may not know everything about your life, but I do believe you deserve a chance to get back into the service. And I know we need you to go after the Byzantine Cross."

"How do I know you'll let me stay in after I'm done?"

"Because I want you back," he said. "For good."

Sarah opened her mouth to protest, but he continued. "Listen, Sarah, it comes down to this: are you happy locked up a lab, or would you rather be out there in the field? The decision is yours."

Sarah didn't say anything. Albert's question resonated with a feeling deep inside her. A question she'd asked herself too many times to count. She was only existing in New York. She had no friends, no family, and, after her outburst at the office, she may not have a job on Monday.

"What do you say?" He waited for her response.

"Do you promise to tell me who set me up?" she asked, facing him. Searching his stoic expression for a hint of some hidden thought.

He raised a hand in a Boy Scout salute. "On my honor."

"Will I be working alone?"

"We already have a double agent from MI6 in place to help you. A Russian. He'll meet you in Moscow, and we'll have all the documentation ready to get you in and out of the country quickly and safely. We expect the whole mission will take less than a week."

Sarah glanced at the piles of books and empty bottles lined up on the credenza. She thought of Waltz and John Campbell and the lie they expected her to sign off on. But beyond her need for a job, she felt a deepening desire to return to the job she loved most. The thrill of being a secret agent. The excitement and intensity inherit in the danger of a mission. It made her senses come alive and she craved it, even now after all these years. Sarah considered all these things together and knew she had buried her passion for far too long. There was no denying it—she *needed* to do this.

"When do I leave?" she asked.

Albert smiled, raised his glass in a toast, and nodded at her. "Tomorrow morning."

Chapter Eight

Twenty-four hours later, Sarah stared out the airplane's small window. The rising sun cast a warm glow over Italy, transforming Tuscany's lush vineyards into a glorious burnished gold landscape. She checked her watch. A quarter to seven. *Only an hour left before we land in Rome.*

Albert slumbered on in the seat next to her. In all their years working together, Sarah couldn't think of a time or place where he couldn't fall into a deep sleep in minutes—a skill he'd once told her he'd picked up as a private in the army during World War I.

Sarah, however, slept only a couple of hours. Ever since last night in her apartment when Albert swore her in, nervous energy electrified her—tempered by doubt.

Her finger tapped against her armrest impatiently as memories of Moscow ran on a loop inside her head. It'd only been two months after the war ended when she'd visited the Kremlin. At the time, the Allies were dedicated to working together to create a new Europe, and as a diplomatic gesture, museum curators gave her a tour of the Armory Museum. Although an amazing experience, the trip was heavily monitored and only showed her what Stalin wanted outsiders to see. This included her tour of the museum. Curators directed her every move and allowed few questions and no independent exploration of the exhibits.

This trip would be very different. She would be playing a part, sneaking into one of the world's most secure compounds and stealing a national treasure. If caught, Soviet authorities would indict and convict her as a spy, with little hope of the CIA even acknowledging her existence.

That realization came to her late last night as she hovered over her suitcase, wondering what to pack. She'd told Albert everything she knew about the cross, and he already had agents stationed inside the Kremlin who could do the job, so why did they need her?

Sarah finally concluded that as much as they needed her knowledge and experience, they needed her anonymity even more. They wanted an expendable. An unknown agent they could use as cover for their involvement. Someone they'd deny any knowledge of if something went wrong. They'd claim she'd gone rogue, and they had her history at OSS as proof.

"Is the coffee ready yet?" Albert said, clearing his throat as he sat up.

"Almost," Sarah answered through a yawn.

"Did you get any sleep?"

"A little."

He reached down to pick up the newspaper that had slipped off his lap. "Too rocky for you?"

"Yes. The seats may be better, but these planes still fly like they're hauling equipment."

"We're the equipment now," Albert quipped. "You can relax at your hotel after the meeting at the Vatican. We'll need time to get your travel documents in order." He fished a handkerchief out of his jacket to wipe off his glasses.

"Who am I meeting?"

"Cardinal Maximilian Schafer, director of the Vatican's secret archives." He shuffled through the briefcase at his feet and produced a file. Albert handed it to Sarah and she picked through the contents. She found a photo and a one-page brief inside.

The black-and-white image shocked her. "What's he doing with Hitler?"

The cardinal was a tall, strikingly handsome man with a square jaw and a broad smile. His perfect posture put him a few inches above the Nazi party leader, yet he showed no sign of humility or adoration as he gazed down into the face of the Führer.

"The cardinal met with Hitler regularly in the '30s in his role of assistant to the bishop of Berlin. When war broke out, the Vatican brought him back to Rome." Albert handed over the cardinal's dossier.

1905 - Born in Munich.

Royal lineage: Otto the I, Holy Roman Emperor, 962 – 973.

1926 to 1931 - Parish priest, Cologne, Germany.

1931 to 1937 - Secretary to the Bishop of Berlin.

1939 - Ordained as a cardinal.

1940 - Became part of the Vatican's Roman Curia.

1943 - Named director of the Secret Archives.

"Impressive."

"He sure is. He's climbed the Vatican hierarchy faster than most but has never been able to break into the Pope's inner circle."

"And he's related to royalty?"

"Yes, he's very connected throughout Europe."

Sarah closed the folder and stuffed it inside her attaché case. "What's my schedule?"

"A car is waiting at the airport to take you to the

Vatican. After your meeting, you'll have the rest of the day to review any information the cardinal has for you. When we meet at your hotel later this evening, you and I can go over the details."

"Do you have any idea what he has for me?"

"More information on the cross. I spoke to him briefly to find out what the Vatican knew, and he mentioned documentation dating back to the Crusades." Albert glanced at his watch. "I'm sorry I can't join you there, but I've got to coordinate with the Brits. I want their agent ready for you. We can discuss your findings tonight when I bring your passport and tickets."

"I'll be ready."

Albert glanced up the aisle, then lowered his voice. "I have a favor to ask."

"Yes?"

"I don't want you coming by headquarters while you're in Rome."

"Why?"

He glanced away, unable to meet her questioning gaze. "Marco's been pulled out of the field."

"Marco?" Sarah sat up, surprised to hear her old lover's name. "What's he doing there?"

"The higher-ups reassigned him to a desk about six months ago."

"Why?"

Albert sighed. "Marco is the one who stole the maps."

"The maps that got me fired?"

"Yes."

Burning anger erupted inside Sarah. "That snake!"

"We found out a few months ago."

"Why didn't you tell me back in New York?"

"I wanted you to take the job—" Albert said with a smirk. "—and I thought your pride might get in the way."

Sarah frowned at his sarcasm. "How did you find out he was responsible?"

"As it turns out, his connections run pretty deep. The agent who replaced you at the Louvre discovered one of their curators received the stolen maps."

"The one I worked with?"

"That's the guy."

Sarah remembered Claude. An intelligent man, but secretive by nature. "Why did Marco want the maps?" she asked.

"Real estate. The curator owned an estate in the Italian Alps, and Marco used the maps to convince the curator to lower the cost. He showed him where our troops were planning to face off with the Germans and convinced him the whole area would become a battlefield, ruining the property value of the estate. Then Marco offered to buy the property at a steep discount. Unfortunately, the whole affair wasn't discovered until years after you'd been let go."

A steward walked up the aisle and offered them coffee. Sarah waited for him to move on before she spoke. "Why didn't they fire him too?"

"Italy is flooded with communists right now," Albert explained. "We need people who have access to the government. The CIA can't afford to lose any more people there." He took a sip from his cup and shrugged. "I guess the higher-ups decided his motives were purely self-serving, and no real damage was done, so they just swept it under the rug."

"No real damage." Sarah scoffed. "And Marco didn't say *anything* when I was let go? Even knowing it was his fault?"

"I'm afraid not."

She didn't say anything for a while as she took in this new information. Finally, she asked, "What's he doing now?"

"What do you think?" Contempt permeated Albert's words. "Living off rich war widows with a string of compliments and lies. He has his job at headquarters, of course, but he gets most of his income from his relationships." Albert shook his head and frowned. "He sure knows how to play the cards he's been dealt."

"Those cards are pretty easy to play when you're handed all aces in looks and charm." Knowing Marco had used her so easily was somehow worse than being let go from the service.

"Don't be surprised if he comes knocking at your door. He was working toward a promotion, but that disappeared after they found out what he'd done. He's tried to find a way back to his old position ever since."

"Does he know I'll be in Rome?"

"I'm afraid so."

Sarah thought about the man she'd once believed she loved. *I should have known he would throw me under the bus. He has no loyalty.*

Lights blinked on in the front of the cabin. Then the middle lit up, then the back, until the entire interior of the plane was illuminated.

"It looks like we're landing soon," said Albert. "Are you ready?"

Sarah took in a deep breath and said, "Ready as I'll ever be."

Chapter Nine

Vatican City

"Here we are," the guard announced. "The Vatican Library." Holding the door open with one hand, he stepped back to let Sarah enter.

The library was quiet at this early hour. No patrons searched the shelves or strolled the aisles. Light streamed in through six windows that stood two stories high. It shone across the marble floor and over two rows of dark mahogany study tables. Ten-foot-tall shelves holding hundreds of leather-bound books lined the other three walls, and an iron spiral staircase led to a second level with more bookshelves.

At the far end of the room, a tall man stood next to a table with his back turned to them. Thick gray hair peeked out from under his red skullcap, and the red sash worn by Vatican cardinals was tied around the waist of his black tunic. His perfect posture replicated what she'd seen in the photo Albert gave her.

The cardinal's attention remained focused on the upper gallery. As they approached, Sarah noticed a metal box with six holes cut into the sides sitting on the table next to a file folder and two books.

The guard cleared his throat to get the cardinal's attention. "May I introduce Agent Sarah Kraft, Your Excellency."

The cardinal spun around and offered his hand. His

warm smile and the crinkles at the corners of his eyes eased Sarah's nerves. "Hello, Agent Kraft. I'm Cardinal Maximilian Schafer. Welcome to my library."

My library?

Her hand disappeared inside his large fist. "It's a pleasure to meet you, Cardinal Schafer," she said. His fluid movements and the pleasant, steady tone of his voice made him seem much younger than his sixty-eight years.

"Please, call me Cardinal Max," he said. "I trust your travels went well?"

"Very well, thank you."

The cardinal nodded to the guard, who stepped away.

"Please, have a seat." He gestured to a chair opposite him at the table. "I understand you were recently called out of retirement." His English was refined and tinged with a German accent.

"Yes. I worked in the private sector for a while."

"And you were stationed at the Vatican during the war?"

Sarah nodded. "Yes. I worked with the Grand Duchess Militza while she was a resident."

The cardinal smiled at the mention of her name. "The duchess was one of our favorite guests," he said. "I'm a bit of a history enthusiast, and I must admit I asked many questions about the Romanov court. She probably grew quite tired of me, but she was very generous and indulged my interrogations."

Sarah remembered the demure, elderly woman sipping her tea as she sat on her plush velvet couch. "She did enjoy reminiscing."

"She certainly did," the cardinal agreed, then he

gestured to the books on the table and said, "Shall we begin?"

****

The lieutenant stood up from his desk and strode to the window. "Would you look at this one?" A mountain of a man dressed entirely in black was climbing the steps to the Vatican police station.

"Oh, he's a beauty," the second guard commented as they watched the man open the door and step inside.

A minute later, the office door opened, and a large man dressed all in black stood before them.

"I have an appointment at the archives," he said. His tone was gruff and his Russian accent piqued the guards' interest further.

The lieutenant held out a hand. "ID, *per favore*."

The man reached inside his jacket and retrieved a small card. The man in black passed it to the lieutenant, who took it and glanced at the picture, then passed it to the younger officer while he kept watch on strange man.

"Sir?" the young officer said. "This is an all-access pass."

"Let me see that." The lieutenant took the card and flipped it over to examine the front and back. It appeared authentic. And new. "Where did you get this?"

"Is it official or not?" The man's voice took on a low growl.

"You didn't answer my question."

"And I'm not going to."

The lieutenant stared at the card again.

"Hurry up." The man thrust his hand out. "I'm late for a meeting."

The lieutenant reluctantly handed the card back to the man and opened the door. "Would you like someone to escort you?"

The man in black left without answering.

Chapter Ten

"You'll need these." Cardinal Max handed Sarah a pair of white cotton gloves before putting on a pair of his own. "The items are very delicate. They're typically stored in a more secure area, but with such short notice, bringing them out here is easier than going through the process of giving you access to visit the vaults."

Sarah slipped on the gloves as Cardinal Max spread a white cloth across half the table and then picked up the books and the box and laid them neatly on top of the cloth.

"Where would you like to begin?"

Sarah glanced at the books and the metal box. "I guess my first question would be, why is it called the *Byzantine* Cross? Our research only connects it to the Romanovs."

The cardinal reached across the table and picked up the first book. "I believe this will help answer that question."

It can't be! Sarah tingled with surprise when she recognized the double-headed eagle on the cover. *Is that the same book I rescued from Montecassino during the war?*

When she'd handed the record of Byzantine relics to the monk back at headquarters, she never expected to see it again. To know the book made its way into the Vatican Archives was very satisfying.

The cardinal pried the book open, taking his time to ease it through several cracks of the spine. "Our crusading brothers carried this record of holy relics to Europe when they returned from Constantinople in 1261."

Sarah nodded along with the story, but her attention remained focused on the book.

The centuries had taken their toll on the leather-bound record. Its vellum pages were brown and brittle with age, but the drawings and text inside remained clear.

The crown of thorns, bones of the saints, the holy grail? These are the most legendary holy relics known to man! I can't believe I didn't look through this book before I gave it to the monk at Montecassino!

"Our knights occupied the city for twenty years," the cardinal continued. "During that time, this inventory served as their checklist to recover nearly every known relic found in churches throughout the Holy Land." His hand hovered over the open book. "As you can see, it was a very extensive collection."

"Yes, very extensive," Sarah repeated as she studied the ancient text. Written in an early form of Greek script, she worked to decipher the text with words she remembered from artifacts she'd studied in college. She'd lost most of what she'd learned over the years but could still read a few simple phrases.

"Through the efforts of the Crusaders and with information recorded in this book, we've been able to fill our cathedrals with fragments of the true cross, the sacred shroud, bones of the saints…" His gaze followed her as she eased through the pages. "I'm sure you're familiar with all this." Reaching across the table, he turned to a page bookmarked with a strip of red silk. A drawing of a plain black cross covered the upper third of the page. "Here we are." His finger hung suspended over the illustration. "This is what we're looking for—the Byzantine Cross."

The image depicted exactly what the grand duchess had described. Black with squared angles on all sides. No carvings or jewels. No embellishments at all. Just a simple wooden cross.

"The Crusaders searched every church in the land, but the cross has never been found."

"Does the book say anything about its origin?" Sarah asked.

"Right here." He pointed to a line of script. "See this word?"

"Genesis?" She translated a word in the text. "I don't understand. Why the Old Testament? Crosses wouldn't hold any significance before the crucifixion."

The cardinal placed the book to the side and picked up the metal box. "I believe this will shed light on that question." He took a key from his pocket and unlocked the lid. Inside, a weathered papyrus scroll was curled around a wooden rod suspended on two supports.

"Are you familiar with the *Chaldaica*?" the cardinal asked as he lifted the scroll from the box and set it on the table.

"Berosus's history of Babylon?"

"That's right." He stopped to look at Sarah. "I'm surprised. Most people only know his work through its later interpretations."

Sarah's mind traveled back to her ancient history course in college. "Berosus was one of our earliest historians, and his *Chaldaica* is considered the most accurate record of early Mesopotamian civilization."

"Very good," said the cardinal. "The *Chaldaica* is comprised of three scrolls. The first contains the region's mythology and laws, the third records the history from the first king to Berosus's time, and—" He carefully unrolled the scroll over the white cloth. "—this one, the second in the series, records events that came before that time, stretching all the way back to the time of Genesis."

"Extraordinary!" Sarah murmured.

"He completed the scrolls during the age of Alexander the Great. Centuries later, they passed on to the rulers of Byzantium."

"Then brought to the Vatican by the Crusaders," Sarah finished the story. She gazed up at the cardinal. "Why doesn't the church acknowledge the *Chaldaica's* existence so the document can be studied? The text must contain information that could fill in the blanks for so many unanswered questions."

He lowered his chin to look down his nose. "It's one of our most precious documents—not something to be handled by scientists."

"Of course." Sarah decided not to argue that ethical question, and she directed her focus back to the scroll. "But I don't understand how the history recorded on this document connects to the Byzantine Cross when crosses didn't become an important symbol of the church until after Christ's resurrection. Those thousands of years…"

The cardinal's genial smile encouraged Sarah to work through the problem.

"Are you suggesting the Byzantine Cross dates all the way back to the earliest period of recorded history?" she asked.

"Yes!" Cardinal Max clapped his gloved hands

together. "A sacred treasure like none other."

"How could something so small and made of wood survive intact for more than five thousand years?" Sarah asked.

"Amazing, isn't it? Nearly as old as mankind, yet perfectly preserved as if created only yesterday. That is the mystery of the Byzantine Cross."

"And the tsar had possession of this cross?"

"Indeed. When the tsar wore the cross at his coronation, we were all elated," Cardinal Max continued. "As far as we know, it's the only relic from the Old Testament still in existence."

"No wonder the Byzantines held the cross in such high regard," Sarah mused.

"The Romanovs too. They believed it was a gift from God and one of the most important relics in their collection."

"Do you know how the cross got into their hands?"

"Sadly, no. I asked that question of the duchess, but she had no knowledge of how the cross found its way to court."

Sarah scrutinized the simple sketch in the Byzantine record. "I still don't understand why a cross existed long before Christ's crucifixion."

The cardinal stretched across the table for the second book. "This will tell us the story." He was just about to open it when a shuffling noise floated down from the upper gallery. Startled, his head jerked toward the sound.

Sarah ignored the disruption and kept her attention focused on the drawing of the cross as the cardinal quickly rolled up the scroll and placed it back inside the box and locked the lid. "If you'll excuse me for a moment, I'm going to check on that noise. This is a closed room. No one is allowed in here without my consent."

Sarah nodded to him as he left the table, then stared at the books before her as she considered the grave responsibility she'd taken on.

"A relic from over four thousand years ago," she murmured. "From as far back as the Old Testament's Genesis—and it still exists!"

Chapter Eleven

Yuri pulled a handkerchief from his coat pocket and held it up to his nose. Smeared with a pungent smelling vapor cream, he inhaled the healing scent deep into his lungs and waited for the wheezing to subside before tucking it back into his pocket.

Footsteps on the iron staircase told him the cardinal was near. Yuri pressed himself further into the shadows of the alcove as he watched the cardinal walk down the center aisle between the bookshelves before finally retreating back down the stairs.

Yuri stepped away from his hiding place, relying on his boxer's training to keep his steps light and silent, and crept to a bookcase near the balcony. Downstairs, the cardinal returned to the table and sat down opposite the woman.

Sarah Kraft.

She looks like women in American magazines. Blonde, wholesome, the perfect picture of health. A woman unlike any he'd known before.

His tongue flicked out to lick his lips as he leaned forward to hear the conversation going on below. Although he could speak English well, their words didn't make much sense to him. Something about Noah's ark and a cross, but nothing that explained why he was about to risk going back into the U.S.S.R.

His handler hadn't told him much about the job. He

only knew he must return to Russia to follow this woman, Sarah Kraft. Only the Vatican seal on the folder he found inside a locker at the train station told him the man who'd hired him was powerfully connected at the highest levels.

And powerful men always mean money.

He smiled at the irony. In all the years Yuri had been involved in organized crime, he never imagined his biggest job would come from inside the Vatican. But after a life spent in and out of prisons, it was surprisingly fitting that his first religious experience would come to him this way.

Chapter Twelve

Cardinal Max sat back down at the table and asked, "Now, where were we?"

Sarah surveyed the items spread across the table. "We know the cross is connected to Genesis, but why? Why would a cross, a symbol so strongly associated with Christ's crucifixion, exist centuries before the time of Christ?"

"Ah, yes. An excellent question." The cardinal gathered up the second book. Small and primitive compared to the Byzantine record, it was made of two wood panels bound by three leather straps.

"This journal comes to us from a remote cliffside monastery near Mount Ararat called Khor Verap. There isn't much activity there now, and only one monk maintains the compound, but in the early days of Christianity, pilgrims used the monastery as a stopping-off point when traveling to visit Noah's ark." He opened the book to a drawing of a small fortress perched on the edge of a cliff. An arched gate with a cross centered in its keystone marked the entrance to a courtyard where a small chapel sat in its center.

"The existence of the ark came into question only after the first Christians left the region." The cardinal turned to a drawing of a large cone-shaped boulder. Its sides were smooth, and a hole was carved through its top. A small cross was embedded in the rock below the hole, and three people knelt in prayer at its base.

"This is an anchor stone," the cardinal explained. "Ancient sailors used them as nautical tools to steady ships in large or rough bodies of water. This one is significantly larger than most used at the time."

"And it's at this monastery?"

"No, this one and several more stones are found along a trail on Mount Ararat. At the time the monks created this book, several of these stones were used as markers along the trail. No one we've spoken to can offer any reason why a nautical tool such as this would be found on a mountainside far from any body of water."

"Interesting," Sarah said. The simple details and proportions of the cross drawn in the monastery's book appeared identical to the drawing in the Byzantine inventory. Plain, with squared edges, and no carvings or adornments. "And the cross was considered holy?"

"Not just holy, but miraculous," he said as he gazed upon the image in the book. "Pilgrims traveling to the ark stopped at the foot of the stone to pray near the cross. They considered the cross a direct link to God."

Sarah glanced up as a new revelation took hold. "And that's how the legend of the Byzantine Cross as a miracle worker was born?"

His smile widened into a huge grin. "Yes! Life-saving miracles attributed to the cross gave it a reputation on the same level as Noah's ark. The faithful traveled from across the Christian world to pray at the rock's base, just as you see depicted in the drawing." He gestured to the record of holy relics. "Some didn't even bother to go to the ark. Their belief in the cross grew so strong, they felt they could communicate with God through the cross alone."

"And they believed the Byzantine Cross could save lives?" she asked.

The cardinal rose to his feet and strolled across the room to a window to stand in the morning light. "They not only believed in the cross's healing capabilities. They had an unwavering faith that it could bring people back from the brink of death." His voice tapered off to a whisper.

Just like Rasputin.

Sarah glanced back at the documents spread out before her. "Is there any documented evidence of these miracles?"

Sarah half expected a rebuke for blasphemy or maybe a vague account from a mystic who lived centuries earlier. Instead, the cardinal reached for a manila envelope, the last item on the table. He opened it and removed two photos.

"The monastery's book gives some accounts of answered prayers, but our most recent evidence comes from our friend, the duchess."

The first photo captured Russia's last emperor, Nicolas II, and his wife Alexandria. Clothed in ceremonial dress, they stared blankly into the camera's lens with flat, stiff expressions and vacant eyes. The Byzantine Cross was pinned to the tsar's lapel in the same place seen in his coronation painting. It took up most of the upper left side of his military jacket, with his many medals stacked together on the right side.

In the second image, a tall, thin Rasputin stood before a white background with two fingers raised in blessing. His greasy black hair was again parted in the center by a broken, uneven line, and his piercing light eyes glared aggressively out from the photo.

He looks alive. A chill ran up Sarah's spine. *I can almost see him breathing.*

The same chain she'd shown Albert back at her apartment swooped across his chest, only this time, the end hung outside Rasputin's robe, and a small, unadorned black cross dangled at the end.

It's just like the one in the tsar's photo.

"Their expressions are quite different, aren't they?" the cardinal remarked. "Very appropriate for the relationship they shared. Rasputin, so powerful even in a photograph, and the tsar and tsarina, stiff in posture and expression as they stare off into the distance. Frozen in time." He traced the chain with his finger all the way down to the cross. "This is the Byzantine Cross. The duchess told me the tsarina gave it to Rasputin, and she shared these photographs to prove it."

Sarah scrutinized the photo of Rasputin. "I've never seen this one."

"It comes from her own collection and has never been reproduced. She told me the tsar hid the fact they'd given Rasputin the cross from the public. They didn't want to fuel the unsavory rumors about the tsarina's relationship with the Mad Monk. But insiders knew, and rumors of the gift spread to the tsar's inner circle."

Sarah's eyes flitted from one photo to the other. "The crosses do look the same."

The cardinal relaxed back in his chair. "The tsarina held an unwavering confidence in the power of the cross, and in Rasputin's ability to utilize it to heal her son's uncontrollable bleeding."

"Hemophilia," said Sarah.

"Yes. Rasputin used the cross as a sacred tool and proved its power was more effective at healing than the doctors who treated the boy."

"Did the Romanovs ever try to figure out how? I mean, there must have been someone who was curious."

"Miracles are often the victims of skeptics and many of the relics believed to have these powers have been destroyed by their lack of faith. But in Russia, if the tsarina believed in its power, the Russian people had to believe as well, and that protected the cross."

Sarah examined the Byzantined Cross on the tsar's lapel again. *Such a simple thing holding so much power.*

After a few moments, Cardinal Max glanced at his watch. "That's all I have for you, unless you have any other questions."

"I don't believe so," Sarah said. "This is a lot of information to take in."

"Indeed." He stood and signaled for the guard to escort Sarah out. "If you do have questions, please don't hesitate to contact my office."

"Thank you," she said as she picked up her attaché case and stood to leave. "Your help has been very enlightening."

"It has been my pleasure." Cardinal Max shook her hand. "I'll pray for you."

"Thank you," Sarah said before she followed the guard out of the library.

Chapter Thirteen

Cardinal Max walked through the door to his office as the clock struck ten. He smiled. Not yet noon, and already, his carefully laid plan was underway.

A cigarette case lay on the corner of his desk. Max picked it up and took out a cigarette, tapping it against the back of the case before sitting behind his desk. He threw the case down and picked up a butane lighter. The top flipped back, and a blue flame hissed to life. He touched it to the end of the cigarette, then stuck the opposite end in his mouth and took a long drag, savoring the heat passing back and forth inside his throat.

Three loud knocks at the door interrupted his thoughts.

"Come in," he ordered.

The door swung open, and Yuri Feodorov filled the empty space.

Max inspected his visitor. The old prize fighter presented just as he'd been described. Broken and scarred. A brute. Max nodded to a chair on the opposite side of the desk, and Yuri sat down, filling the seat to capacity. "I see you arrived just in time for my meeting with Agent Kraft."

"Bad instructions," the Russian grumbled.

"I hope this isn't an indication of your abilities. Your handler said you could follow this woman into the Soviet Union without her knowledge." He took another drag on the cigarette, then pointed at the Russian. "You can do that, correct?"

Yuri gave a curt nod as he glared out from under a heavy brow.

"Be more careful from now on. I could hear you shuffling around in the upper gallery." He tapped the cigarette on the edge of an ashtray. "We're lucky the woman didn't hear you."

Yuri lifted his chin in defiance. "I was quiet. She—"

"Quiet!" Max cut him off. "It sounded as if you were only a few feet away." The cardinal scowled at Yuri from across the desk. "I won't be there to keep you from getting caught next time, and I don't want her to know she's being followed until after she has retrieved the cross. Understand?"

"*Da.*"

"English! English!" Max pounded his fist on the desk. "I don't want that commie talk in here."

Yuri grunted his reply.

"Your passport is inside." Max slid a manila envelope across the desk. "She's leaving tomorrow morning on the express train to Berlin. Follow her and pay off the ticket agent to get a cabin in the same car." He pulled on his cigarette and let the smoke seep out between his words. "She'll switch trains to get to Moscow. Make sure you know where she is at all times." He tapped the cigarette on an ashtray and then pointed to the envelope. "You'll find a thousand rubles in there. That should cover your expenses while you're in Russia."

"What about the five hundred thousand American dollars?" Yuri asked. "That is the deal I made with Ivan."

"You'll get the money when the cross is in my hands." Max's focus shifted to a spider crawling up the desk lamp on his left. "Until then," he said, bending forward and taking the cigarette from his mouth, "you'll have to settle for the rubles." He touched the burning ember to the spider. A soft hiss was heard as the heat seared the spider's tiny body, then the burnt remains fell to the desk in a pile of loose ash.

"And the girl?" Yuri asked.

Max waved his question away. "Do what you want with her. All I want is the cross." A cruel smile appeared on Yuri's mangled face, and the cardinal added, "Just don't expose yourself to the authorities. It won't do either of us any good if you're caught inside the Soviet Union. I want the cross, and I'm sure you wouldn't want to spend your remaining years inside another gulag."

Yuri's head snapped to attention.

"Oh, yes." Max smiled. "I know all about your past. Sixteen years inside Stalin's worst prison." A smirk lifted the corners of his mouth. "You must have been a pretty little piece for the convicts at the age of fifteen." He dragged on his cigarette, blowing out smoke as he talked. "Once you're inside, you have just as much at stake as I do." He made eye contact and pointed his finger at Yuri. "So don't fuck up."

Yuri held his stare, refusing to show any submissiveness.

Max pushed back his chair and stood up. The meeting was over. He walked to the door, and Yuri followed, but before they reached the exit, Max turned around and poked his finger into Yuri's chest. "Don't even think about double-crossing me, Feodorov. My connections reach farther into your world than you could ever imagine."

"*Da,*" Yuri spit out as he shoved past him and disappeared down the hallway.

Cardinal Max returned to his desk and sat down. He took another long drag on his cigarette as he picked up the lighter. The papal seal was bonded to its metal case, and he ran his finger over it. Two keys—one silver, one gold—were crossed over a shield with three crowns stacked above. To the Catholic faithful, the seal represented the unique transcendent relationship between the Pope and God. To Max, it represented a power more incredible than even Adolf Hitler could have imagined.

He opened his desk drawer and found a ring holding two skeleton keys the Führer gave him eleven years ago. He held them up to watch the light flicker across their surface.

The gold key represented the heavenly realm, while the silver key signified the earthly kingdom of man—Hitler's Third Reich. Together, they represented a unique promise between himself and the Führer.

The same promise Pope John XII gave my ancestor Otto the Great on the day he was crowned Holy Roman Emperor.

The promise dictated that on the day Germany declared victory over Europe, he would sign a decree deposing the current pope and hand the title to Max. In return, Cardinal Max would bless Hitler's reign during his papal coronation and declare him ruler of all Europe, validating his authority and setting him up to expand his influence around the world.

Max ran a finger over the two keys and smiled. He placed his dreams in Hitler's hands, only to have them dashed by the Allied victory.

But once I have the Byzantine Cross, I'll perform miracles just as Jesus did two millennia ago, and I'll be seen as the second coming of Christ. I will rule not only Europe but the entire Christian world, and no person or government—not even the pope himself—will be able to stop my rise when the faithful witness what I can do with the cross in hand.

Max glanced at the door. *If only that bumbling ox can deliver.*

Max's nature would normally not allow him to leave a task of such importance to others, but now, he had no choice. As a man of the cloth, he would not dirty his hands with the blood of another.

Those things must be left to the dregs of society. To bloodthirsty animals like Feodorov.

Fortunately, he'd convinced his contacts at the CIA to get involved. With their agent's expertise and the hit man's brutality, he should have the cross in his possession in a matter of days. After that, he'd hold the power to give or take life on a whim. He'd be both loved and feared as he delivered the Lord's justice to the masses.

His thoughts drifted back to Sarah. When Albert Phillips first suggested her, Max hadn't been impressed. However, after their meeting in the library, he understood why Phillips insisted she was the best person for the job. Just as the duchess had assured him, Agent Kraft was the only other person he'd met who knew anything about the cross besides the few remaining Romanovs. He could see she had both the knowledge to identify the cross among the Kremlin's collection and secret it out of the Soviet Union and into his hands.

He only hoped Yuri could keep up with her. The Russian hadn't impressed him nearly as much as the woman. The prizefighter's handler assured him Yuri could travel easily through Russia without drawing attention, but after the episode in the library, Max wasn't convinced.

He held the keys up before his face, watching the light flash across the metal. One for God, one for man. And he, Cardinal Maximilian Schafer, would hold agency over both. With the cross in his possession, he would become the undisputed link between the faithful and their God.

A healer.

A destroyer.

A modern-day miracle worker just like Jesus Christ himself.

"Two weeks." His hand swooped down to catch the keys inside his clenched fist. "I will hold the fate of the world in my hands in two weeks."

Chapter Fourteen

Sarah scanned the documents laid out on the blue damask bedspread. A train ticket to Moscow, her falsified East German passport, a photo of her contact in Moscow, and some notes she'd scribbled after visiting the Vatican. Tomorrow morning, she'd become Katarina Russman, a Russian name with a German address to give her legitimacy in both countries.

Sarah picked up the black-and-white photo of the British agent in Moscow. Nicolai Rodzyanko, age forty, a Russian-born double agent. The photo showed him relaxing outside a café, reading a newspaper, his legs crossed, and an arm thrown over the back of his chair. He was a handsome man with a square jaw and deep-set eyes. In the photo, he appeared relaxed, as if he hadn't a care in the world. An unusal pose for a double agent. She balled up the photo and her notes and threw them into the fireplace before heading to the bathroom.

As Sarah brushed her hair, she studied her reflection in the mirror. She looked tired. Her skin had lost its vibrant hue and a few more wrinkles had settled into the corners of her eyes over the last few years. And yet, a spark glowed in her blue eyes that she hadn't seen in a long time.

Her reverie ended with a jolt when Sarah heard the click of a patio door opening in the bedroom. A breeze blew into the bathroom carrying the scent of cypress trees. She stepped to the door and peered through the opening. The back of a tall man in a perfectly tailored gray suit stood next to her bed. Even with his back to her, Sarah recognized him immediately.

Marco D'Amico.

"Just couldn't stay away, could you?" she said, stepping into the room. Marco spun around.

Dammit. He's still gorgeous. He hadn't changed a bit in the last six years. Beautiful smile, black wavy hair, and skin tanned by the Mediterranean sun. His gaze roamed casually over her body, scrutinizing her with the same heat she remembered from five years ago.

"Hello, Sarah," he said. "It's been too long."

The mention of her name on his lips made her grimace.

"Spying on me?" she asked.

He laughed. "Of course not. When I heard you were in Rome, I couldn't resist seeing you again." He stepped toward her and opened his arms. He held the train ticket Albert had given her in his hand. "You look beautiful."

"Oh please." Sarah rolled her eyes as she walked across the room and snatched the ticket from his hand. She nudged past him and picked up the rest of the items from the bed. "How did you hear I was in town?"

His hand slid down her back and around her waist, pulling her backward into him. He pressed her body against his and kissed her neck. A long-forgotten impulse sparked to life inside her, stoking a desire that had been dormant for too long.

No! He's not going to win this time.

"I've missed you," Marco whispered.

"I'm sure you have." Sarah slipped out of the embrace and shoved him away. "You've probably been pining away like a lovesick teenager." She gathered up the rest of the papers on the bed.

He chuckled. "Now I wouldn't go that far, but I have thought of you often."

Sarah ducked past him and picked up her attaché case, then walked across the room to lay it on a desk. As she passed the balcony, she sensed the light from outside illuminating the curves of her body through her silk robe and felt exposed. She tugged the sash tight around her waist.

"No need to be shy." Marco's voice deepened with passion. "I remember how beautiful you are."

She clenched her fists. "You're leaving."

"Come on, Sarah. Let's not miss out on this moment."

She jabbed her finger at the door. "Now!"

He picked up a bottle of red wine from the nightstand. "Let's at least share a drink." He waved the bottle around, grinning. "Your favorite vintage."

"Do you honestly think you can just waltz in here with a bottle of wine, and I'll forget everything you've done?"

"You're not still mad about Dominique, are you?" He clicked his tongue disapprovingly. "Jealousy is not good, Sarah. It'll only make you bitter in your old age."

"Jealous? Don't flatter yourself."

"Then what is it? That I haven't called. I haven't written?"

"Don't play me for a fool, Marco. Albert told me about the maps. He told me you were the one who set me up."

"You don't believe him, do you?" He waved the accusation away as he flopped into a chair.

Sarah remained standing, arms crossed. "You've told so many lies in your life, you don't even know what the truth looks like anymore."

"Maybe in the old days, but the CIA has me beat now. New people are running the place, and everything has changed since the war."

Sarah again pointed to the door. "Out."

"Come on, *mi amore*. Sit down. Share a drink with me while I tell you my side. I promise I won't try anything." He waved the bottle at her again. "I'm not leaving until we share a glass."

He kept pulling the same old strings, and she felt her resolve breaking.

"Fine, one drink, and then you're going," she relented. "And don't call me your love."

Marco retrieved a corkscrew from his pocket. "That's more like it."

Chapter Fifteen

This time, when Sarah went to the bathroom to get the glasses, she avoided looking in the mirror.

Marco. I should have known you'd find a way to slither back into my life.

Memories of waking up in his arms came flooding back. The intensity of his touch. His body entwined with hers. The sweet words he'd whispered that made everything seem wonderful despite the war, despite the death, despite the threat of leaving this life without ever knowing true love. Those things hadn't mattered when she and Marco were together. Their time together centered around living life to the fullest, finding adventure and fun along the way—and making love.

And the lies. Don't forget the lies.

Marco couldn't be trusted—a fact Sarah couldn't ignore. Still, she couldn't let him walk out of her life without asking him about the night that upended her life.

He stood poised, ready to pour when she returned from the bathroom. In a brief unguarded moment, Sarah noticed a strained expression on his handsome face. It disappeared when he noticed her standing in the doorway.

"You really do look beautiful, Sarah." He took the glasses from her.

"Thanks." She sat in the chair opposite him.

"How've you been?" He poured wine into a glass.

"I heard you're living in New York now?"

"Yes, that's right."

"Married?"

"No."

He handed her a glass, then raised his own in salute. "Then I still have a chance."

"A wedding ring never stopped you before. You must be slipping."

He laughed. "See? We can still be friends."

A comfortable silence settled over them until Sarah said, "I heard you're at headquarters now."

"I'm sure you've heard many things," he said before taking a sip of wine.

"That's true."

Marco set his glass down and slid to the edge of his seat. He took her free hand in both of his and said, "Sarah, I never meant for you to get embroiled in that map business. I hope you believe me."

"As a matter of fact, I don't." She tried to jerk her hand away, but his grip tightened.

"Why not?" His eyes widened with confusion, and he seemed genuinely stunned.

"Why didn't you tell them the truth when they fired me?"

"I would have, but you were already gone when they realized I was the culprit," Marco said.

Sarah shook her head. "You could've gone to them and cleared my name. That's what a decent person would do."

"It was a delicate situation."

"A delicate situation?" Sarah yanked her hand free. "You said you were going to tell me your side. Get on with it then."

"Alright." Marco relaxed back in his chair. "When word got back to me that you'd been fired, I went to Phillips and tried talking to him, but he wouldn't listen."

"That's a lie," she said. "Albert knows me well enough to know I wouldn't have stolen those maps. If you went to him, he would have at least listened to you."

"There was a lot more going on at the time than any of us knew. And now, new people have taken over, and Phillips wants to hang onto his job like everyone else."

"What are you talking about?"

"Do you know you were the first of fifty-four agents let go within six months after the war? They were cleaning house, Sarah, and the women went first."

"How do you know all this?"

"It's common knowledge—now."

"I don't believe you."

"Look around. You won't see one female agent at headquarters. Maybe that's the reason they've kept you away from there."

"That's not the reason. You're just spinning more lies, and I'm tired of you wasting my time. Besides, that doesn't explain your actions. You stole those maps, and you let me take the blame."

He glanced down at his glass and then back up to Sarah. "They knew it was me all along, Sarah," he said softly.

"No." Sarah shook her head. "If they knew you stole them, they would've just fired you like they did me. Come on, Marco. You can do better than that."

"They couldn't get rid of me," he countered. "There are communists all over the Italian government, and the CIA needs access to my connections."

That's the same thing Albert claimed, too.

"Okay, then. Tell me what happened."

He slumped in his chair and heaved a big sigh before speaking. "I went to the map room early in the morning at the end of the night guard's shift. Everyone knows they sleep down there. I slipped by him without signing in, but he must have woken up as I was leaving. Later, when they questioned him, he called me out." He shook his head as he reflected on that night. "I guess my luck ran out."

"*Your* luck?" Sarah laughed. "Your luck didn't run out. Mine did."

"However you want to say it, that's what happened."

"That's not what I heard."

"What? From Albert?" he asked, swirling the wine around in his glass. "I wouldn't trust him if I were you. He's one of them."

Sarah stood and walked to the window, staring out into the darkness.

"I'm really sorry, Sarah," Marco whispered as he came up behind her. This time, she didn't move away when she felt his hand on her hip.

"You ruined everything for me," she whispered.

"I know, and I'm sorry."

"Sorry won't erase what you did."

"Then let me make it up to you." His hand slid up to caress her hair.

"You need to go." Her voice was laced with an awakened passion.

"Don't you want to say goodbye like we used to?" he whispered into her ear.

"No, I don't." She moved to step away, but his arm fell to her waist and drew her back against his chest. "Let me go." She struggled against his grip.

He slid his arms around her body and hugged her close. She felt his kiss on the back of her neck, and she trembled under his touch. Sarah tried to put space between them before her body reacted, but his hold only grew stronger.

"You remember, don't you?" His hands roamed over her body.

Stop! Sarah screamed inside her head, but the words would not come.

"Oh, yes. You remember how good we are together." He spun her around and pressed his lips to hers in a lingering kiss.

Sarah kissed him back, their bodies melding together, hungry for each other. One hand slid up his chest, and the other curled around his waist. She leaned into him. His heartbeat pounded against her own, and she was transported back in time to the last embrace they'd shared.

"Oh, yes, Marco," she said when the kiss ended. "I remember." Gazing up, she smiled. When he smiled back, his grip relaxed, and Sarah wiggled out of the embrace. She shoved him away and hurried backward toward the balcony doors. With one hand on her hip and one behind her back, she said, "Time to go, Marco."

He put out a hand to take hers, but she recoiled. "But what about us?"

"Us?" Sarah laughed. "There never was an us. Only a you."

"That's not true. I always cared for you. I still do." He approached her, but she backed away, out of his reach.

"Stop lying to me! You care about me only enough to find out what I'm doing here." Sarah went to the balcony doors. When she spun back around, she said, "This mission must be pretty important for the CIA to bring me back after you ruined my reputation, don't you think?"

"You mean more than that to me. You know that."

"Do I?"

He stepped closer, his arms open wide. "Of course, I—"

Sarah held her hand up to halt him.

"You really need a new routine, Marco. This seduction act is getting pretty stale." She gestured at the door. "You need to leave. Now."

"But Sarah—"

"Not ready to go? Maybe I can motivate you." Sarah opened one of the balcony's doors, then turned back to Marco holding his brown leather wallet in her hand.

"What are you doing?"

He took a single step toward her but froze when Sarah opened the wallet and removed a slip of paper. "Baroness Bianca Lombardi?" She waved the note at him. "A baroness, Marco? I thought your aspirations were much higher."

He shrugged.

"Let's see how important she is to you, shall we?" Sarah crumpled the paper into a ball and tossed it out the open door where it was caught by the wind and disappeared.

"Wait!" He rushed toward her but stopped again when she held out several hundred-dollar bills.

"What do your communist friends in the Italian government say when they see you carrying around this much American money?"

"Don't!" He closed in, but she opened her hand and

let the wind take the bills.

"Are you leaving yet?" Sarah unzipped the wallet's inside pocket. Marco remained silent, scowling as she took out a key. "Who does this belong to?"

"Give that to me." He tried snatching the key from her hand, but she jerked it away before he could grab it.

"Are you leaving?"

He sighed. "I'll leave. Just give me the damn key."

She slipped the key back inside the pocket, then tossed the wallet over the balcony's railing. "You can leave the same way you came in, Romeo."

As he passed by her on his way out the door, she grabbed him by the arm. "This is over, understand? If I see you again, I'll turn you in."

Marco tore his arm away and went outside to the balcony. "You've changed, Sarah." "Believe me when I tell you the CIA has changed too," he warned her. "Don't trust anyone. Not even Phillips." With that, he threw a leg over the railing and flung himself over the balcony.

Sarah shut the doors and strolled back to her chair. She lifted her glass and swirled the wine around a few times, savoring the sweet smell, before taking a drink.

Don't trust anyone, she mused. *Especially you, Marco D'Amico.*

Chapter Sixteen

Sarah arrived at Rome's Termini train station the next day at nine in the morning. Families, military men, and other travelers milled about the station as they awaited the next arrival. Sarah scanned the room as she set her bag on the floor next to a bench. There was no sign of Marco.

Maybe he gave up after I threw away his wallet. Sarah smiled, remembering the horrified expression on his face.

In the center of the terminal, the numbers on the station's arrival and departure display rolled over as the times updated. Sarah read down the list and realized the express train to Berlin had already arrived, so she walked out the door to join the crowd on the platforms.

A huge man dressed completely in black followed her through the crowd. Sarah didn't notice his presence until he coughed. It was a loud, hacking cough that drew the attention of several people. He pressed a handkerchief to his nose and Sarah smelled the pungent aroma of menthol vapor emanating from it. The man noticed Sarah watching him and smiled at her. A familiarity in his gaze resonated inside her and she felt the pinpricks of perspiration crawl up the back of her neck.

Do I know him?

The conductor called the announcement to board.

Sarah glanced once more at the man, noted the feeling he gave her, then picked up her suitcase.

Time to get to work.

****

Marco hid in a doorway behind her, spying as Sarah boarded her train. He took note of the carriage number and jogged back inside to the ticket booth.

"One, sir?" the clerk asked.

"Yes, *per favore*." Marco put his face close to the barred window. "I'd like a cabin in Car 2201, if possible?" He lowered his voice. "My wife is in that car. We had a fight."

"Oh?"

Marco flashed him a knowing glance. "You know how jealous women can be."

The old man squinted at him over the rim of his glasses. "Let me see." He thumbed through the logbook. "Yes, there is one cabin left."

"I'll take it."

The old man counted the money before tearing the ticket out of his book and handing it to Marco. "You'll have to hurry. They're loading right now."

"Grazie."

"Sir!" the clerk yelled after him. "Don't you want your change?"

"Keep it," Marco called over his shoulder as he ran to the waiting train.

Chapter Seventeen

Service was already underway when Sarah arrived in the dining car later that evening. A waiter beckoned her with a smile, and she followed him down the center aisle between men and women dressed in their finest traveling clothes. The tables on either side were covered in white linen, with a red carnation standing in a vase in each center, dancing to the sway of the train's carriage.

The waiter pulled out a chair for Sarah, and she sat down at a table for two. "Tonight, we are serving a delicious beef béarnaise, roasted rosemary and garlic potatoes, steamed carrots, a green salad with herb vinaigrette, and a lovely crème brûlée for dessert." He spread the napkin across her lap.

"Thank you. That sounds wonderful," she replied.

"May I get you something to drink?"

Sarah ordered a coffee, and the waiter moved on as her attention shifted to the passing snowy landscape outside. After eight hours on the train, they chugged along deep inside the Italian Alps. It was a beautiful sight, but Sarah's attention drifted as she thought about the mission.

"Remember our weekend at Monte Bondone?" a familiar husky voice whispered in her ear. "I'll never forget the night we spent on that train."

Marco's reflection materialized in the window.

"I seem to recall buying two tickets to Alvera once."

Sarah shrugged, pretending that his appearance on the train hadn't surprised her. "Was that you?"

Marco grasped his chest. "You break my heart." He pulled out the other chair and sat down across from her as the waiter approached their table.

"Good afternoon, *signore*. Would you care for something from our bar?"

"I'll have a scotch. The *signora* will have a glass of your best pinot noir." He gave Sarah a wink as the waiter glanced her way.

"I'll just have the coffee, thank you." The waiter nodded and moved on.

"Your cheeks are flushed, darling." Marco ran a finger down her cheek. "Just like after we make love."

Anger blazed inside Sarah, and she smacked his hand away. "My patience has run out with you."

Marco shrugged. "I'm only here to help."

"I'm sure you are," she snapped, "but what you don't seem to understand is that your help is not wanted. Nor is it needed."

"You're wrong about that."

Sarah scoffed. "What an ego you have."

Marco's expression suddenly hardened. "Listen to me. You don't know who you're dealing with."

"Oh, and you do?"

"Yes." Marco lowered his voice. "I've seen things you haven't. The Soviets don't play the same way the Nazis did, boasting about everything to anyone who would listen. The Russians don't talk at all. We don't know what the hell is going on behind their borders. If you are caught, you'll disappear without a trace, and no one at that damned CIA is going to lift a finger to help you."

Sarah waved him away. "You don't know what you're talking about. You've done nothing since the war except wine and dine politicians on the weekends and service their wives during the week."

"I know more than you think," he insisted.

Sarah shook her head. "No. This is my assignment, Marco, and I don't need your enormous ego telling me what to do."

"You don't believe me?" Marco asked. "Why don't you ask that *bastardo*, Albert Philips, about Joseph Avery?"

Sarah remembered Joe. They worked together several times during the war. He was respected in the OSS and dedicated to his work.

"The director sent him into Berlin's Soviet sector last year to coordinate with one of his people. He was only supposed to be there overnight, but he disappeared immediately. Gone, just like that." Marco snapped his fingers. "And they've never done anything about it. It's like he never existed at all. The CIA sends agents in, hoping they accomplish something, but they can't always get them back out and they have no idea what to do." He shook his head and added, "Now they're going to do it to you too."

"You think they're setting me up?" Sarah asked.

"That's exactly what they are doing."

"Just like you did?"

"You know that wasn't my plan. You just got caught up in it." He slid his hand across the table and wrapped it around her clenched fist. "Let me help you. Please. I'm worried about you."

Sarah yanked her hand free. "You? Worried about me? Don't make me laugh." She glanced around the dining car and noticed people staring. "You forget," she whispered, "we were both trained at the same time, in the exact same way. What makes you think you'd do any better than me?"

"I'm not questioning your skills. I'm just saying I know what the current situation is. You've been out for too long."

"Thanks to you."

Marco sighed. "I told you I was sorry last night. Can't we move on?"

"No," she said with a finality meant to end the conversation.

Marco turned away to gaze out the window. Tension etched lines into his handsome face. "I'm only looking out for you."

"You don't look out for anyone but yourself."

Sarah picked up her purse and started to leave, but Marco grabbed her wrist. "We were too good together for it to end like this."

"Really? I guess I don't remember." She yanked her hand away. "I hope you have your passport in order, Marco. We arrive in Berlin in the morning, and I don't think you'll fool the Soviets any more than you're fooling me."

"Don't trust them," Marco called out as she strode to the exit. "Don't trust any of them."

Chapter Eighteen

"Yes, sir!" The steward gave the bar a little tap with his knuckle before reaching for a bottle of scotch on a shelf behind him.

Why are they always so happy? Marco mused as he reached inside his dinner jacket for his pack of cigarettes.

His mood had turned dark. This was the second time Sarah thwarted his attempt to get involved.

What is she up to? They'd worked together several times during the war and she'd trusted him completely back then.

Marco caught himself smiling in the mirror behind the bar as he remembered the woman he'd known then. Sarah had been carefree, adventurous—exciting. Always up for anything he suggested. They'd had an unspoken partnership that started during their time in training. Now, she only saw him as an enemy.

Dammit!

The steward set Marco's drink down, gave him a nod, and moved on to the next customer.

The evening was still early, and only a few passengers relaxed in the lounge car. A jazz tune played over the loudspeaker, and a couple at the other end of the car attempted to dance, but the shaking of the train made it impossible. They laughed, their friends laughed, everyone laughed but Marco.

"Did your woman kick you out of bed?" a deep

voice with a foreign accent asked.

Marco turned around to find a large man stuffed inside a black coat and hat hunched on the stool next to him. A black scarf covered the man's head under his hat. *"Scusi?"* he asked.

"I saw you in the dining car."

"Oh, that." Marco reached across the stranger and picked a matchbook up from an ashtray. "Women," he said in an annoyed voice. He lit his cigarette and blew out a thin line of smoke.

"Mind if I join you?" the man asked, offering his hand. "Yuri Feodorov."

"Marco." His hand was swallowed up inside the other man's fist. "Your accent—Russian?"

"Finnish," Yuri lied before ordering a vodka.

"Sounds cold," Marco said.

"It is. I like Italy much better." He drank the vodka in one swallow and asked for another. "You had a fight with the *signora*?"

"A fight, but not with my wife."

"Ah, I see." Yuri chuckled. "She's a pretty one. I'm sure the apologies later are worth it."

Marco smiled. "You could say that."

****

The conversation continued long into the night. Current events, the state of Europe, the weather, and Sarah. Always back to Sarah. The liquor acted like a truth serum on the arrogant Italian as he bragged about his relationship with Sarah and his plan to follow her to Moscow. Yuri kept ordering drinks, and Marco kept talking.

By one o'clock the lounge car had emptied and Marco gestured to a clock on the wall. "The bar is closing," he slurred.

Yuri coughed as he scrutinized the younger man. He swayed on his stool, drunk.

Time to end this.

"It was good we met, I think." Yuri raised his glass in a toast. "And now, back to your woman to beg forgiveness?" He swallowed the last of his drink, set the glass on the bar, and stood.

Marco slid off his barstool and stumbled a few steps as the train lurched to one side. "I don't think she wants to see me right now."

"No, I don't think so." Yuri said. "Let me help you."

"I can manage." Marco tried to walk upright but the movement of the carriage kept him off balance, and he grabbed the bar.

Yuri smiled. "You don't want to fall off the train, do you?" He took Marco's arm and wrapped it around his shoulder. The extra weight pulled his right side down, triggering a tickle in his throat that expanded into a suffocating urge to cough. The cigarette smoke he'd inhaled throughout the night had irritated his lungs, and he was anxious to get to fresh air.

I better make this quick. He picked up his pace as the flutter in his chest grew inside him.

They passed through the gangway connection and entered the now-empty dining car. When they got to the next door, Yuri slid it open, and a blast of cold air hit him in the face.

Marco, shocked into clarity, struggled to push Yuri's arm off his shoulders, but he was weak, and Yuri's grip was too strong.

"I think I can walk now," Marco yelled into the wind.

"I don't think so." Yuri placed Marco against the car and held him there with one hand as he unhooked the chain blocking the exit stairs with the other.

The train's whistle pierced the air as the engine approached a bridge. The noise drowned out the sound of Yuri's cough and he hacked violently until the phlegm rose from his chest to his throat and he spit over the side of the train's handrail.

When he turned back to Marco, he noticed the Italian's eyes were half closed and his breath labored under the pressure of Yuri's hand on his chest. He was mumbling words Yuri couldn't understand.

A jarring bounce rippled through the train when it rolled onto the bridge and Yuri peered over the edge. The train had entered a deep canyon.

He took Marco by the shoulders, spun him around, and thrust him toward the exit.

"What are you doing?" Marco yelled over the noise of the train.

"You've got an early departure."

"What? Why?" He struggled, but Yuri blocked him.

"You should have listened to the woman," Yuri yelled. He held Marco over the edge by his jacket collar. "You should have left her alone!"

"Stop, please!" Marco wrapped his arms around the handrail.

A cruel smile distorted Yuri's face. He loved it when they begged.

Yuri let go of his jacket and delivered a kick to Marco's kneecap. His body flew out from underneath him and slammed against the outside corner of the train. The look on Marco's face made Yuri laugh. Panic, confusion, fear.

Dena Weigel

"Not so sure of yourself now, are you? You cocky little shit!"

Yuri kicked Marco again, this time in his chest. It knocked the breath out of him, and his arms slipped, but he caught the railing in both hands and held on tight.

Yuri placed his hands over Marco's, holding him there as he peered past him at the fog obscuring the canyon's floor. "Don't worry," he said. "You won't even see it coming."

He bent Marco's fingers back and watched as the Italian's inebriated mind finally understood his fate. The first hand came free, Yuri mouthed, *"Arrivederci,"* then he pounded his fist down on the other hand and, with a last panicked, helpless gaze, Marco's body flew away from the train. A whistle from the engine drowned out his cry for help.

Yuri stepped back from the edge and held the handkerchief up to his face as Marco's stories of Sarah played on inside his head.

A cruel smile spread across his face.

Soon, she'll be begging me too.

Chapter Nineteen

A newspaper and a carafe full of piping hot coffee waited on the floor when Sarah opened the door of her cabin the next morning. Her stomach growled. After leaving Marco in the dining car last night, she'd been too angry to eat, and she'd awaken with her stomach growling. The coffee would have to do for now. She tucked the newspaper under her arm and was about to pick up the carafe when a voice further down the car caught her attention.

"Sir, sir?" A porter tapped on a door three cabins down from hers. "Are you there, *signore*?" When no answer came, he noticed Sarah and called to her. *"Signora?"*

"Yes?"

"Scusi, per favore, but do you know the man assigned to this cabin?"

"I'm afraid not. Is there a problem?"

"I noticed the door is ajar, and I can see his things scattered all over the room." He scratched his head. "Are you sure you don't know the gentleman? I saw you with him at dinner last night."

Marco? Anger jolted to life inside her. *Damn him! When will this end?*

"I'll take a look," she told the porter, stepping between him and the door. The room was a mess, the wall bed remained untouched in the bench position and

Marco's suitcase lay open on the floor, its contents scattered around the room.

"You haven't seen him this morning?" Sarah asked the porter.

He shook his head. "I only now noticed the door. Do you know him?"

"Yes," she said. "I know him." *But this isn't like the Marco I know.* He'd always been a vain man who took great pride in his designer clothes.

She faced the porter, blocking his view. "You're right. I dined with him last night. I didn't realize his cabin was in this car."

"Do you know where he is? This room must be cleaned before we reach Berlin." He craned his neck to see around her, but Sarah put an arm on the door to stop him.

"I'll pick up his things."

The porter shrugged his shoulders and rolled his cart to the next cabin as Sarah got to work. First, she picked up the suitcase and ran her hand around the interior. A broken seam behind the handle caught her attention. She peeled a flap back and discovered a small piece of paper folded inside. When she unfolded it she realized Marco had written down all her travel information in his distinctive scrawl.

Is he really trying to follow me all the way to the Kremlin? She crumpled up the paper and threw it out the window. *Reckless, but that's Marco.*

She gathered the rest of the clothes together and dropped them in the suitcase. Only a white handkerchief remained on the floor. Sarah scooped the cloth up and grimaced at the smell. A strong menthol scent emanated from it, triggering a memory.

The man in black from the train station?

Sarah turned it over. The distinctive D'Amico family crest was missing on the cheap cloth.

Marco would never own something so common.

She glanced around the room again but found nothing else unusual or out of place. When the train reached Berlin, she'd rent a locker for the suitcase and call headquarters to let them know Marco had followed her. Hopefully, it was the last time she'd have to deal with him.

Sarah suddenly felt ice cold when she remembered his warning.

Can Albert be trusted, or is Marco just manipulating me again?

Sarah shook the thought away and stuffed the handkerchief in the suitcase and closed it.

Marco probably met up with someone to spend an evening drinking and found the next target of his manipulation.

She couldn't waste time thinking about that. Marco wasn't her responsibility, and she had a job to do. When they arrived in Berlin, Sarah Kraft and her problems would cease to exist, and she would become Katarina Russman.

Chapter Twenty

Moscow

Twenty-four hours later, with a bump and a jerk, Sarah's train came to a stop inside Moscow's snow-covered central station. People on the platform waited for passengers to disembark and Sarah studied each of their solemn faces through the window of her cabin. No one resembled the MI6 agent, so her focus shifted to seven policemen strolling through the crowd with rifles hanging from their right shoulders.

The sight of Stalin's armed men sent a shiver through Sarah. *No turning back now.*

She closed her eyes and thought of the photo of Rodzyanko. *Broad mouth, deep-set eyes. An athletic build.*

The conductor's announcement to disembark echoed down the car. Sarah picked up her bag and joined the other travelers shuffling toward the exit. With every step, the ruse she was about to take on felt like a weight lowering over her shoulders.

What if we don't recognize each other?

A porter met her at the exit, an older man with a thick, Stalinesque mustache and a stooped back. He offered an outstretched hand as she stepped onto the platform. She followed a woman and her daughter walking through the doors to the station's lobby as a loudspeaker squawked a message in Russian over the entrance. The garbled words came too fast for Sarah to understand.

Inside the terminal, a group of benches filled the center of the room and kiosks selling snacks were spaced out around the edges. Sarah searched faces in the crowd for Rodzyanko's likeness as she moved through the crowed to sit down.

A shrill whistle blew outside and Sarah glanced back at the Berlin train one last time.

That's it. If he doesn't show up, I'm on my own.

As the train moved out of the station she thought of Marco. He hadn't reappeared since their fight in the dining car, so she'd be surprised if he suddenly showed up in Moscow now. He'd attempted to manipulate her and failed—twice. Maybe he'd finally given up.

But he's a desperate man, and desperate men do desperate things. She scanned the terminal in a sweeping glanc*e, half expecting him to appear.*

She shook her head to rid it of the thought.

A man walked past the bench, but his balding head didn't match the photo. Sarah scanned the upper floor gallery and noticed two men in gray suits. They stood next to the balcony and silently scanned the room as people came and went from the platforms.

KGB? Probably.

Sarah's stomach rolled over and tied itself into a knot at the thought. *What if this Rodzyanko doesn't show up?*

She took a seat on a bench under an oversized Soviet flag hanging from the ceiling. Nervous energy coursed through her body and exited through a rapid tapping of her foot.

If he doesn't show up, I'm on my own. Dropped into

this pit of vipers waiting to strike.

She scanned the crowd again for Rodzyanko, and still, there was no sign of him. But she noticed two more men who lounged next to an office door and stared in her direction.

He'd better get here soon.

"Katarina!" Relief washed over her when she heard a deep voice say her pseudo name from the other side of the bench. Sarah glanced toward the voice and saw Nicolai Rodzyanko striding toward her.

"So good to see you again!" he said in Russian-accented German. When he got to the bench, he swept Sarah to her feet and into an embrace. "Relax," he whispered in her ear. "You're safe with me." He gave her a quick kiss on the lips, and then stepped back and held her at arm's length. "You look beautiful."

He was undeniably handsome. Wavy brown hair, caramel-colored eyes, and a lopsided smile that gave him a disarming, boyish look.

That black-and-white photo didn't do him justice.

He handed her a bouquet of flowers.

"Danke," she thanked him in German.

He picked up her suitcase. "Are we ready?" Then he took her by the arm and guided her toward the exit. "My car is waiting outside."

The parking lot was full outside. Nicolai led Sarah to a boxy, black Soviet car that sat alone in the corner of the parking lot and opened the passenger side door. The hinges groaned and creaked when he slammed the door shut behind her. Sarah settled in and waited as he walked around the car, opened his door, and tossed her bag into the backseat before sliding in behind the wheel. He had a natural vitality and confidence in the way he moved—

a characteristic that eased her anxiety.

"I was surprised to learn they were sending a woman," he said in perfect English.

The statement caught Sarah off guard. "Is that a problem for you?"

"Of course not. My intelligence told me the CIA had—" He paused and searched for the right word. "—released?" She nodded and he continued. "I'd heard they released all their female agents after the war."

Her smile waned when Marco's warning came to mind. *Don't trust any of them.*

"All except one," she said. "My name's Sarah Kraft. I'd shake your hand, but our relationship seems to have already moved beyond that point."

He chuckled. "Nicolai Rodzyanko. I'm sorry I couldn't think of a better story. It is the best I could offer on such short notice."

"No need to apologize." Sarah scrutinized the unfamiliar knobs and levers on the dashboard. "It's safe to talk here?"

"I have a man in the motor pool. He sweeps the car every morning before I get to the garage." Nicolai pressed a button on the dash, and the engine sputtered. "It's the only place we can talk openly. My apartment is wired." He pushed the button again, and the engine rolled over and came to life. "The whole building is. We must be very careful." He revved the engine a few times, and a cloud of black smoke escaped from the tailpipe as the stench of gasoline filled the interior. "I've been anticipating your arrival. I haven't met many Americans."

"Thanks for taking this mission on," Sarah said. "I hear MI6 has been a big help."

He threw his arm over the seat and backed out of the parking spot. Snow crunched under the tires as the car rocked back and forth over the uneven ground.

"Have you been at the Kremlin long?" Sarah gripped her seat to keep from toppling over.

"Five years. British intelligence recruited me after the war when I was stationed in Berlin. After a few months, I secured a post at the Kremlin inside the defense department." Fumes filled the car as he gunned the motor to crest a snowdrift blocking them from the main road. "Is this your first visit to the Kremlin?"

"My second. I took part in an official tour for the war department at the end of the war."

A traffic guard waved them through an intersection, and Nicolai turned right to enter the flow of traffic. Cars and horse-drawn carts crowded the icy street, and people waited in long lines outside stores as street merchants walked back and forth selling black-market goods from handcarts. Nicolai stopped at a corner, and five uniformed men in heavy, gray wool coats crossed in front of the car, the last one limping behind on a crutch.

Sarah shifted her attention back to Nicolai. "What's our plan for tonight?"

"Stalin is hosting a state ball at the Kremlin's Grand Palace to welcome the president of Belarus. You'll accompany me as my date. I've arranged to have the alarms silenced at ten o'clock. That's when we'll make our way to the museum."

"What are our chances of running into trouble?" Sarah asked.

"There's always a chance," he told her. "But I know a route that will take us through the palace all the way to the museum without having to step outside the buildings."

Sarah gave him a curious glance.

"Stalin lives at another residence a short distance from the Kremlin, so the palace is only used for official events. The guards are busy at the event, so we should get in without meeting any resistance He glanced sideways at Sarah. "They told me you know the museum well enough to find what you're looking for."

"I should be able to, as long as there haven't been any changes to the floor plan since the war."

"There's little chance of that. Any money meant for those projects is being used to rebuild the city."

He twisted a knob, and the right turn signal flashed red as they entered another busy street. They rounded the corner, and the Kremlin, with its tall brick walls and gold-capped onion domes, came into view. It was a formidable place. Nineteen towers crowned the outer wall, and Sarah saw the silhouettes of armed guards stationed at intervals behind the crenelations.

"After you find what you're looking for," Nicolai continued, "we'll return to the ball without anyone knowing we were gone." He pressed the gas, and the rickety car chugged up a hill. "I've been told the item is small enough to hide inside our clothes."

"Only about six inches long," Sarah said, "but I didn't bring a ball gown."

"A seamstress is waiting at my flat. I asked her to bring several gowns for you to try."

Nicolai veered left and cruised alongside the riverbank until he neared a gate to a modern, constructionist-style apartment building that occupied the entire block.

"Once we're inside the Kremlin, we won't be

searched. I'll put the cross inside my jacket and walk out. The police are only concerned with people going in, not leaving."

"Sounds simple enough," Sarah said.

"I have found that simplicity is the quickest route to success." Nicolai gunned the engine. Sarah gripped her seat as the car climbed the last snowdrift into the parking lot. It landed on the opposite side with a thump and a loud chorus of creaks and groans. "Things tend to get complicated enough on their own."

"I completely agree," Sarah said as she held onto her seat to steady herself.

He pulled in behind another car idling in front of a guardhouse. "This is a government building," he whispered. "We must remember the parts we are playing at all times."

"Are you expecting trouble?" Sarah asked.

Nicolai nodded to the guard waving him through. "In Stalin's Russia, you must always expect trouble."

Chapter Twenty-One

Sarah swiped a hand across the frosty windshield and peered out at Red Square.

The police are everywhere!

Parked patrol cars clogged both sides of the street and policemen stood alert between each one all the way from St. Basil's Cathedral to the Kremlin's main gate.

Dressed in a red silk gown, white fur wrap, and diamond jewelry provided by Nicolai, Sarah gripped the edge of her seat as her foot tapped nervously against the floorboard.

Nicolai noticed. "Calm down. Everything will be fine."

Sarah sat back and laid her hands in her lap. "Sorry. I haven't done this in a while."

"It's a quick job. One of the easiest I've ever been given. You'll do fine."

He drove up to the first checkpoint, and a guard came up to the driver's side window. He asked for their identity cards as he flashed a light around the interior. When it landed on Sarah, he paused, and she held her breath.

Nicolai answered the policeman's question and gave him a wink and a smile. The guard handed Nicolai back his cards with a slight smile and waved them through the gate.

Sarah waited until Nicolai rolled up his window and

then asked. "Is he one of yours?"

"No."

"But he let me go so quickly. I thought we'd have a much harder time."

Nicolai smiled. "This isn't the first time I brought a woman to the palace."

The police presence disappeared as soon as they passed under the gate's tower, replaced by dozens of Kremlin guards with rifles slung over their backs. Six spotlights swept the rooftops of the compound in circular patterns, four on the ground and two more on the rooftops. One beam landed on a cathedral's rooftop, and its gold dome burst into brilliance like a lit candle on a birthday cake.

"Do they always have this much security?"

"It's an exhibition. Stalin wants to remind people of his power."

Nicolai drove the car onto the avenue leading to the Grand Palace.

"There's the museum," he said, "Tonight's target."

Sarah followed his line of sight past the palace to the Kremlin Museum at the end of the street. Dark and foreboding, its yellow façade stretched the length of an entire block. The windows were dark and the building appeared empty.

It'd better be. At least for tonight.

The car pulled up to the entrance to the palace, and Sarah's door opened. A young soldier stepped forward to help her out of the car. Her gloved hand shook as she took his, but when she stepped onto the red carpet and took Nicolai's arm, her fears subsided as her new persona took hold. Her hands stopped shaking, and her breathing relaxed as her training and instincts kicked in.

Check your breathing. Look them in the eye. Smile. All the tricks she'd learned during the war came flooding back as Nicolai introduced her to people at a dizzying rate. It was a clever strategy that curtailed her conversations to a polite nod.

"Where do you find such beautiful women?" Sarah overheard one young man ask.

Nicolai smiled. "They seem to find me somehow."

"You must bring a lot of women here," Sarah mused when they were alone.

"A man needs outside interests, doesn't he? What is the American saying—'All work and no play makes Jack a dull boy'?"

Sarah laughed. "That goes for Jills too."

Across the room, a group of high-ranking military men caught Sarah's attention. Deep in conversation, all their attention was focused on a short, bald man with a cleft chin and bushy eyebrows. When he noticed her looking at him, he broke away from the group.

A server passed by, and Nicolai picked up two wine glasses, handing one to Sarah.

"Have a drink," he said. "We're about to be interrogated."

"*Comrade!*" The man's booming voice dominated every other sound around them. "So good to see you tonight." He shook Nicolai's hand and then scrutinized Sarah. His gaze was penetrating, but Sarah smiled demurely and played her part well.

"And who is this beauty?" the man asked.

Sarah felt Nicolai's hand at her back. "Katarina Russman, may I introduce you to Deputy Leonid Baranov of the Commissariat for Internal Affairs. Katarina is visiting us from East Berlin."

"Ah, our German outpost," he said in fluent German. "How wonderful!" Baranov lifted Sarah's hand and placed a lingering, wet kiss on her wrist.

"It's a great honor to join you tonight," she replied as she fought the urge to wipe the feeling of his lips off her hand.

"I imagine Moscow is a wonderful respite from the conditions in Germany. I understand the cities are still quite deplorable."

His intrusive gaze never eased, and Sarah felt naked under his intense scrutiny.

"And you met while you were stationed in Berlin?"

"Yes, during my time there after the war." Nicolai gestured to Sarah. "Katarina was interested in learning more about our country," he explained. "She is Russian born. Her family moved to Berlin during the last days of the Empire."

"You must have been a baby at the time."

"Only two years old," she said.

"And your father's name?"

"Viktor Russman."

"Are they still living in Germany?"

"They did not survive the war."

Baranov raised his glass in salute. "Then, may I be the first to welcome you to your homeland once more." After that, Nicolai directed the conversation to more mundane topics until Baranov excused himself and rejoined his group.

Sarah let out the breath she'd been holding. "How did I do?" she whispered.

"With him, you never know until it's too late."

"He was staring at me as though he could see right through me. Do you think he bought my story?"

"Bought?" Nicolai asked.

"Never mind."

Nicolai nodded toward a service entrance. "That's our exit. When the master of ceremonies announces the start of the banquet, we'll slip through the door and use the service corridor to get to the apartments."

"How much time do we have?"

"Thirty minutes. We'll have to run."

"I don't know how fast I can run in this dress."

"Maybe it'd be better if you took it off," Nicolai teased.

"Is nudity standard practice when you gather intelligence?" Sarah teased him back.

He laughed. "You'd be surprised."

A waiter approached to take away their empty glasses as the orchestra began another waltz. After he left, Nicolai bowed deeply. "Would you care to dance?" he asked before bringing Sarah into his arms.

"I haven't done this in years," Sarah told him as they glided across the room in time with the other dancers.

He spun her around in a circle. "Yet it comes naturally to you."

Sarah smiled as she lost herself in the dance, and they made small talk as Nicolai led her gracefully around the room. When they passed by a group of five elderly men talking in hushed tones, he said, "You see those men?"

The tallest man leaned far into the group, and he struck his chest with a balled-up fist. "Who are they?"

"Scientists from the state security department. Your government has targeted them since the end of the war."

"Why?"

"I don't know, but the tallest is so valuable to the

Soviets, his name has been scrubbed from all the records." He paused. "Or at least, I haven't found it yet."

"And he's at a diplomatic dinner? That seems odd."

"They've been away from Moscow for most of the year working on a top secret project. They must be in town to update Stalin on their progress."

The Byzantine Cross?

"Do you know what the project is?" she asked.

"Rumors are they have developed a new weapon, something that has never been attempted before, but I haven't found any proof."

The orchestra quieted, and the master of ceremonies stepped onto the stage. He cleared his throat.

"Ladies and gentlemen," he announced. "Please welcome our supreme leader, the General Secretary of the Communist Party of the Soviet Union, Joseph Stalin."

Whispers rippled through the crowd as everyone drew a collective breath. Sarah strained to see the man through the crowd and clapped with the rest of the guests.

He isn't nearly as impressive as I thought he'd be. Short, soft in the middle, and a little hunched over. The war had taken its toll on him.

Baranov appeared by his side to shake his hand as the orchestra struck up the first notes of the next waltz.

"Let's keep our mind on the job, shall we?" Nicolai whispered as he drew Sarah back into his arms. "Don't forget. Baranov is watching."

He checked his watch. "Almost time. Are you ready?"

Energy surged through her body, an excited vigor she remembered well from her missions in the war. She smiled at Nicolai. "Ready when you are."

Nicolai spun her around in a circle as he guided her toward the service exit. As the orchestra's last notes faded, they slipped through the service door.

Chapter Twenty-Two

Yuri steered the limousine into Cathedral Square and followed the guard's directions to an empty parking spot. A second guard approached the car with a clipboard and motioned for Yuri to roll down the window. Without saying a word, Yuri handed him the documents Cardinal Max had given him, and the man aimed a flashlight at Yuri's face. "Have you been to the palace before?"

Yuri squinted into the bright light. "Once," he grunted.

"Who did you bring tonight?" he asked.

"The minister of the MGB."

"Security, eh? Want to stand watch with us tonight?" The guard chuckled as he gave him the clipboard to sign.

Yuri ignored the question and scrawled Boris Lermontov, the name Max gave him, on the line before handing it back to the guard.

"Follow the signs and stay in your area," the guard instructed. "You can come and go from the lounge to the cars but nowhere else." Yuri nodded, and the guard moved on to the next car.

So far, this assignment was one of the easiest he'd ever taken on. Max provided everything he needed to cross the borders quickly and without any questions. The only obstacle he'd faced so far was that cocky Italian, Marco, but he was lying at the bottom of a ravine now.

Yuri reached down between his legs and unhooked his gun from the seat's frame. He released the clip to check the bullets before popping it back in and slipping the gun into the shoulder harness hidden under his coat. He searched under the seat a second time and removed a silencer, dropping it into the side pocket of his coat and then he retrieved a map of the Kremlin Max had drawn for him.

A route was marked in red on the map for him to follow. It wove through the Grand Palace all the way to a skybridge connecting the palace to the museum. Max assured Yuri it was the same route Sarah would take, so Yuri picked a stairwell along the route to hide in until she returned with the cross. A quiet place, with nowhere to run and no one to hear her screams.

Yuri slipped the map into his pocket and climbed out of the car, glancing back to the six guards standing at attention at the entrance to the lot. Two more were marching to the lounge, and he'd counted more than fifty soldiers on his drive into the Kremlin. Not good odds if something went wrong.

It's only twenty-four hours. Just get the cross and get out.

Yuri wiped his mouth with the back of his hand.

The money is worth it. And so is the woman.

Chapter Twenty-Three

"Your gown. Be careful." Nicolai's tone took on a new intensity.

A line of carts heaped with dirty glasses took up half the hallway. Sarah gathered her gown to squeeze past and followed Nicolai around a corner. He halted at a small, unmarked door.

"One of my people stashed some clothes here for you," he whispered.

They stepped inside, and Sarah closed the door as Nicolai pulled a cord overhead. A ceiling light flickered on and gave off just enough light to show they were in a linen closet. Nicolai stretched his arm up to the top shelf to shove aside a stack of towels. He reached toward the back and fetched a pile of dark clothes. "I hope these fit. I guessed your size."

Sarah took the clothes and said, "As long as the shoes stay on, I'll be fine." She stepped out of her heels and into the black trousers. No time for modesty. She let the dress drop to the ground in a red heap as she pulled the black turtleneck over her head and slipped into the loafers.

A bit tight, but perfect for the job.

"Ready to go?" Nicolai picked up her ballgown, wrap, and her shoes, rolled them into a ball, and placed them back on the shelf.

Sarah opened her mouth to answer but stopped when

she heard footsteps on the other side of the door.

She froze, and Nicolai switched off the light. The room went dark. They waited in the closet as the sound grew louder, and then gradually faded away. The loud bang of a door closing signaled the threat had passed.

Nicolai cracked open the door and scanned the corridor. "Let's go." He took off at a jog, and Sarah followed.

****

"Where are you going?" asked one of the men at the table. "You can't leave when you're winning."

Yuri glanced at the clock on the wall. "I've got to get some air."

Another driver took a drag on his cigarette. "At least stick around long enough to give us a chance to win back our money." He blew smoke in Yuri's direction.

"I can't breathe." Yuri wheezed and pressed his handkerchief to his nose. The other players grumbled as he pocketed his winnings and left the room.

Out in the hallway, Yuri braced himself against the wall and breathed in the vapor. After the attack subsided and he could breathe normally again, he stuffed the handkerchief back in his pocket and checked his gun before screwing on the silencer. When he finished checking the chamber, Yuri opened the door to the palace and took off down the hallway.

****

Nicolai rarely slowed down, veering left, then right, then right again before merging with a larger hallway. Sarah fell into step behind him.

Another right, and they stopped at a door. Nicolai opened it, and Sarah recognized the ceremonial staircase she'd seen on her visit.

We made it to the palace's royal apartments!

They raced down the stairs and crossed the room to a set of double doors. Nicolai hunched down and bent the toe of his shoe back. A flat piece of metal fell on the floor. He picked the tool up and inserted it into the lock, rotating the improvised key back and forth a few times until the tumblers fell into place, and the door clicked open.

Light from outside filtered in through east-facing windows, landing on priceless paintings covered in dust and furniture scattered around the room, but Sarah noticed none of it.

They ran through seven more rooms and halted at another set of double doors. Nicolai opened one and peered through. Cold air blew in, telling Sarah they'd reached the skybridge connecting the palace to the museum.

Sarah snuck a glance through the arches supporting the bridge's peaked roof and saw three palace guards in the garden below. The tips of their burning cigarettes glowed bright red in the night.

"I'll go first," Nicolai whispered. "Wait for my signal and stay low." He stepped outside and hid behind the first arch. Sarah's gaze followed him as he slipped from one shadow to the next, switching between tracking his movements and the movements of the guards. When Nicolai reached the other side, he checked the guards, then motioned for Sarah to make her move.

Sarah ducked behind the balustrade and ran the length of the bridge to Nicolai, who was already picking the lock on the museum's door. He pushed it open and swiped a hand across his brow. "You're in charge now."

Sarah's mind raced. *Focus, focus!* She took a deep

breath and said, "We need to get to the first floor."

Nicolai indicated a stairway heading down to the first floor. Sarah took the lead. They sprinted down the steps two at a time and entered a large gallery at the bottom.

A red carpet took them past several glass cases housing a collection of headless mannequins dressed in seventeenth-century clothes. Gilded carriages crowded the next gallery, and in the third, they found the ceremonial regalia of the Russian Orthodox church. Sarah slowed her pace as she searched for the cross.

Silver chalices and trays.

No crosses.

Bronze lamps and incense burners.

No crosses.

One more right turn, and they stopped in front of a row of six cabinets containing *dozens* of crosses.

"This is the case," Sarah announced, scanning the shelves.

"Which one is it?" Nicolai asked.

Every cross was highly decorated with gold and jewels. Not a single one among them resembled the plain cross Sarah saw in the Vatican archives. She panicked.

"It's not here."

"Are we in the wrong room?" Nicolai's gaze swept around, searching the other cases.

"No. All the crosses are in this room." Sarah read the labels sitting on the shelves next to the crosses. "And all these are from the sixteenth century, just like the one we're looking for."

Nicolai checked his watch. "You've got eleven minutes."

The flash of red on a gold box on a lower shelf

caught her attention. Rubies set in a design of a two-headed eagle covered the top. No information or card explained the presence of the box on the shelf, but the craftsmanship in its detail was far above the level Russian jewelers had mastered at that time.

The style, the artistry—it's not Russian. It's Byzantine.

"The cross is in there," she said. "How do we open the case?"

Nicolai moved around to the back and found two locks, one at the top and one at the bottom.

"Does that tricky little piece of metal work on glass cases?" Sarah asked.

"We're about to find out." Nicolai went to work on the top lock, but the sliding glass door didn't move.

He tried the bottom lock. Still nothing.

"We have to break the glass," he finally said.

As Sarah searched for something that could crack the case, a spotlight from outside flashed through the window and landed on her hand. A sparkle caught her attention.

Nicolai's diamond ring! He'd given the ring to her, along with matching earrings, to wear with her ballgown.

Nicolai grabbed Sarah's hand, but she yanked it back.

"Let me." Sarah scowled. "You'll break my finger."

She slid the ring off and gave it to Nicolai, who dropped it on the ground and stomped on it until the diamond broke free of the setting. He traced a circle on the glass, tapped his knuckle against it twice, and the glass inside the circle fell backward into the case and shattered. The hole was just large enough for Nicolai's hand to go inside and grasp the box.

"Here you go," he said, removing the box through the hole and handing it to Sarah.

Sarah didn't respond. She blew a layer of dust off its lid and ran her finger over the double-headed eagle to see the rubies flash red in the light. She lifted the lid and lying inside on a cushion made of purple silk was the Byzantine Cross.

No decoration, no jewels—just a simple wooden cross.

"That's what you're after?" Nicolai glanced over her shoulder. "Rather plain, isn't it? The box is worth more."

"You would think so, wouldn't you?" Sarah murmured.

Nicolai glanced at his watch again and said, "We should get going. The power will be back on in nine minutes." He took the box from Sarah and carefully put it back on the shelf. "Hopefully, this will go unnoticed until you're back in Rome."

Sarah tucked the cross into the waistband of her trousers and pulled her sweater down as she jogged back through the galleries behind Nicolai. When they got to the main hall, they rushed toward the stairwell but stopped when she heard the click of a gun behind them.

"Stop where you are, or I'll shoot!"

Chapter Twenty-Four

Yuri huddled in the stairwell with his gun loaded, thinking of Sarah. Hair like spun gold, eyes as blue as the ocean. He licked his lips. She was just the kind of woman he hoped to find in every whorehouse he'd ever been in.

He held his handkerchief up to his face and took a deep breath, filling his lungs with the healing vapor until the congestion cleared and the wheezing quieted.

Loud footsteps on the other side of the door told him to get ready. Two pair. One heavier than the other.

The cardinal said she'd be alone.

They grew louder as they came closer to the door, and a third pair was clearly heard in the distance.

Two men and one woman?

"Kremlin Garrison! Don't move!" a voice bellowed in Russian from the other side of the door.

A Kremlin guard!

Yuri shrank further back into the shadows as another cough formed in his chest.

They're caught. Dead. They'll never make it out alive.

The man was talking to the guard now. The woman was silent.

As quietly as his big frame would allow, Yuri retraced his steps back to the skybridge.

Chapter Twenty-Five

"Kremlin Garrison!" a deep voice yelled again a few feet behind them.

Sarah sucked in a breath and held it. *No! Not now!*

"Pizdets!" Nicolai swore next to her as he raised his hands above his head. "Follow my lead," he whispered as they pivoted to face the man.

"Stay where you are." The guard stalked them, his gun aimed at Nicolai's chest. He appeared twenty years younger than Nicolai, and bigger in size.

This won't be easy.

"What are you doing here?" the guard asked in Russian.

"I can assure you there is no need for weapons," Nicolai replied with feigned confidence.

"What's your name?" the guard barked.

"Nicolai Rodzyanko, secretary to the chairman of defense. I have my credentials in my pocket if you'll allow me." He moved to reach inside his dinner jacket but froze when the guard took a step forward.

"Keep your hands up!"

The guard closed the short distance between them in three steps and reached out to search Nicolai for weapons.

"I work in the intelligence office," Nicolai said. "We're guests at the ball tonight. My date wanted a tour of the museum." He waved his hand dismissively. "It has all been authorized."

"By whom?"

"The director of intelligence. He arranged for the alarms to be turned off."

The guard waved the gun at Sarah. "What about her? Why is she dressed that way if you're coming from the party?"

"She's…she's," he stammered and glanced helplessly at Sarah.

"I'm an American spy," Sarah blurted out in English. "Here to steal the Kremlin's treasures."

This unexpected admission, spoken in American English, surprised the young guard, and he froze in place. Nicolai sprang forward and grabbed the gun, twisting it around until the guard lost his grip. The gun flew from their hands, slid across the floor, and disappeared under a bench.

The guard made a move to retrieve the gun but was stopped when Nicolai landed an uppercut to his diaphragm. He doubled over and fell into Nicolai, grabbing him around the waist as he gasped for air. The pair fell to the ground with the guard landing on top. He drew a knife from his belt and scrambled up Nicolai's body, pinning his chest to the floor with a forearm.

Sarah ran to them. She pulled back her foot and kicked the guard in the right temple. His head flew back, and he let go of the knife. It fell on the floor and Sarah kicked it away.

The guard shook off the assault and wrapped both fists around Nicolai's throat, squeezing tight until his face went pale.

Sarah primed a second kick, but the guard whipped his arm around and grabbed her ankle. With a twist of his wrist, he flipped her backward onto the bench and a sharp pain shot up from her ankle. She hit her head on the windowsill and slid down the bench crumpling into a heap on the floor.

Flashes of white light obscured Sarah's vision as she struggled to stand. As her sight cleared, she saw the guard bend over Nicolai, cradling his head in both hands and slamming it into the floor repeatedly.

Dizzy from hitting her head, Sarah staggered backward into the velvet drapes covering the window. She clutched the fabric, pulling the cord that opened them at the same time. Bright lights from a roving spotlight burst in and flooded the room.

Wrapping the cord around her hand, Sarah opened the curtain all the way. She glanced at the two men rolling on the floor two feet away. The guard had the advantage, his hands still wrapped around Nicolai's throat. Nicolai struggled to breathe as he dug his fingers into the guard's hands.

As the pair moved toward Sarah, she leaped onto the guard's back and drove her knee into the space between his shoulderblades. She looped the cord three times around his neck and leaned back with all her weight, trying to wrench his body away from Nicolai's.

The guard moved to stand and Sarah hung on tight to the cords. He staggered closer toward the window, clawing at his neck as he fought to free himself, but Sarah hung on with both hands. The cord tightened around her palms until she thought her bones would break.

Nicolai lay at their feet, gasping for air.

"Open the window!" Sarah shouted as the guard reared backward like a wild bronco. "Open the window!"

Louder this time, to break through Nicolai's addled mind. He stumbled to the window, unlocked the lowest pane, and opened it.

Sarah felt the guard weakening under her. His steps faltered, and he tilted to his right side. She drove her knee deeper into his back and pulled the cord tighter until his body arched backward and she slipped off his back.

Nicolai opened the window wide and Sarah maneuvered the guard to it. She wound the cord around the guard's neck several more times, and then pushed him forward into the window.

The guard lurched forward, fell halfway through the open window and doubled over with his head left to hang outside. Sarah and Nicolai grabbed his legs, lifted them up, and heaved him out the window. The cord snapped into a tight line as the guard's body hit the outside wall with a thud, then it rolled back and forth a few times across the windowsill before it stilled.

"I thought he was going to kill me." Nicolai sat on the bench to massage his throat.

"Me too." Sarah rubbed the red line where the rope had pressed into her hand. She glanced out the window. The guard's head tilted at a lifeless angle below her.

She glanced across the Kremlin. The six spotlights continued grazing the rooftops at a steady pace. "We've got to get him in before a spotlight hits him."

"Is he dead?" Nicolai asked.

She leaned out of the window and gave the rope a couple of tugs. "He's gone. Hurry, before someone sees him."

Sarah tugged on the cord to test it, but it didn't budge. She yanked the line again, harder this time, but it barely moved. "He's caught on something."

Nicolai tapped his watch. "We have to leave him. We've only got three minutes before the alarms come back on."

Sarah wrapped her hand around the Byzantine Cross still tucked into her pants and said, "Let's go."

Chapter Twenty-Six

Yuri cracked open the door to the skybridge. A spotlight swept the sky above, but the Kremlin grounds remained quiet. He ducked behind the first column and peered over the balcony. The guards stationed in the garden below were gone.

They must be with Kraft.

He waited for the spotlight to pass, then stepped into the shadow of the next column. As he did, he heard a thump against the museum's exterior wall. He turned toward the sound and spotted a man dressed in a Kremlin guard's black jacket, hung from an open window on the second floor. His legs kicked under him as he fought for the last moments of his life.

The guard?

A moment later, Sarah leaned out of the window and tugged on the rope—it didn't budge. She disappeared back inside.

She killed the son of a bitch! He'd never seen a woman kill a man before and the thought stayed with him as he slipped through the palace door and retraced his route through the palace.

The door to the apartments was left open, and Yuri entered the room as a spotlight hit the windows of the palace. It lit up everything in his path and he slowed to stay out of its beam.

Yuri exited the first room and entered a second only

to stop halfway through when he heard the sound of voices in the next room.

Did they find the body?

He waited, straining to hear what they were saying.

If they found me inside the palace, I'll be tortured and killed. Or worse, sent back to the gulag for the rest of my life.

Yuri ran a finger along the barrel of his gun.

Death is the better option.

The voices grew louder as they approached the entrance into the next room. Yuri hurried to a small door in the back of the room, opened it, and stepped inside a closet.

Chapter Twenty-Seven

Nicolai bounded up the stairs, and Sarah limped behind him on her twisted ankle. When they reached the skybridge, he opened the door and they stepped outside. A spotlight landed on the bridge, and they dove to the ground just before it swept over them. Sarah peeked over the railing. The guard's body hung out of the window, a dark blot against the yellow facade.

When the spotlight moved on, they entered the palace and ran at full speed to the next door. Another spotlight beamed through the window and chased them into the next room. Sarah grabbed Nicolai's sleeve.

"Something's happened," she said. "There weren't any spotlights on this side of the building before."

Nicolai took her hand. "Hurry!"

They ran through the rooms of the royal apartments and were almost to the main room when Nicolai came to an abrupt stop. He pointed to a light coming through the keyhole, and Sarah heard a woman's voice on the other side say in Russian, "It has been pried open. Look at those scratch marks."

"Is it locked now?" a male voice asked. The doorknob jiggled as the person on the other side tested it.

"Yes," the woman replied. "I'll get the key."

Sarah and Nicolai backed away from the door and searched for an escape.

A large fireplace on the other side of the room

caught Sarah's attention. The interior of the hearth was dark with soot and large enough to hide two people. She tugged Nicolai's sleeve, and without a sound, they crept across the room and entered the fireplace.

A cloud of ash curled under their feet as they stepped inside the dirty hearth. Sarah ran her hand over its soot-covered interior and found a row of bricks protruding from the wall in a spiral pattern. It was a ladder the builder made for maintenance.

"Help me up," she whispered, bracing herself against the wall.

Nicolai cupped his hands, and Sarah clambered up into the dark shaft. She found the first brick with her right foot and braced herself against the wall to search for the next one. As she leveraged her way higher, Nicolai followed, lifting his feet out of sight at the same moment a light flicked on in the room below. They both froze in place.

"Check that side of the room," one man said to the other.

Nicolai adjusted his footing on a brick, and bits of charred stone cascaded down the shaft. They landed with soft thuds in the ashes below.

"Did you hear that?" the man asked.

Sarah's breath caught in her throat.

"I don't hear anything," another man answered.

"A thumping noise."

Silence.

"I still don't hear it. Probably just a mouse."

"Mice don't thump, stupid. They scratch."

Nicolai shifted his footing on the brick, and a chip fell to the hearth.

"Shine your flashlight in the hearth," the man said.

A beam of light flashed inside the hearth below Nicolai's feet.

"You need a chimney sweep in here. The fireplace is filthy," one of the men said.

"These rooms haven't been touched in years," the woman replied.

Silence again. Dust tickled Sarah's nose, and she stifled a sneeze.

"I see nothing out of place," the guard said. "Let's check the drawing room."

Sarah and Nicolai waited a few minutes longer to climb down to the hearth.

"What do we do now?" Sarah whispered as she rubbed at the creosote on her hands.

"Pizdtz!" Nicolai said under his breath.

"What?"

He tapped his dinner jacket's lapel, and a cloud of dust floated away. "I can't go back to the ball like this. Even if we make it to the linen closet to get your gown, all this coal dust on me will have people asking questions. We'll have to find another way out."

"How? The guards are everywhere."

"I know a way," he said, feeling around for something to wipe his hands on. "The bigger problem is getting out of Russia."

"Why?"

"Stalin will close the borders as soon as they realize a guard's been killed." He rubbed his hands on a tablecloth. "Going south through Ukraine to Istanbul is probably our best chance."

"How are we going to—" Sarah stopped midsentence when she heard a scraping noise coming from a closet.

They rushed back into the hearth, and Nicolai again cupped his hands, sending Sarah back up the chimney. They climbed higher this time and had almost made it to the top when the rumble of coughing filtered up from below. Sarah squinted into the dark and glimpsed a hulking black form moving inside the hearth.

The chimney's metal crown was a few feet above Sarah. She climbed to the top of the chimney and laid her hands on the frost-covered crown. She pushed against it, but it didn't budge. A burst of pain shot through her injured ankle, and her foot slipped. She fell forward, slamming her head against the brick wall, and slid down onto Nicolai's shoulders. Loose soot and brick cascaded down through the chimney's long shaft.

The click of a cocked gun's hammer resonated up from far below.

Sarah fumbled around with her foot, searching for another brick to stand on. She found one, steadied herself, and tried again to push the crown free of the chimney.

Nicolai squeezed up the chimney to stand beside Sarah, bracing himself against the brick wall. Together they pushed on the chimney's crown. An awful grinding sound of metal on metal echoed through the chimney as they worked to separate the crown from its casing.

Laughter floated up the shaft from below. "You won't get out that way, little lady. Come down here so we can have a little fun."

"One, two, three!" Nicolai whispered behind her. They pushed again, and the crown moved an inch.

"One, two, three!" It moved another inch.

"Again," he whispered. "One, two, three!" The crown popped off, and cold air rushed in through the opening. It blew through the chimney and stirred up more loose soot.

Sarah stifled a sneeze as they heaved the metal cap to the side.

Nicolai climbed out the top of the chimney first.

Sarah heard a distinctive cough coming from the hearth below. The same unmistakable hacking sound she'd heard at the train station in Rome.

The man in black? He followed me all the way here?

Nicolai's hand appeared through the top of the chimney and Sarah grasped it as a muted pop echoed up the shaft.

He's got a gun!

Chapter Twenty-Eight

"Take my hand!" Nicolai yelled as a second bullet embedded itself into the brick. A third bullet dug into the wall next to Sarah's head as he lifted her out of the chimney and onto the Grand Palace's frozen rooftop.

"Who is that?" he asked, holding her close until she gained her footing.

"I don't know," Sarah gasped, shivering from the cold. "But he followed me from Rome."

"Why didn't you tell me?"

"I didn't know he was in Moscow until now."

Nicolai nodded toward six Kremlin guards marching in formation across the inner courtyard below. "They haven't found the guard yet."

Sarah stared past the Kremlin's walls to Moscow. The city streets surrounded the Kremlin in ever widening circles. Cross streets lit by dim yellow streetlights intersected each ring to create a spider web pattern all the way to the four corners of the horizon.

And we're trapped in its center.

Nicolai pointed across the courtyard. "The Terem Palace!" he yelled into the wind.

Directly opposite from their position on the Grand Palace, Sarah recognized the Terem Palace, the ancient brick home of the early tsars. It was five stories tall and topped by a smaller building surrounded by a rooftop terrace.

"There's a tunnel underneath. It runs all the way to the river," Nicolai shouted. "Follow me and do exactly as I do."

He counted the spotlights—eight now. After one beam passed below them, Nicolai let go of the chimney and slid down the roof's metal plates. He landed next to a parapet running along the bottom and crouched down inside a shadow.

Sarah glanced past him to the ground far below, and fear washed over her.

"Come on!" Nicolai waved to her with his arms open wide. "I'll catch you!"

She took a deep breath and let go of the chimney. Arms flailing, she searched frantically for a way to slow down. She flattened her body over the metal plates, but, with every inch she slid, her speed increased. She braced herself for impact. Faster and faster, she raced to the bottom, slamming into Nicolai's body. He helped her stand and placed her hand on the railing. "Hang onto this!"

Sarah peeked over the side of the parapet. A big mistake. There was a sixty-foot drop between her and the cobblestones below.

More guards arrived in the courtyard below. Light from their flashlights bounced on the stones before them as they sprinted toward the museum.

They found him!

"Come on!" Nicolai yelled.

Shivering from the cold and limping on her sore ankle, Sarah followed Nicolai along the base of the roof past the central dome to the corner connecting the palace to the cathedral. They ducked down in a shadow and glanced back at the museum where a spotlight was aimed at the guard's body.

"Pizdtz!" Nicolai cursed. "They found him." He wiped the sweat from his brow and waved at three observation towers around the perimeter where an ominous orange glow stood out from the dark. "They're warming up the rest of the lights. We've got to move fast."

At the end of the palace, they jumped onto the next roof and another stab of pain traveled up Sarah's leg. She followed Nicolai as he crept halfway to the next building, stopping only to lift his head and nod to a tower directly above them.

Another spotlight was warming up. The silhouettes of men moved around inside the glass room.

Twelve spotlights now!

Sarah crouched down and followed Nicolai to the next rooftop. When they reached it a spotlight positioned inside a tower on the opposite side of the Kremlin swung around and landed on Sarah, blinding her. She dropped to her stomach and waited as the spotlight grazed the base of the observation tower and continued its path across the roof.

Nicolai was hiding in a shadow, waving Sarah on. She checked the position of the other spotlights and waited as the next one passed overhead. Down in the courtyard, more guards were running in several directions.

They must be searching inside the buildings.

She ran to Nicolai, favoring her twisted ankle, and he took her by the hand as they wove their way through a series of smaller domes to an iron railing surrounding the rooftop terrace of the Terem Palace.

Sarah was about to climb over, but Nicolai grabbed

her by the arm to pull her back down. He pointed to eight spotlights taking sporadic paths in every direction.

"They're all over the place," she said. "There's no cover."

"Follow their path," Nicolai instructed, "and wait until it's clear to run."

Sarah studied the lights' trajectories as she calculated her next move. Once the lights passed over them, Nicolai jumped from the cathedral roof to the Terem's rooftop terrace a few feet below. He landed on his feet and crouched down inside a shadow.

A siren wailed.

Below them, Sarah spied several guards running across the inner courtyard toward the museum. She moved to the edge of the roof and jumped to the terrace, landing in a kneeling position next to Nicolai. He held up his hand, motioning her to wait as two spotlights crossed paths overhead, then he pointed to one of the Terem Palace's turrets.

"You see that door?"

She nodded. He waited for a light to pass, then darted across the roof and slammed his foot into the door's aged wood. It broke open and he disappeared inside.

Another beam of light swept the terrace. It landed on the palace, paused for a moment, and then swung back to the empty space where the door had been.

Sarah took a deep breath and sprinted to the light as another siren began to wail behind her.

Chapter Twenty-Nine

"B'lyad!" Yuri swore as he stared up through the chimney at the black sky outside. He unscrewed the silencer and slipped it back into his pocket. He tucked the gun into the holster and stepped out of the hearth. Clouds of soot flew out around him, coating the inside of his nose and mouth with a thick layer of dust. His chest tightened, and he fumbled for his handkerchief.

She's heading to Istanbul, is she? He recalled the conversation heard through the closet door.

There was still a chance to finish the job. He had a few connections there, and a blonde American woman should be easy enough to find.

Outside the window, a bright light caught his attention. It crawled along the Kremlin wall and out of sight.

B'lyad! The guards must have found the body.

A sound came from the next room, and Yuri retreated back inside the hearth. A guard entered the room, snapping on his flashlight and moving around the room. Yuri's gaze followed him as he passed in front of a window.

He was young. Probably twenty. A big kid. His rifle hung from his shoulder, and a pistol was sheathed at his hip.

Yuri pulled out his own gun and quietly checked its chamber. One bullet left. Just one chance to take him out.

He retrieved the silencer from his pocket and quietly screwed it back into place.

The guard, only a few steps away now, walked casually, stopping to look at things in the room, picking up a book or running his hand over a velvet settee.

Yuri hunched down. As the guard neared the fireplace, he lunged at him, grabbing him around the knees and thrusting forward, and the guard toppled over to the ash-covered floor. The flashlight flew from the guard's hand, spinning across the floor.

Before he could roll over, Yuri crawled up the young guard's body and pushed the barrel of his gun under his chin. One muffled pop, and the boy crumpled beneath him, dead.

A perfect kill.

Yuri rolled off the body, stood, and took off his chauffeur's jacket. He pulled the guard's coat off and shook out the soot before squeezing into it. It was a tight fit, but it would work. He tucked his handkerchief into its side pocket before tossing his own jacket into the fireplace, then he picked up the guard's hat and pulled it down low over his head, hiding the black headscarf the best he could.

A smirk contorted Yuri's face as he studied the body lying at his feet. He chuckled at the sight.

Send a boy to do a man's job.

Yuri placed his gun back in his shoulder holster, and the silencer in his coat pocket. He knew this guard's death would anger the cardinal, but at the moment, he faced a much more dangerous situation. It would be a lot harder to get out of Russia now, but he knew where Kraft was going, and that information made him much more valuable to the cardinal.

Yuri picked up the guard's rifle, pistol, and his flashlight, and headed for the service entrance.

Chapter Thirty

Nicolai rammed his foot against the heavy inner door of the Terem Palace when Sarah hobbled into the turret. On the third try, the lock broke, and the door swung open. They entered a large room with low vaulted ceilings and blood-red walls covered with murals of Orthodox saints with vacant black eyes. Triangles of light—yellow, pink, and purple—danced around the room as spotlights from outside rolled over the stained glass windows.

"There's a secret tunnel in the throne room leading to the river," Nicolai said. "If we hurry, we can beat the guards." Sarah ignored the pain in her ankle and followed him down the grand staircase to the lower floors.

The rooms grew darker the deeper into the palace they went, and the air changed, becoming thick and hard to breathe. A crushing pain grew inside Sarah, constricting her lungs until she gasped for breath.

Something strange was happening to Sarah. The atmosphere in the room was heavy, as if she were underwater and her attempts to yell failed. Her words came as whispers, soft and unintelligible. She struggled to move or even breathe, and she fell behind Nicolai.

Outside, sirens screamed like banshees all around the Kremlin. They penetrated the room until she could no longer hear anything else.

When she crossed the threshold into the next room, Sarah's vision blurred, and the space around her spun. Objects morphed into shapeless forms and light and shadow blended together until she could no longer determine where one began and the other ended. With outstretched arms, she felt her way through this strange place.

As she struggled to find her way into the next room, an invisible force gripped Sarah's twisted ankle and yanked her leg backward. She fell face down on the floor. Her fingers dug into the tattered carpet and broke the brittle fibers apart under her fingernails as she struggled to crawl to the door where Nicolai had exited.

The sense of being underwater faded away, and Sarah heard voices. Many voices. The spinning sensation gradually slowed to a stop and, as her vision returned, a strange sight appeared before her. Dozens of elaborately decorated velvet shoes shuffled around her. She lay on the floor as a cacophony of brass bells filled the room.

What's happening to me? She shook her head to rid herself of the strange feeling, but it didn't go away. She got to her knees, then forced herself to a standing position.

People dressed in royal clothes gathered around her, ignoring Sarah to see past her to a man and woman kneeling before an Orthodox priest. The woman wore a white damask gown with fur cuffs and collar, and the groom wore a dark green kaftan. His long white beard shook every time he nodded his head.

Sarah strained to see through the crowd to a vast mural on the wall and realized it depicted an exact replica of the ceremony taking place before her. The Orthodox priest, the woman in white damask, and the bearded groom in his green kaftan were all represented in the mural. Even the faces of their guests were seen in the painting, and Sarah realized she was seeing the spirits of the people who had witnessed this ritual hundreds of years ago.

The priest stood over the woman and her groom, his hand raised in a blessing as he announced, "Ivan and Sophia, Emperor and Empress of all of Russia." His voice was deep and somber, and he spoke in a language foreign to Sarah, yet one she somehow easily understood. The groom lifted the bride's veil, and her luminous dark eyes searched the room until she found Sarah in the crowd.

The woman studied her, and Sarah found she couldn't speak or move under the woman's intense gaze. It was the only real connection she felt in this surreal world.

Sarah moved through the crowd toward the bride, drawn to the mysterious woman. No one else seemed to notice.

An icy sensation flooded her body, and the powerful stench of a decomposing body filled the room. Sarah feared she'd pass out. She tried to scream, but nothing came out.

Everyone in the room—the priest, the emperor, and the woman with the black eyes—screamed "Nooo!" at the same time, then they all vanished in a flash and Sarah found herself alone in the room.

The invisible hand returned, now on her back. It pushed her forward, and she tripped and crashed to the floor. A moldy stench flowed over her, and an unseen force crawled up her body to pin her to the carpet. It poked and prodded her until she felt she'd been stabbed a hundred times over. She strained to break free, but the evil force held her down.

"Sarah!" Nicolai's muffled voice cut through the fog in her head. "Sarah!"

"I'm here!" Her own voice was muted and distant.

"Come on!" he yelled, the sound broke through her muddled senses and she glanced up to find Nicolai standing in the doorway to the next room.

"I found the tunnel!" He called to her.

Sarah's head cleared as the hands ceased their torture and dissipated into nothingness. She got to her knees, stood, and limped to the doorway.

When she entered the room, Nicolai was holding open a small door wide enough for only one person to pass through at a time. Hidden behind a curtain hung behind the royal throne, it was a secret escape for the ancient tsars.

"Quick, in here."

Nicolai disappeared through the opening, and Sarah followed as the sound of the guards stomping across the floor could be heard in the next room. She had just enough time to glimpse a staircase descending into a dark tunnel before the little door clicked shut behind her, and they were cast into darkness.

Chapter Thirty-One

Vatican City

"I don't want to be disturbed. Understand?"

The young nun nodded and lowered her gaze as she handed Max his dinner tray. Barely fifteen, the novice was the youngest yet to serve his household. As she walked away, he imagined her unclothed body underneath her habit. The cuts from her last punishment must have scarred by now.

Max set the tray and the newspaper on his desk and sat down. The steak appeared overcooked again. He picked up his knife, stabbed the tough meat, then pushed the plate away in disgust.

A headline on the paper's front page caught his attention: *"Two Bodies Found Murdered during Kremlin State Reception."*

Yuri and Kraft?

He scanned the rest of the article, but no details were offered. He hadn't heard from the punch-drunk fool for nearly a week, and he was worried. If the Russians caught either of them, there was no doubt the cross would disappear forever, and Max would miss his second chance at the papacy.

The phone rang, startling Max back to the present. He picked up the receiver. "Yes?"

"Cardinal?" a gruff voice said.

"Have you got the cross?" Max recognized Yuri's

voice. "I saw a headline about two murders. I was afraid you'd been caught."

"No, those were guards."

"You killed two Kremlin guards?"

"Only one. Your woman took care of the other one."

"Kraft?" This surprised Max.

"She had help."

"Who?" he demanded. "She was supposed to be alone."

"She has a boyfriend."

Max ignored this new bit of information and moved on to what he really wanted to know. "Did you get the cross?"

"Not yet," Yuri wheezed.

"What do you mean?" Anger darkened his voice.

"She has it, but I know where she's headed, and I can get the cross from her there."

"You lost it?" Max exploded. "You idiot!"

Yuri went silent for a moment. When he did speak, his words came low and threatening. "Listen, you arrogant bastard, I told you. You'll get your little trinket. Just shut up and do as I tell you."

"How dare you—"

"Do you want the cross or not?"

The finality of his words checked Max's anger. No one had ever spoken to him like that, and Max sensed he was losing his control over Yuri. "What do you want?"

"You will meet me in Istanbul with the money you owe me, plus a million American dollars. I'll get the cross from her there."

"No, absolutely not!"

"You've got two days," Yuri continued, ignoring his outburst. "Bring me the money, or you can forget the cross."

Max took a moment to consider Yuri's demands. "What guarantee will you give me? You've already let her slip through your fingers once."

"You'll get it," Yuri assured him. "You forget there's another prize for me. I want the girl."

Max was both disgusted and intrigued by the thought. "Contact me tomorrow, and I'll let you know where we'll meet."

"Two days," said Yuri, and the line went dead.

Max slammed the receiver down in the cradle. *That lowlife. That peasant! He thinks he can tell me what to do? Blackmailing me—ME!* He swept his arm across the desk, scattering everything onto the floor. Dishes, food, and papers littered the room.

Max stomped to the door and ordered the young nun into the room. He grabbed her by the shoulders and pushed her toward the desk.

"You see that pile of garbage you served me?" He forced her head down to view the mess on the floor, and her white coif fell off. Thick auburn hair fell in waves around the girl's shoulders. Max grabbed a fistful and yanked her head backward against his body, exposing her neck.

"Is this why you've come to my house?" he whispered into her ear. "To tempt me?"

"No, Your Excellency," she said through tears.

Max shoved her to the floor. "Clean it up."

She gathered the papers and nudged the food back onto the plate. When she finished, she stood up and faced him, her gaze downcast, whimpering.

"Put it on the table," Max murmured, and she did as she was told. "Now, lift your skirt." Slowly, the young nun lifted her black robe. "Higher." She pulled the hem up past her knees and exposed an elaborate pattern of scarred tissue covering her legs from the knees down to her ankles.

"It has healed nicely. Don't you think?" Max pointed to the center of the room. "Someday, I hope I won't need to do this."

The nun shuffled to the middle of the room and stood on a metal heating grate. When she turned to face Max, tears filled her hazel eyes.

"Be brave, little one." Max smiled. "It's only through our penance that we come to know the true grace of God."

Her head bent again, and Max waited as she studied the lines of the grate. They matched the marks on her legs.

"Kneel."

The girl reluctantly dropped to her knees, and Max watched the pain in her face grow as the full weight of her body pressed down on the thin metal brackets. She bent her head to pray, but her Hail Mary was broken by the sound of her crying.

Max walked across the room to the thermostat and twisted the dial. A whoosh of hot air rumbled through the floor to the grate, and he smiled as the girl's dress filled with air.

It's as if she were a flower blooming in the middle of my room.

He only wished he could see her face.

Chapter Thirty-Two

Ukraine

Frost coated the boxcar's door, but Nicolai didn't notice when he grabbed the latch. After spending the night bouncing around inside the freight train, his whole body was numb.

He bumped against the door, and the seal broke. It slid open, and cold wind blew in, stirring the leaves into a little tornado inside the empty car. He braced himself against the door as he watched the world roll by outside.

The rising sun colored the clouds orange and pink. A river cut through golden wheat fields and curved around a rise in the land before disappearing into a birch forest. A beautiful sight, but one that only served to darken Nicolai's already bad mood.

He checked his watch. If this train was on time, they had crossed Russia's southern border about an hour ago. Nicolai searched for landmarks he might recognize.

Seven years ago, he and his brother Jakob fought the Nazis near here at the Battle of Kursk. Memories of that terrible time still haunted him, and he leaned out of the train and peered back down the tracks. His brother Jakob's grave lay out there somewhere. He'd died taking a bullet for Nicolai, leaving his older brother the last surviving member of their family.

Nicolai took a deep breath of the cool early-morning air, but it did nothing to lighten his darkening mood.

I have nothing now. No family, no home. And for what?

Nicolai glanced back at Sarah asleep on a pile of dirty tarps.

She'd surprised him during their escape from Moscow. She found the delivery truck they'd used to speed across the city and then acted as lookout as they skirted the authorities. They'd raced through backstreets and alleys to a freight yard on Moscow's south side, where they hopped a train heading south to Odessa on the Black Sea. Hidden inside an empty boxcar, they settled in for a restless night of travel.

Now, he only saw Sarah as an annoyance. An obstacle he wanted to leave far behind as he figured out what to do next.

He turned back to the fields, gliding past the open door.

Moscow is out of the question.

The KGB would have gone through his apartment by now, gathering names, finding his cache of photos and everything he'd worked for over the last five years. All of it gone so some rich collector could have a dead emperor's little cross—something a peasant could have made.

The thought had rattled around inside his head for hours, triggering his resentment toward Sarah and feeding his anger. He knew the situation they were in wasn't her fault, but all he could think about was getting as far away from her as possible.

"Where are we?" Sarah's voice cracked behind him.

Nicolai glanced over his shoulder and watched Sarah stumble toward him, fighting against the sway of the train. He pointed outside to a bridge further down the tracks next to a town with a church capped by bright-blue onion domes. "The train will stop there. Can you jump?" he yelled over the noise of the train.

Sarah nodded. "My ankle barely aches anymore."

"Good. We need to get off before the bridge. The engine will have to pick up speed on the other side to get up the hill."

"I can do it," Sarah said.

When the train neared the bridge, Nicolai pointed to a flat patch of tall, deep grass along the tracks ahead. He grabbed Sarah's hand and shouted, "One, two—" They jumped on three. Their hands separated when they hit the ground, and they rolled into two heaps next to a field.

Nicolai lay flat on his back with his eyes closed, listening to the train rolling down the tracks. The grass was cool and wet with dew, and when he ran his fingers across the blades, they slipped through his fingers like silk. It felt good to be still again.

"Nicolai?" A shadow passed over him. "Are you okay?"

He opened his eyes and Sarah stood above him. He rolled over onto his side and stood up.

"Yuck!" She ran her hand over the old wool coat he'd stolen at the train station and given to her. She held up a dirty hand. "I landed in a mud puddle."

"Think of the dirt as a souvenir," Nicolai said as he flicked his hands over his own coat and brushed himself off.

"What now? I guess we hike around the city and get back on another train?"

"That's what I would do."

"I wonder how many more miles until we reach Odessa."

Nicolai bent over and swept his hand through the grass to find his hat. "Once you get to Kyiv, look for a fully loaded train. They won't stop for freight along the way, so you'll travel faster with less chance of getting caught."

He couldn't meet her eyes, and the realization irritated him, so he kicked around at the grass. His hat had to be here somewhere.

"You should avoid towns if you can," he went on, "They're all small around here, and people will recognize a new face."

He stole a glance at Sarah and saw alarm on her face. "You're leaving me?"

"Yes."

"But you were supposed to get me out of Russia." Her hands went to her hips. "That is your assignment."

"And I have." He stretched his arms wide. "Welcome to beautiful Ukraine."

"But I don't know where I'm going. I have no money, no passport. All my papers are in Moscow!"

"You're smart. You'll find your way there." He kicked at the grass until he glimpsed the brown felt brim of his fedora. He picked it up and slapped the hat against his thigh a few times to shake off the dirt.

"I'm sure the CIA will pay you whatever you want."

"Pay me?" He laughed. "I've lost more than money on this little adventure of yours."

"What are you talking about?" Sarah asked.

"I'll never be able to go back to Moscow now. I'd be lucky if MI6 will have me." He closed the space between them in two steps, tapping at the cross inside her coat pocket. "My entire network, exposed because of that damn cross." She backed away, so Nicolai grabbed her by the arm and spun her around. "Tell me!"

"Tell you what?"

"Why is the cross is so important," Nicolai pressed. "Tell me!"

Sarah's face went blank. Emotionless. Nicolai recognized the look as the expression of a professional agent. One that gave no hints about the secrets locked inside her head.

Sarah wrenched her arm free. "Thanks for getting me this far." She pulled up the collar of her coat, shot one last defiant look at Nicolai, and took a step to leave.

Nicolai gripped her arm and pulled her back. "You're not going anywhere until you tell me why your people want the cross. You owe me that much."

"I don't owe you anything!" Sarah's blue eyes blazed with anger. "You're doing your job, just like I am! You know the risks. There's always a chance something could go wrong." She twisted her arm to wrench it free of his grip, but he held on. "Let me go!"

Her voice reached a desperate pitch, but Nicolai didn't care. *I lost everything. She owes me an explanation.*

They remained there, eyes locked, until her body finally relaxed.

"I've got to know why," he said again.

"I can't. I'm sorry, but I just can't right now." He loosened his grip and she pulled her arm away. "But if you help me, I'll tell you as soon as the cross is safe. I promise."

"Why should I believe you?" he challenged.

Sarah glanced away, then back to Nicolai and sighed. "Because I understand what you've lost. I lost the same thing once too."

"You?"

"You were right when you said the CIA got rid of all their female agents. They only brought me back for this job. If I'm successful, they'll bring me on permanently, and I'll do my best to get you on with the agency too." Her words were tinged with hope.

Nicolai felt the weight of her stare as she waited for him to react. *Can I trust her?* Her gaze met his without flinching. She seemed sincere.

Sarah needed his help. *Maybe I need hers as well.*

He gazed back up the tracks—to Russia, his home. His past. There was no future left for him there.

If Sarah can get the CIA to take me on as an agent, I might have a chance to start over.

He sighed.

What choice do I have? If I can get her to Istanbul, at least I'll be able to prove my loyalty to the Americans.

"All right, you win," Nicolai finally relented. He faced the small village ahead, his back to Russssia—his homeland. "I'll take you to Istanbul."

Chapter Thirty-Three

Sarah heard the noise first. The crunch of footsteps on dried leaves littering the forest floor. The sound came from behind but caught up to Sarah and Nicolai in seconds until it surrounded them on three sides.

"On the left," she whispered to Nicolai.

He nodded to his right. "Over there, too."

They'd entered the heavy cover of a leafy birch forest, following a path through a dense stand of trees. The route felt much safer after the anxiety of crossing too many open fields, but after an hour they found themselves the prey of an invisible threat.

"What do you think it is?" Sarah asked.

"Vagabonds. Outlaws, maybe," Nicolai said. "Let's keep walking and see what they do. Is there any bread left?"

Sarah searched her pocket and found the loaf Nicolai had purchased with his last ruble. "This is the end of it." She tore the crust in half and handed him a piece.

"It's enough," he said as he took a bite.

Nicolai barely spoke to her since they left the train. It was an uncomfortable existence. She sympathized with him about losing the life he must have built in Moscow. *But what's done is done.* She had the cross to think about now. It was her responsibility to get it to safety, and she couldn't fail. Even when things went sideways, they still had a job to do, no matter the consequences. They were professionals, after all.

Sarah bit into her half. It had no taste. She was tired and knew Nicolai was too. They'd walked ten hours since they jumped from the train. Her feet were throbbing and their fight from earlier still bothered her. Despite this, Sarah's twisted ankle was no longer painful. Within hours of their escape from the Kremlin, the throbbing in Sarah's ankle dissipated completely as if the injury never occurred.

Maybe this cross really does have the power to heal.

The crunch of a broken twig drew her attention to their left. Sarah's hand instinctively tightened around the cross inside her pocket. "Did you hear that?"

"I heard it."

"I count ten," Sarah said. "They move so fast." A new noise came from the right. A feigned bird call, amateurish in its execution, but when another high-pitched chirp answered, Sarah and Nicolai knew they had to act.

They froze and turned back-to-back. Nicolai called out in Russian, and a chorus of giggles materialized all around them.

A flash of red ran between the trees, and a girl suddenly popped out onto the trail to block their path. Around twelve years old, she wore a bright red, floor-length skirt and a long-sleeved, dark green blouse under a patchwork vest. A tangled braid held back long black hair and swung behind her every time she moved. She scrutinized Sarah and Nicolai up and down, her keen dark eyes taking in every detail. She spoke Russian but had a strange accent, making the words difficult for Sarah to understand.

"What did she say?" she asked Nicolai.

"She's asking if we are snow people."

He asked the girl a question, then translated for Sarah. "Her name is Meera. She belongs to a camp near here."

Nicolai asked another question, and the girl answered in her high-pitched voice.

"Ah," he said. "They're from a Romani camp about a mile from here—gypsies passing through the area to clean the fields after the harvest. The children are scavenging the forest for dinner."

"What are snow people?" Sarah asked and Nicolai asked the girl.

Nicolai shrugged. "Us, apparently. She thinks we are people who travel south during winter. We're supposed to bring the snow." He asked Meera a question, then added, "It's a bedtime story their mothers tell them." The girl pointed to Nicolai's arm. "It explains our light skin," he added.

He gestured to the basket in Meera's hand and asked if she would mind sharing the berries she'd picked, but instead of answering, the girl yelled into the woods, and more children came bounding out of the trees. They all had the same black hair and intelligent eyes Meera had, a few of the younger faces smeared blue with juice from the berries they'd been eating.

Nicolai said something to Meera, who answered him excitedly. "She says her mother, Viviana, is the camp leader and would want to meet us. Maybe we can get something to eat from her."

A little boy around five years old wrapped Sarah's wrist in both his hands and tugged her along with him. All the children crowded around them. They talked over each other as they led Sarah and Nicolai through the forest. The bravest of the group took turns touching their skin and hair, investigating whether these strangers were as cold as ice like the story said.

"Let's hope the adults are as friendly as their children," Sarah took the little boy's hand in hers and gave it a squeeze. "I'm starving."

****

The camp was unlike any Sarah had ever seen. Located inside a clearing in the forest, thirteen barrel-shaped wagons painted red, green, and yellow and decorated with landscape scenes formed a circle around a small bonfire. Steps at the back end of wagon led to a porch with a little door.

Meera told them to wait outside the camp until her mother invited them in, so Sarah rested against a tree and watched as the children ran to find their mothers.

"Do you think they'll give us some food?" Sarah's stomach growled loudly as she breathed in the rich smell of spices coming from the camp.

"I hope so." Nicolai sat down on a stump.

The women inside the camp, alerted by their children, straightened up from their work and peered at the strangers. The tallest woman broke away from the group and stormed across the camp. The other women followed, shouting and shaking their fists in the air.

"Let me handle this," Nicolai said, getting to his feet. When the first woman reached them, he took off his hat and bowed at the waist. "Good evening, madam," he said in Russian. "We are tired travelers seeking a safe place to rest tonight."

"No!" the woman shouted. She pointed her finger past them to the forest. "You go now!"

"Please, madam," Nicolai begged. "Just a bit of food and a place to sleep. I promise we mean you no harm."

"No! You lie. You are a government man, and you have taken enough from the Romani."

"No, no, no." Nicolai shook his head. "We're only runaways traveling to the coast."

The word *runaways* caught the woman's attention, and her eyes narrowed as she scrutinized both of them closely. "The farmer gave us permission to stay here while our men clean his fields," she insisted, but Sarah sensed a hesitation in her words.

"We only ask for something to eat and a place to lay our heads. We'll leave before sunrise."

The women glanced at each other, then back to Sarah and Nicolai until, finally, the tall woman shook her head again. "No. We want no trouble. You must go."

Sarah ran her hand up and down the lapel of her coat, and her fingers caught on something hard sticking out of the fabric.

The diamond earrings.

Nicolai gave them to her to wear to the ball. During their escape, she'd pinned them to the back of her collar for safekeeping and forgotten them.

Until now.

"We can trade," she said, unpinning one and holding it up to the women. "For food and a bed for the night."

All the women surrounded them to examine the jewel in her hand. "Stolen?" one woman asked.

Sarah shook her head. "A gift." She didn't dare look at Nicolai.

The woman reached out to pluck the diamond from her hand, but Sarah snatched her hand away before she could pick up the earring. The woman grimaced and turned away to consult with the group.

Sarah caught sight of Nicolai's brooding expression and shrugged.

He can't be mad at me. He may have loaned her the jewelry, but he destroyed the matching ring.

"I believe you," the woman said when the group broke apart. She nodded toward Nicolai and smirking, said, "A government man wears his jewels on the outside and his dirt on the inside." She brushed a hand across Sarah's filthy coat. "You wear your dirt outside and hide your jewels inside." The woman cackled with delight at her observation, and the Romani women laughed with her.

"You can share our dinner and sleep in our camp." She held up a finger. "One night, then you must go."

Sarah opened her palm, but as the woman picked up the diamond, her fingertips grazed Sarah's hand, and a strange expression came over her face. She snatched her hand back with the diamond and squinted at Sarah.

"First, you must have a reading," she said. "Follow me."

She pushed her way through the crowd and into the camp, and the women trailed after her.

Sarah whispered to Nicolai, "What just happened?"

"It seems you just gave my diamond away."

"Oh, I'm sorry," Sarah quipped as they fell into step behind the group. "Were you planning to wear them to another ball?"

"Well, don't give the other earring away so fast. We may need it to buy passage when we get to Odessa. That diamond the only thing we have that's worth anything."

Sarah's hand slipped into her coat pocket and wrapped her hand around the cross.

Chapter Thirty-Four

The woman led Sarah and Nicolai across the camp, past the bonfire to a rickety old wagon.

"Wait here," she told them when they reached the porch. She climbed the steps, knocked, and then disappeared inside.

"What's going on?" Sarah whispered as the other women gathered in a circle around them. Nicolai could only shrug before the woman reappeared in the doorway to wave them inside.

The wagon creaked and swayed as Sarah climbed the steps. Smoke from burning incense filled the interior, nearly choking her when she stepped into the cramped space. A lantern burned low at the opposite end of the wagon. It provided enough light to view the stoic faces of Romani ancestors in black-and-white photographs hanging on each side of the wagon. They swayed on their hooks as the wagon's carriage shifted under Sarah's feet.

Just like a haunted house.

A bench built into the left side of the wagon led back to a platform where a tiny, withered body rose like an apparition from underneath a pile of patched quilts. Sarah recoiled at the sight. The figure moved, and a woman, crippled and wasting away, faced them. Gray hair twisted into a long, thin braid fell over her left shoulder and coiled in her lap. Tired green eyes gazed out from a face crisscrossed by wrinkles, and when she spoke, her voice came as no more than a whisper.

The younger woman closed the door behind them, and the light in the room dimmed. Sarah heard the click of a lock, and as her eyes adjusted to the dark, she saw the old woman pick up a half-smoked cigarette from an ashtray and put the butt between her dry, cracked lips.

"Sit," the woman ordered as she lit a candle next to the bed. "My name is Viviana, and this is Grandmother Rosa." She blew out the match and sat down across from Sarah. "She has the gift of sight and can see into the past. She will begin your reading now."

"My reading?"

"Shh!" Viviana quieted her. "Let her speak."

The old woman grimaced in pain as she settled back against a stack of pillows. A cough racked her frail body, and she wrapped her arms around her chest as she shuddered in pain. Sarah could almost see bones in her tiny body break with each cough. After recovering, she held out an arthritic hand to Sarah.

"Give her your hand," Viviana instructed.

The old woman clasped ice cold fingers around Sarah's wrist and rotated her palm up. She huddled closer, and her eyes glazed over as she mumbled a torrent of unintelligible words.

Faster and faster the words came until, as if in a dream, and Sarah felt her consciousness slipping away. Her vision blurred, sounds echoing from far away, and her thoughts changed to nothing more than a jumbled mass of disconnected words. Alarmed, Sarah drew her hand back, trying in vain to break the hold this old woman had on her. But her body was too weak to move. The Romani grandmother had complete control over her.

Sarah panicked.

"Sophia!" the old woman screeched. A tremor swept through the wagon, like a bell had just been rung. The sensation collided with Sarah's body, vibrating inside her and making her shiver uncontrollably.

"My name is—"

"Shh!" Viviana hushed her. "Only Grandmother speaks now."

"Sophia, Sophia, Sophia!" the old woman chanted. Her voice grew stronger, louder, each time she said the name.

A breeze blew through the wagon and caught the candle's flame, sending it into a spasm of sparkling light. It flickered across the photographs around the wagon and animated the grim expressions of the Romani ancestors.

Sarah felt disconnected and weightless, as if her body was split into a million tiny pieces flying freely around the room. The wagon and everything around her faded away, and a black void swallowed her whole.

"What's happening?" Her voice sounded thin and distant to her own ears.

When the light returned, Sarah found herself standing in a large, blood-red room with low arches and images of Orthodox saints painted on the walls. Diamond-shaped lights dotted the floor beneath her feet, and Sarah recognized the room instantly.

The Kremlin's Terem Palace. The room was decorated exactly as it had been during their escape from Moscow. The thought of those invisible hands clawing their way up her body made her want to run, but she couldn't move.

"Princess Sophia," a voice whispered, but the pitch and tone had changed from the old woman's smoky whisper. Instead, the words came clear and strong—

young and robust.

"Princess Sophia?"

Sarah's back straightened into a regal pose, and she heard herself say, "Yes. Come." Her own voice no longer sounded familiar, and the words she spoke were of an ancient language she only understood intuitively, as if she'd spoken the words all her life. Subconsciously, Sarah realized her reality had merged with the spirit of Princess Sophia, the first empress of Imperial Russia.

A young woman appeared beside her and said, "Princess Sophia." Sarah recognized her, somehow, as the spirit of the old woman, now in the body of a servant. "The tsar awaits your arrival. The wedding ceremony will start soon."

"I am ready," she answered as the princess.

"You will become Russia's first empress, my lady."

"Yes. To a young and flourishing empire."

"Your marriage will legitimize the crown."

"And secure the legacy of my ancestors."

Sarah felt herself walking across the room to peer out the window. Through the eyes of the princess, she surveyed the peasants in the snowy courtyard below as they waited for their first glimpse of their new empress.

"With this crown, I will build a New Byzantium!" Sarah's fist hit her chest as Sophia made her vow. "An empire built on the shoulders of my children!"

Sophia, in Sarah's body, moved to a table where a gold box with a two-headed eagle made of rubies sat in its center.

The box from the Kremlin Museum!

Sophia—and Sarah within—ran her finger along the sides of the gold coffer and lifted the lid. There, on the pillow made of purple silk, lay the Byzantine Cross.

"Noah's cross," Sarah heard Sophia say. She picked up the cross and cradled it in her hands. "He rebuilt the world from the wood of his ark, and with his cross, I will rebuild the greatest empire man has ever seen."

"The tsar awaits," the servant reminded her gently.

Sophia handed the cross to the servant, who wound a length of gold cord around its cross section and then tied the cord around Sophia's neck.

"You are ready, my lady," the woman announced.

The time had arrived.

"On this day, I will become empress of Russia, the deliverer of Byzantium to a new imperial realm." Sophia's words rang inside Sarah's head.

As the scene played out in Sarah's mind, a heavy weight lowered down upon her shoulders. She glimpsed a flash of white and peered down, and instead of the frayed, woolen coat she'd been wearing, a white tunic with an elaborate pattern sewn with silver threads flowed around her.

"Your descendants will become rulers of a great land," the servant declared as she placed the crown of the new Imperial Russia on Sophia's head. Its heaviness caused her neck to bow, but when Sarah reached up to adjust it, her hand met nothing but empty space.

The servant stepped back so Sarah could view herself in the mirror, but it was Princess Sophia's reflection who gazed back at her. A tall, regal woman with black hair, full lips, and intelligent, luminous dark eyes.

"God walks beside you on your journey," the servant said.

An icy wind blew in, and a jarring, pulsing vibration overtook the room. The tremors rattled through the

164

wagon and then faded to stillness, and everything went black.

Sarah hung in the void again. Suspended in a dark, empty space. Floating in nothingness—becoming nothingness itself.

Sharp pain inched up her body. Piercing talons, poking and pinching her flesh in the same way the invisible fingers had dug into her skin in the Terem Palace. Sarah cried out in pain.

"Rasssputin!" The old Romani grandmother's face floated before her and then vanished. Sarah screamed for help, but the words were swallowed up inside the void.

"Rasputin!" the grandmother hissed again. "Rasssputin!"

The servant's face materialized in front of Sarah, only to morph into something else. Someone else. The angles of the woman's cheekbones grew sharp, and her nose lengthened. Greasy whiskers appeared on the face and grew into a beard, and stringy, dirty hair framed a skeletal face. The apparition's eyes popped open, and two vibrant, glowing light-blue orbs stared unblinkingly out from the darkness.

Rasputin!

Before Sarah could react, the apparition inhabiting the grandmother's body reached into Sarah's coat pocket and grabbed the Byzantine Cross with the old woman's withered hand.

"No!" Sophia yelled through Sarah. "He must not have it!"

"It belongs to me!" Rasputin bellowed, his words faint and garbled as if spoken underwater as he fought to wrestle the cross away from Sarah's grasp.

"It must go back to the ark!" the princess wailed

from somewhere in the void.

The cross scraped against Sarah's palm as her fingers were forced closed around the hard wooden shape. Heat radiated from the cross and burned her skin until she cried out in pain.

"It is you who must return the Byzantine Cross!" Sophia commanded.

The invisible hands pried and clawed at her fingers, but she gripped the cross tighter, refusing to let go.

"The cross is mine!" Rasputin's voice echoed inside her head.

Sarah's consciousness spun wildly in the void, untethered to reality, trapped somewhere between the past and the present. Unable to break the spell.

Scuffling sounds filtered into the trance from far away, and Sarah fell against a soft, unyeilding surface. She heard rhythmic beating, faint but strong, as her body soared high into the air. A bang reverberated through her body, and a cool, soothing breeze blew over her.

"Sarah!" a new deep voice called out to her. "Sarah!"

The faint beating grew louder until it drowned out all the other sounds.

A heartbeat? The fog she drifted in lifted, and her confused senses settled upon Nicolai's worried face above her.

"Sarah!"

Light flashed across her face, and her fingers dragged through the dirt. She looked around, dazed. She was outside,on the ground with the shattered door of the wagon scattered in pieces all around her.

"Sarah?" Nicolai smoothed her hair back from her face. "Are you okay?"

She nodded weakly and relaxed into his arms. She was safe.

Nicolai is here—with me. Out of the old woman's trance and back in the camp with the Romani.

He lifted her hand still holding the cross and eased open her fingers. "It's the cross, isn't it? We stole the Byzantine Cross."

Before she could answer, the old woman peered down from the steps of the wagon, her bony hands grasping the broken doorframe to hold up her fragile body. Her breathing was strained and her voice cracked when she said, "You must take the cross back."

"To Russia?" Sarah asked.

"No!" She nearly choked on the word. "To the ark. The ark! It is the only way to rid the Byzantine Cross of its curse."

"What curse?"

"Rasputin's curse. His spirit attached itself to the cross and corrupts its powers. If you do not return the cross to its home, his power will grow until no one can stop his cruelty."

Sarah opened her mouth to protest, but the woman raised a hand to silence her.

"You must rid the cross of his evil, or you will be the one who is cursed."

Chapter Thirty-Five

"Sarah!" Nicolai called as he followed the path to the river. "Sarah!" He almost tripped over her, sitting alone in the tall grass next to the river. "There you are. I've been looking for you."

"The women wouldn't stop staring at me after what happened in the wagon, so I came out here." Sarah scooted to the edge of the blanket and Nicolai sat down next to her. "They were looking at me as if I had two horns sprouting out of my head."

"The men gave me some of their vodka." He unscrewed the lid from a glass jar and handed it to Sarah. "It's strong but not too bad." After two glasses of the homemade liquor with the men, Nicolai already felt a warmth settling over him. *Perfect on a cold night like tonight.*

Sarah grimaced as she took a sip, then handed the jar back. "I hope you like camping. The women are so scared of me they don't want me near their wagons."

"I like it here by the river better." Nicolai propped himself on his elbow, stretched out his legs, and glanced up at the sky. "Look at all those stars. I'd forgotten how many you can see in the country."

Sarah didn't speak, so he handed her the jar again. Even in the moonlight, he could see the tension on her face. "How are you doing?"

"Better." Sarah swirled the liquid around before

taking another drink. "This helps."

"They said their vodka could solve any problem."

She handed the jar back without meeting his gaze. "I don't know if it'll solve mine."

"Do you want to talk about what happened?" He screwed the lid back on the jar and set it in the grass, then plucked a stem to roll back and forth between his fingers.

Sarah blew out a deep sigh. "I wouldn't know where to begin."

"Just tell me what you saw."

"It's all so muddled." She closed her eyes. "I was in the Terem Palace. The red walls, the colored windows—everything was the same, just newer. Like it'd just been built. And other people were there. Servants, I think. But the strangest part—" She shook her head and frowned. "I don't know—I felt like I was myself but also someone else at the same time. A woman named Princess Sophia."

"You were mumbling something," he prompted. "Do you remember what you said?"

"I remember a conversation. With a servant. She was dressing me—but it wasn't really me." She flopped back down on the blanket. "The whole thing is so confusing."

"The old woman said something about a wedding."

"That's right." Sarah sat up. "To Ivan the Great."

"He married a Byzantine princess named Sophia," Nicolai rubbed the stubble covering his jaw. "Do you think that's who you're talking about?"

"Yes!" Sarah sat up. "She was the one who took the cross to Russia, and she wanted to use the cross to rebuild the Byzantine empire. She said she'd rebuild her empire like Noah rebuilt the world after the flood."

"Noah?" He waited for her to go on, but she

remained silent. "What do you think she meant?"

"I don't know." She paused, then shook her head. "It just doesn't make any sense. I know the legend of its power to heal, but how could a little cross rebuild anything?" She rubbed her eyes. "It was all so strange."

She was silent for a moment and Nicolai could see she was struggling to recall the details.

Sarah glanced up at the stars. "There is something else I haven't told you."

Nicolai threw the blade of grass to the side and sat up to face her. "What?"

"When we were in the Terem Palace and I fell just before we reached the escape tunnel, and I felt something. Something I felt again in the wagon."

"What did you feel?" Nicolai asked.

She ran a hand down her side where the feeling of the stabbing talons still lingered. "Something was digging into my sides. Fingers, maybe." She shook her head. "I don't know what it was, but it grabbed me and held me down."

"And you felt the same thing happening during the trance?"She nodded, and Nicolai saw a tear sparkle in the moonlight and roll down her cheek. He resisted the urge to reach out and wipe it away. "What else happened?"

Sarah sat up as another memory from the Terem Palace resurfaced. "I saw the same woman from the trance! The princess! And she saw me too. I'm sure she did!"

"What was she doing?"

Sarah grew quiet as she thought about the scene. "She was getting married. There was a roomful of people, a priest, and the tsar, but she was the only person who could see me. She stared right at me."

"Did she say anything?"

"No. She vanished with the others as soon as those invisible hands started their assault on me."

"Do you remember what happened at the end of the trance? The woman said something I couldn't understand just before your whole face changed…right before you screamed."

"Yes, she kept repeating 'Rasputin, Rasputin, Rasputin' over and over." Sarah remembered the glowing blue orbs floating in the dark void. She closed her eyes and buried her face in her hands, unable to finish the thought.

Did I say something wrong? Nicolai pulled her close and wrapped his arms around her. She laid her head in his shoulder.

"You're shaking." He stroked her hair, letting the silky strands slip through his fingers. She felt so small in his arms. So vulnerable. Yet she'd shown him how tough she could be. She'd faced every challenge and surprised him each time with her courage and resolve. She'd even killed a man twice her size to save his life.

Nicolai didn't pressure her to say anything more. Instead, he held her close and waited until her body relaxed. It didn't take long. Her body grew limp as she fell asleep in his arms. He continued to cradle her for a long time, hoping she felt safe in his arms.

There would be another time to talk about the cross.

And I hope more time to get to know Sarah too.

Chapter Thirty-Six

Istanbul

The cobblestone streets of Istanbul's Old City were empty when the taxicab drew up to the cathedral. Max paid the driver, grabbed the briefcase at his feet, and stepped out of the car. He was already angry.

How dare Feodorov demand I meet him? He failed at his job, and he wants more money? No! He'll get what we agreed on, and that's all. Nobody is going to blackmail me.

Max entered the dark chapel and crept along a corridor deep into the main chamber. When a shadow appeared as if by black magic from behind a column, Max stepped backward, ready to run, but when he saw the ghostly white face of Yuri Feodorov, he stopped.

"You have my money?" the huge man asked.

Max raised the briefcase to his chest.

"Open it."

Max unlocked the briefcase to show him the stacks of hundred-dollar bills. Yuri picked one up. "Where's the rest?"

"Half now, half later when I have the cross in my hands."

"*Nyet.*" Yuri spat out the Russian word. "I want all the money, now."

"I need more time," Max said. "A million American dollars is a lot of money. You'll have to wait for my bank in New York to wire it."

Yuri snatched the briefcase and stomped to the door.

"Wait!" Max raised his hand.

Yuri stopped but didn't turn around.

"You said you could get the cross. But you haven't done delivered on the promise."

Max took a step toward Yuri but halted when the Russian wheeled around to face him. The unbridled hatred in his deep-set eyes frightened Max.

He wants to murder me.

Max changed tactics. "I can get the rest of the money in a few days."

"You said you would have all the money today. Now you want more time? No more games!"

"But remember, that's not all I promised you," Max reminded Yuri. "Don't forget the woman. You want her, too, don't you?"

"You should have brought all the money."

Enough with his demands! He's already getting more than he deserves.

Max struggled to keep his voice low. "You should have brought the cross to me, but you haven't. Instead, you let it slip right through your hands." Max jabbed a finger at Yuri. "You don't deserve a million."

Yuri stepped closer to Max, his huge frame dominating the thinner man. "A million is not enough after Russia!" he shouted into Max's face.

He thinks he can intimidate me? Never! "I can't help it if the guards found them before you did. Besides, maybe you alerted them. From what I've seen, you—"

Yuri seized him around the neck, choking off the sentence before he could finish. Max's hands scrabbled at his throat, gasping as his windpipe closed off.

"I want the rest of the money or no cross. Understand? No more waiting, no more games, or I kill you right here, right now."

Max nodded. Yuri released his grip, and Max dropped to the floor. The thud echoed around the empty chamber.

"Fine," Max choked out as he rubbed his throat. "I'll have the money ready for you tomorrow morning."

"Kraft should arrive here tomorrow. I'll come for you when I find out where she's staying."

Max nodded again.

Yuri emitted a low growl, picked up the briefcase, and lumbered back into the shadows, leaving Max collapsed on the floor.

Chapter Thirty-Seven

Nicolai found Sarah alone in the hotel's empty lounge sitting next to a window. Her head was bent over her coat and her blond hair shone like spun gold in the early morning sunlight streaming in from an open window.

"I'd hoped I hadn't missed you," he said as he crossed the room to her.

"Good morning," Sarah glanced up and smiled. "I didn't want to leave the city without saying goodbye to you." She wound a thread around the needle to anchor a knot in the fabric.

Goodbye. The word sounded so final. "I woke up early and went to the market to buy some new clothes." He opened his arms wide and showed her his new clothes. "What do you think?"

"It takes a hundred miles off you," Sarah joked before she bit the thread and freed the needle from the coat.

"Did you get any sleep?"

"A little."

Nicolai walked to a bar across the room and pulled a bottle from the shelf. "Would you like a drink?"

"What is it?"

"I'll surprise you." He filled two glasses, strolled back to Sarah and handed her the glass. Then he sat down and stretched out in the chair opposite her. "What are you working on?"

Sarah flattened the lining of the old coat over her leg to show him the outline of the cross. "I'm not taking any more chances of losing it."

"Good idea."

She picked up the glass and took a drink. "Whiskey?" she asked.

"Not just any whiskey. The best scotch I've ever had." He took a sip. "The manager told me a Scottish regiment stayed here during the war. I guess they left a little piece of home for us."

"A little early in the day for whiskey, isn't it?"

"Don't American cowgirls drink whiskey?" he teased.

"I only said it was early," she said with a smile before she took another drink.

Her eyes look teal in this light. This was the third time he'd noticed the strange way the blue in her eyes could darken or take on a green shade when her mood shifted. He'd never seen this color before. And he'd never seen her so relaxed before. Happy, even.

It was the exact opposite of what Nicolai felt. Ever since they'd arrived in Istanbul, an unexpected dread plagued him. The mission was over, and soon she would fly back to Rome, and he to London to report to MI6.

Nicolai caught himself staring, so he turned to gaze out the window at Istanbul's skyline. "Such a beautiful city."

"The innkeeper said you're checked in until Friday." Sarah asked as she returned her sewing.

"I think I deserve a vacation. Don't you?"

"Definitely." She pulled the thread tight and looped it back into the coat's lining. The hotel's laundry did a decent job getting most of the dirt and grime off the coat, but its cleanliness didn't make up for its worn and patched look.

"Well, you did it." He held his glass up in a toast. "You got what you came for."

"Don't congratulate me yet," Sarah said. "I've got a lot of miles to cover before I'm rid of this cross."

"Are you leaving right away?"

"Not yet. I need to call my contact at the CIA and arrange a few things before I leave."

"Why don't we go out to lunch, then?" he said, "My treat. I just came from the bank, and I feel rich."

"The bank?"

"MI6 has a bank account set up for me here in case I ever needed it." He gestured out the open window. "I stopped there on my way to the market."

"Well, then, lunch sounds wonderful," Sarah answered, holding up the coat to examine her stitches.

Nicolai's nose crinkled up in disgust. "You're not wearing that dirty rag home, are you?"

"Of course! It's the perfect disguise. Everyone will think I'm too poor to rob."

"*Da,*" he agreed with her logic. "They'll think you're a beggar and run away." He sipped his drink, swirled the glass around, and watched the amber liquid sparkle in the sunlight. "Why don't you let me buy you a few things while we're out?" he offered. "We can go to the Grand Bazaar."

"That's very nice of you," Sarah said. "But you've done so much for me already. I couldn't ask more from you."

"You're not. I just can't stand the thought of you wearing that filthy coat another minute, so, please, let me get you some new clothes for your trip back to Rome."

Sarah laughed. "Well, maybe just a couple of things." She paused a moment and then laid her hand upon his knee. "Thank you for all you've done for me."

An unfamiliar rush of heat flooded Nicolai's cheeks. "Of course," he stammered. The feeling of her hand on his knee remained long after she returned to her sewing.

Sarah pulled the thread tight, whipped it around in a circle, and bit the thread free of the needle. "What do you think?" she asked, holding up the coat. "Do you think anyone will see it?"

The shape of the cross was visible near the left-hand pocket inside the coat's lining but invisible on the outside of the coat. "No one will ever know." He paused, thinking, then added, "It exists, you know."

"What?"

"The ark, Noah's ark."

Sarah's hands dropped in her lap. "Now, how would you ever know a thing like that?"

"Because I've seen photos of it."

Sarah stared at him in shock. "You've seen pictures of Noah's ark? The Bible's ark?"

"*Da.*"

"Where did you ever find those?"

"When I worked in the archives at the Kremlin, I found a report by a lieutenant named Roskovitsky. He was a pilot in the Russian Imperial Army. One of the first. He flew a reconnaissance mission over Ararat in 1915 and reported seeing the ark. The last tsar even commissioned an expedition to locate it. This happened right before he abdicated the throne."

"And they found it?" Sarah's gaze stayed on his face as if mesmerized.

"Not only did they find it, they mapped it, measured it, and took pictures," he said. "It's all in the file."

"And it's still there?"

He nodded. "The images were blurry, but the shape of a large ship on the mountain was clear in the photo."

Sarah smoothed the coat over her knee again, scrutinizing the shape of the cross through the fabric. "How long were you in the defense department?" she asked.

"Almost three years."

"Did you ever hear anything about the cross?"

"No. Why?"

"I'm just wondering why the cross was in a museum."

"What do you mean?"

"My contact suggested scientists were conducting experiments on it. He theorized they could use the cross to create a new weapon."

"That would make sense. I know they've been developing many different types of weapons to compete with your government." He paused before asking, "What are you thinking?"

"If they were experimenting on the cross," Sarah said, "it shouldn't be in a museum; it should be in a lab. You saw for yourself how much dust was covering it. Nobody's touched it in years."

"Are you suggesting your contact lied?"

Sarah stared out the window as she considered the question. "I was just remembering something someone once told me. A warning about trusting my contact. I didn't believe him at the time, but—" Sarah hesitated. "It just doesn't add up. They have agents embedded inside the Kremlin, yet they brought me in from the outside.

Why?"

"Do you know what your government wants with the cross?"

"No. I only know they received a report from a British agent stating the Soviets were experimenting on it. My handler mentioned they could be experimenting with nuclear technology."

"That's interesting," Nicolai mused. "Yet it was your government that dropped atom bombs on Japan—twice."

"Do you think the CIA might weaponize the cross?"

"It's the next logical step, don't you think?" He leaned forward and rested his elbows on his knees. "Scientists in both nations are creating larger and more destructive bombs. They're desperate for it. If the cross does have some magical power, wouldn't your government want to utilize it before Stalin's scientists can?"

"But would the CIA send someone inside the Kremlin to steal something when there's only a chance at finding a new science?"

"It's a possibility."

"But they already can wipe out an entire city. Why would they need anything more?"

Nicolai settled back in his chair and stretched his legs out before him. "There's a new kind of war starting," he told her. "It won't be fought on a battlefield. It'll be in laboratories, and scientists will be the soldiers." He motioned to the coat lying in Sarah's lap. "The cross and whatever you felt in the Romani woman's wagon may be just what they need to create a new weapon." Nicolai picked up Sarah's hand and ran his finger across her palm. "We both witnessed the power it contains when it burned your hand during the trance. There's no telling what the cross is capable of." He reluctantly let go of her hand.

"But I only saw visions. There were no explosions."

"Maybe that's the weapon they're developing."

"Visions?"

Nicolai shrugged. "Maybe the cross can be used to confuse the enemy."

Sarah gazed down at the shape of the cross sewn into her coat. "It certainly confused me when I was in the trance."

"Psychological tools are the next weapon of war. The scientists may be testing the cross to see if it can plant false memories or direct the actions of soldiers, commanders, even a world leader."

"That's an interesting idea." Sarah studied the cross's outline inside the coat. "If this cross does hold the power of God like the records at the Vatican claim, then it shouldn't belong to any government." She glanced up at Nicolai. "But what am I supposed to do with it? I can't carry a holy relic around inside my coat for the rest of my life."

"No, but it wouldn't hurt to learn why your government has gone to the trouble of stealing the cross before you hand it over."

"No, I suppose it wouldn't." Sarah remained silent for a moment. "I'll see what my contact says when I call him."

She held the coat up in front of her again, and Nicolai ran his hand over the outside of it. "I don't think anyone will ever guess you have a holy relic hidden in there."

"Great," Sarah said. "I'd hate to lose it now."

****

"That's her," Max said, squinting through his binoculars from a car across the street. They'd been watching the hotel for over an hour, waiting for Sarah to emerge.

He lowered the binoculars but kept his eyes fixed on Sarah. "Follow her until we can get her alone."

"What about the rest of my money?" Yuri asked.

"You'll get the money when I have the cross," Max snarled. His attention swung back to the hotel's front door when Nicolai joined Sarah at the curb.

"When we get her alone, you'll hold her while I question her. She can't get away from both of us."

"Da."

"Is that him?" Max asked as he peered through the binoculars.

"Da."

They watched the pair as a taxi pulled up to the curb. The man opened the door, and they both crawled into the backseat.

Max lowered the binoculars. "Give me your gun."

"Nyet."

"You can't grab her and hold the gun." He held out his hand. "Give it to me."

Yuri handed it to him, grumbling through gritted teeth. Max checked the chamber. Six bullets.

The taxi swerved out into traffic and drove off, and Max said, "Let's go."

Chapter Thirty-Eight

"*Sayı, lütfen,*" the telephone operator greeted Sarah in Turkish.

"The international operator, please."

"What country?"

"Italy."

"One moment." The phone clicked once and went silent.

Sarah rested against the booth's cool glass wall and watched Nicolai's tousled brown hair recede into the crowd of the Grand Bazaar, Istanbul's busiest indoor market. *Straight back, head held high, and the same easy stride I've been following for days.* A feeling of loss washed over Sarah as she considered how much she'd miss his company.

"Number, please?" an Italian operator asked in English.

Sarah clutched the phone's receiver close to her mouth and lowered her voice. "Rome, please. U.S. Embassy."

"Just a moment."

The line clicked a few times in rapid succession until an American woman answered, "How can I direct your call, please?"

"Albert Phillips."

"And who can I say is calling, ma'am?" she asked.

"Sarah Kraft."

"Please hold."

Albert picked up next. "Sarah?"

"It's me," Sarah spoke low into the phone.

"Thank God." He sighed. "Where are you?"

"Istanbul," she replied.

"Istanbul?" Surprise was clear in his voice. "How did you end up there?"

Sarah glanced over her shoulder. "I ran into some trouble in the Kremlin."

"I heard about that."

"What did you hear?"

"Two fatalities three days ago."

This news surprised Sarah. "Two?"

"Yes, two." His voice carried a note of concern. "Our informants have been keeping us updated. I was worried something happened. Did you get the cross?"

"I have it." She slipped her hand into her pocket and traced its edges through the lining with her finger.

"Excellent!" Albert said. "I'll have the travel office arrange a flight for you, and we can discuss what happened when you're back in Rome tomorrow."

"Wait a minute, Albert. I need to ask you something first."

"If it's about what happened in Moscow, don't worry. The Soviets aren't publicizing the news, so we're not expecting any prob—"

"Someone's been following me," she interrupted.

"Do you know who it is?" Albert asked.

"No. He's Russian, but not KGB. He followed me all the way from Rome to Moscow."

"What does he look like?"

"Big. Over six feet. Maybe fifty years old. He wears all black and has a black scarf tied around his head under a hat."

"Doesn't sound like anyone I know," Albert said. "I think we'd better get you back here as soon as possible." Sarah could hear papers shuffling in the background.

"Albert?" she asked.

"Yes?"

"What will happen to it now?"

The shuffling stopped. "Excuse me?"

She cupped her hand around the receiver and whispered, "What plans do you have for the cross?"

Irritation laced Albert's words. "That's confidential."

Confidential. Sarah sighed. *The same excuse he used with Marco and the maps.* Her heart sank at the realization. *Marco was right—she really couldn't trust him.*

"That excuse won't work this time," she stated.

He sighed in exasperation. "I'm sorry, but I can't tell you. You've done your job. Just bring in the cross and be done with this mission." His silence awaited her response, but Sarah was done playing games. "You are stubborn, aren't you?"

"Will you tell me, or not?"

"It's part of a diplomatic mission." He brushed the question aside. "That's all I can tell you."

"Diplomacy? *Really?*"

"You know we only give our agents the information they need to know," Albert added. "What's wrong with you?"

Sarah recognized the warning note in his tone. His patience was near its limit.

"Just come in and let's close this file."

Sarah glanced over her shoulder. "I think you're

overlooking one thing."

"What?"

"I still have the cross," she said. "The ball is in my court, and I'm not coming in until you tell me everything—even if I have to take this cross all the way back to where it came from."

"To Russia?"

"No. To Ararat."

"Ararat!" He shrieked into the phone.

"Yes, that's where the cross belongs. Not with scientists, or governments, or even the CIA." Sarah's voice rose in intensity.

"Why are you insisting on this?" Albert snapped.

"Why?" she scoffed. "First, I took the fall for Marco, now I'm being shot at by some stranger. Do you really expect me to trust the agency's motives?" Sarah laughed. "Not on your life."

Albert was silent as Sarah sucked in a deep breath and released it slowly to calm herself. Finally, she said, "Listen Albert, I'm tired of being lied to and I'm tired of you using me as a cover-up for other people's crimes. You owe me an explanation, and I'm not coming in until you tell me why you want this cross."

More silence.

"Albert?"

"You'll need clearance," he finally relented. "I can't tell you anything until tomorrow morning."

Sarah smiled. "I didn't know you were such a company man."

He sighed. "Times have changed."

"So I've been told," she said, then added, "One more thing."

"Jesus, Sarah!"

"Calm down." Sarah glanced around her. "I just want to know if you've heard from Marco."

"Oh," he said, relief clear in his tone. "We got your note from the Berlin office. Nobody's heard from him since the day before you left."

Curious, but Marco was unpredictable. *He's probably in Monaco living the high life with one of his wealthy benefactors. Licking his wounds and drinking champagne while he gambles away someone else's money.* "Okay. I'll call you tomorrow morning. Nine a.m. your time."

"I'll be waiting." Albert hung up.

Sarah set the phone's receiver in the cradle and sighed. *Nicolai is right. Albert is hiding something.*

She opened the phone booth's door and stepped out into the market. A few feet later, two huge hands grabbed her from behind.

Chapter Thirty-Nine

One arm tightened around Sarah's waist as another trapped her right arm against her body and slid up her chest. A huge hand covered the lower half of her face. It smelled of menthol.

The Russian!

Half shoving, half carrying, he dragged Sarah into a small, dark room a few feet from the phone book. The door slammed shut behind her. She struggled to break free, but the man in black held her tight against his broad chest.

A clicking sound was heard, and the room was lit up by a sputtering flame from a cigarette lighter. Sarah saw she was in a storage closet. Shadows, cast by the flickering light, landed on brooms and mops, and shelves with towels.

"You are much more difficult than I'd anticipated, Agent Kraft," a familiar voice with a German accent said from a corner of the room.

The cardinal? Sarah stopped struggling for a moment. *What the hell is he doing here? And with the Russian?*

"When we met at the Vatican," he continued as he lit a cigarette, "I didn't think you'd be much of a challenge for my man, Yuri, but he tells me you are quite a ruthless woman." The scent of burning tobacco filled the air as he took his first drag. "I should have paid more attention when Phillips told me about your skills."

As his words took hold, the wheels clicked into place. *It's a mission for the Vatican—Marco was right! Dammit! Albert did set me up.* Sarah twisted back and forth, fighting to free herself from Yuri's grip.

"You see, Phillips wasn't the one who picked you to find the Byzantine Cross." Max made a clicking noise with his mouth. "No, no, no. The CIA was just a way to get to you." He moved to stand in front of Sarah, the burning ember of his cigarette inches from her face. "Nor was it my idea. Oh, no. You were groomed for this task long ago by our mutual friend, the Grand Duchess Militza." He chuckled. "The afternoon teas, the walks around the Vatican—they served her goal. Not yours."

He blew a puff of smoke in her face, and Sarah felt Yuri recoil behind her.

"You see, she believed the cross belonged to her. A Romanov." He plucked the cigarette out of his mouth and stabbed the air with it. "I disagree."

Sarah felt Yuri's chest convulse against her back as smoke filled the small space.

"The duchess was the first to tell me about you," he continued. "She said you were an extraordinary woman. Someone who could steal the cross right out from under Stalin's nose." He took another drag and let the smoke filter through his teeth as he spoke. "Her faith in you was justified. You got the cross out of Russia, but you were too cunning and escaped my Russian friend. So now we find you in Istanbul." He nodded to Yuri. "Search her."

Yuri's right hand pressed down on her mouth while the left moved under her coat to roam roughly around her body. Sarah fought the assault, but he jerked her backward against his chest and held her tight as his hand ran over her abdomen, up her chest, down her side, and across her hips, just missing the spot where she'd hidden the cross inside the lining.

"It's not here," Yuri said.

"Keep looking," Max ordered.

Yuri's hand crisscrossed her body again. Moving across to her back and over her buttocks.

"It's not here," Yuri repeated.

"Where is the cross?" Max seethed, and Yuri lowered his hand from her mouth.

"Do you think I'm stupid?" Sarah spit out as she gasped for air. "I wouldn't bring something so important to a crowded place like this."

"It's at the hotel?" Max asked, surprised.

"Locked safely away, and nobody can access it but me," she sneered.

Max stepped back and paused before speaking. "You know, Sarah, Yuri isn't here for the cross."

The Russian's hand slid down her breast and squeezed it. Sarah winced in pain. She struggled against his hold on her, but he didn't budge. Instead, he leaned in and let out a low, menacing growl as his hand continued its path down her body.

"My friend has a little crush on you." Max said, then laughed. "Well, maybe not a crush, exactly. You see, the cross is my prize." He grabbed Sarah's chin and drew her face close. "You, my dear Agent Kraft, are his."

Yuri's hand slid down to her pelvis.

"I think you may want to make a deal with me," Max whispered.

****

"How about these, sir?" the shopkeeper asked Nicolai as he waved his hand over a collection of cufflinks displayed in a glass case.

Nicolai removed the last diamond earring from his pocket and showed it to the jeweler. "I'd like a diamond earring to match this one," he said, handing it over to the jeweler. "I, um, lost its match." He smiled, remembering how excited the Romani women became when Sarah showed them the earring.

The jeweler picked the diamond up and peered through his eyepiece. "Very nice," he said, handing the earring back. "Excellent quality. I think I have the perfect match." He disappeared into the back of the store.

The shop, barely larger than a closet, glittered floor to ceiling with gold and gemstones. Nicolai glanced around at the many choices until he spotted a large sapphire pendant on a gold chain. He stopped. In the light, the gem flashed true blue, but as his shadow passed over it, the color changed to teal.

Changing colors. Just like Sarah's eyes.

The thought escaped him before he realized what feelings it brought with it. Over the last few days, he'd watched almost every expression play out in Sarah's beautiful eyes. When she was scared, they were true blue, turquoise when she got angry, and teal when she was relaxed.

I saw the teal for the first time this morning.

"I found it! The perfect match." The shopkeeper beamed with pride as he presented his diamond. "And not a single imperfection."

Nicolai picked the diamond up and studied it through the eyepiece. "Yes. Very nice. Can you put this one into an earring?"

"Of course. If you have a minute, I can do it for you right now."

"Yes. Thank you."

"Wonderful! Is there anything else I can get you, sir? We have a selection of beautiful tie clips." The shopkeeper gestured to another case.

Nicolai handed the stone back. "No, thank you."

The shopkeeper stepped to the register.

Nicolai glanced back at the necklace with the blue sapphire. "Just a moment." He gestured to it. "I'd like this, too."

"Yes, sir!" the jeweler said as he searched his pocket for the keys to the case. "The stone comes from America—Colorado, I believe. An extraordinarily rare find!"

Nicolai smiled, thinking of Sarah. *Yes, she certainly is.*

Chapter Forty

"Move!" Max ordered.

The barrel of a gun bit into Sarah's back as Yuri forced her out of the storage closet and into the bazaar. He held her by the arm as they walked together down the street. Max followed close behind, keeping the gun hidden inside his coat sleeve.

Yuri took Sarah by the arm and guided her toward a busy avenue with shops crowded together under striped awnings. Piles of clothes, household items, and other goods spilled out from their open doors, and eagle-eyed salespeople stood waiting for their next customer. When they spotted Sarah and her kidnappers, they stepped into the street and called to them in broken English, each one eager for their chance to entice them into their store.

Sarah caught the eye of one of the shopkeepers, and an idea popped into her head.

"I've come back with my husband," she called out, "and he has lots of money!"

The man jumped up and hurried their way with an enthusiastic smile and outstretched arms. "Please, come into my shop. I have excellent merchandise from across the seven seas." He gestured to his shop, but Yuri knocked him aside and kept trudging forward, pushing Sarah ahead of him.

More salespeople surrounded them, stepping in between Sarah and her captors. Yuri's grip struggled to hang onto her arm.

"No!" Max barked. He tried to break through the crowd to keep up with Sarah and Yuri, but they blocked his way. "I'm not interested. Leave me alone!"

Sarah twisted her arm back and forth inside Yuri's hand as people pressed forward. When a man stepped in between her and the kidnappers, she jerked her arm free and threw herself into the crowd.

Chapter Forty-One

The crowd in the bazaar had doubled in size when Nicolai stepped outside the jewelers. He dropped the bag with the necklace and earrings into his pants pocket and was about to step into the street when shouts from the crowd a few feet away caught his attention. A moment later, he noticed a flash of blonde hair among the dark heads of the Turkish people.

Sarah?

Nicolai had just processed the thought when Sarah burst through the crowd, and he broke into a run, forcing people out of his way as he yelled her name.

She heard him and yelled back, "There's two of them! Two!"

Two what? The question was cut off by the sound of gunfire and the crowd dropped to the floor. Nicolai backed up into the door of a shop as a tall man with gray hair emerged from the crowd with a gun aimed at Sarah's back. Nicolai rushed forward to get in between the gunman and Sarah, but the man pulled the trigger before Nicolai could reach her. The bullet whizzed past his head and embedded itself in a wall as the gunman raced past him. The smell of sulfur from the discharge lingered in the air.

More shouts, and a second man stepped from the crowd. He was big. Taller than Nicolai with forty more pounds on him. Dressed all in black, he appeared like a hulking black shadow shoving people out of his way as he jogged forward.

Nicolai stepped into the middle of the street and braced for impact, cocking his fist back and waiting for his moment. As the man drew near, he landed a right hook squarely on the man's jaw. It felt like it was made of stone. Nicolai winced in pain.

Stunned, the big man staggered back a few steps and shook his head as Nicolai took a fighter's stance and waited for a second chance to take the man out.

"Ah!" The man in black's mouth twisted back at the corners. "You must be the woman's man from the chimney."

Nicolai recalled the deep, raspy voice immediately. *He's the same man who'd shot at us inside the palace's chimney!*

The big man laughed. "Another boyfriend to fight."

Another boyfriend?

The man was already in a defensive stance, head down, fists in front of his face. He threw a right hook, but Nicolai stepped back before it could connect. He took two more steps to stand behind the man, landing two punches to his kidney before the he could react.

With a swiftness only seen in the ring, the man in black spun around and delivered a blow to Nicolai's abdomen. It knocked the wind out of him, and he stumbled backward. The crowd parted as the strange man followed up with an uppercut to his jaw, and Nicolai dropped to the ground.

The big man glanced down at Nicolai lying at his feet and bellowed with laughter. "You're not man enough for that woman!"

Pain throbbed inside Nicolai's mouth. His legs

nearly buckled when he stood up and blood spilled from his cut lip. He shook his head to clear it, then stooped over and rammed his shoulder into the man's torso. The move threw the man backward into a stack of baskets.

The man crawled out of the mess and bent over, sucking in mouthfuls of air, wheezing and coughing as Nicolai readied himself for a second blow. Just as his right almost connected, the man sidestepped the strike and delivered a punch to the side of Nicolai's head. Flashes of light obscured his view as he dropped to the floor.

The man reached down and grabbed a handful of Nicolai's shirt. He lifted Nicolai up to eye level and wrapped his other hand around Nicolai's neck, squeezing until he struggled for air.

"You should have stayed out of it," the man growled as he shook him roughly. "You should have let her do her job."

The man opened his hand, and Nicolai crashed on the floor. He started to crawl away, but the man stepped on his back and held him there as he bent down, grabbed a fistful of Nicolai's hair and pulled his head back to gaze into his the eyes.

"Now, I have to kill you just like the last boyfriend."

Chapter Forty-Two

Bang!

A bullet shot through the crowd, embedding itself into a wall next to Sarah's face. People screamed, shopkeepers locked their doors—and Sarah ran.

Another shot. This time, the bullet landed right behind her left foot.

He's getting closer!

Sarah ducked down and ran through the Grand Bazaar's complicated maze of dead ends and hidden alcoves until she had lost all sense of direction.

The cardinal fired another shot, and people dropped to the ground around Sarah, leaving her an open target on a long, straight avenue. Tunnel vision took over, and she spotted a group of heavy Persian carpets rolled up and standing on end at the next corner.

The carpet seller's market.

One of the busiest places in the Grand Bazaar, Sarah sprinted toward the corner as another bullet echoed through the street. She crouched down and rammed her body into the first tower, lifting it with her shoulder and pushing the pile into the other carpets, but they barely budged, so she ran on.

The spice seller's market began at the next corner, with ground spices of every color in open bins on both sides of the street. Sarah grabbed a fistful of crushed chili pepper and threw the spice behind her in a cloud a burning dust.

Max jogged straight into it. "You bitch!" he yelled, rubbing the burning spice into his eyes. The pain slowed him down but didn't stop him.

After two more corners, Sarah came to a dead end.

She glanced around and saw dozens of colorful glass lanterns hanging on long chains from hooks on the wall. A few had kerosene-fueled flames burning inside.

The crowd parted, and she and Max stood face-to-face.

"You think you're pretty smart, don't you?" He rubbed his red, watery eyes as he stalked her. "You ran right into your own trap."

Sarah unhooked a lamp, wrapped its chain around her hand, and started swinging it back and forth until the lamp rotated in a circle in front of her. As she increased its velocity, she extended the chain and raised the lantern above her head. Burning oil leaked out of the glass and fell to the floor, encircling her in flames.

"Where is it?" Max demanded as he pointed his gun at her face.

"Step back," Sarah warned.

A crowd gathered around them, blocking the only exit out of the alcove. Max moved toward Sarah but dodged the lantern when it flew past his head.

"Lots of people want the cross, Sarah," he said. "Hand it over and save yourself a lot of problems."

"It doesn't belong to you!"

"It belongs to the church!"

"It belongs to no one!"

She opened her hand and released the chain. It slipped through her palm and straightened out to its full length as the glass lamp came around and connected with

Max's face. A loud crash echoed down the street as the lamp smashed into the left side of his skull and shattered into a million tiny pieces.

Max screamed as glass shards embedded deep into his skin. Burning oil dripped down his shoulders and ignited his clothes before landing at his feet. Two men rushed forward and threw a rug over him to stifle the flames.

His curses followed Sarah as she ducked past him and down the street to find Nicolai.

Chapter Forty-Three

"Did you think you could save her, fool?" the man in black sneered. He twisted the hand holding Nicolai's hair and rolled him onto his back, then grabbed Nicolai's arm and yanked him onto his knees. The man in black stood behind Nicolai and forced him into a kneeling position and held him there with an arm wrapped around his neck. Nicolai fought to free himself of the man's grasp but stopped when he drew a blade from inside his coat and held it to Nicolai's throat. The crowd cried out in horror.

Out of the corner of his eye, Nicolai saw a flash of blonde hair push through the crowd.

Sarah!

She threw herself feet first into the man's right knee. His legs buckled, and he fell on top of Nicolai. Sarah got up as Nicolai pushed the bigger man off his body and scrambled on top of his barrel chest as Sarah stomped on the hand still holding the knife. The man's palm opened, and Sarah scooped the knife up.

Nicolai gripped the man in black's head between his hands and slammed it hard, over and over, into the pavement. He heard the crowd gasp in unison as the black hat and the scarf underneath fell away, exposing his naked, scarred head. Shocked, Nicolai stopped his assault and left him dazed and moaning on the floor.

A voice behind them called out, "Come here!

Quickly! Come!"

Nicolai glanced over his shoulder to the same jeweler who had sold him the diamond waving him into his shop. He grabbed Sarah by the hand and followed the owner into the store.

The jeweler led them through the shop to a curtain leading to a back room. He pushed it aside and lifted the corner of a rug lying on the floor, revealing a trapdoor underneath. He opened, and the musty smell of stagnant water wafted into the room.

"Quick! Down there." The shopkeeper gestured to the dark space. "The Basilica Cistern. There's a boat tied up below. Follow the pillars marked with an *X*. They connect with another cistern. Look for another dock just like this one." He pushed a flashlight into Nicolai's hand. "You'll need this."

"*Da*." Nicolai's fingers closed around the light.

"Thank you," Sarah said as she stepped down onto a ladder.

"Very bad man," the jeweler said, shaking his head with disdain. "Go! Now!"

****

"Where did they go?" Max demanded as he entered the jeweler's shop. He marched toward a voice he heard in the back, stopping momentarily when he caught a glimpse of himself in a mirror sitting on the display case. His face was a mess. His coat still smoldered where the oil had burned the fabric, and blood streaked the side of his face. He touched it with a finger and felt hard shards of glass embedded into his skin.

That bitch!

Yuri limped behind him, holding his handkerchief to his swollen, blood-streaked face.

The jeweler stepped in front of Max, blocking the door to the back room.

"Get out of my way," Max ordered, but the jewerler shrugged, pretending he didn't understand.

Max shoved him, but the jeweler stood firm. Without another word, Max raised the gun to the shopkeeper's chest and squeezed the trigger. The shopkeeper let out a surprised gasp as the bullet hit his heart, and then he dropped to the floor—dead.

Max shoved the jeweler's body to the side with one foot and stepped over him. Yuri followed and stood next to Max as he gazed down into the cistern. Twenty feet below, a beam of light stretched out across the dark water. Muffled voices and the sound of a boat splashing through the water as it rowed away from the dock echoed up through the opening.

****

"Are you okay?" Sarah asked. Her words bounced off the stone walls and amplified across the still water.

"*Da*," Nicolai's voice cracked. "I think so." He rubbed his throat as he aimed the flashlight at the nearest column. It was nealy completely dark inside the cistern, making it difficult to navigate around the dozens of columns supporting the roof from caving it. "Do you see an *X*?"

Sarah followed the beam of light to another post beyond the first. "There's one!" she said. Nicolai aimed the light on the mark painted at the top of the column. Sarah held the right oar steady as she paddled toward it.

"You need to get back to Rome as soon as possible," Nicolai croaked, his voice hoarse from being choked. "When we find our way out, we'll get a taxi to the airport."

"No," she said, blowing out a big breath as she settled into the rhythm of rowing. "Things have changed. I can't go back."

"What happened?" Nicolai dropped his hand from his throat.

"I think you're right; the CIA is involved. I don't know how, but when I called my contact he admitted they've been working with the cardinal."

"The cardinal?"

"The man with the gun."

"How do you know?" he asked.

"Both my contact and Cardinal Max told me," she said. They're working together."

"What is your plan now?" Nicolai shined the light on the next X.

"There's only one thing I can do." She sucked in a deep breath, readying herself to commit to something she knew she couldn't take back. "I'm taking the cross back to the ark, just like the Romani grandmother said."

"All the way to Mount Ararat?"

"To a monastery near the mountain called Khor Verap. It's where the cross was kept safe for centuries." She rounded a corner and aimed the boat toward another red X. "It's where the cross belongs."

"How will you get there?" Nicolai asked as he searched for another X.

"I don't know, but I won't hand something so important over to people I can't trust to protect the cross. And right now, there's no one I trust."

"Do you trust me?" Nicolai asked.

Did she? Maybe, but she knew one thing for sure. As the new mission took shape, she knew she didn't want to go alone. "Do you want to come with me?"

Even in the semidarkness, Sarah could see Nicolai's smile. "I wouldn't miss this adventure for the world."

****

As Sarah and Nicolai's voices faded away, Max glared at Yuri. "Get the car!"

Yuri shook his head. "They're gone. It's over."

"But we know where they're going." Max's fury drove him on. *More insolence from this Russian buffoon!* "We can still get the cross from them at the Mount Ararat monastery. Khor Verap. I know where it is."

"No! I'm done."

Max stabbed his finger into Yuri's thick chest. "If you want your money, you'll do as I say."

"No. This is too much." He gestured to the jeweler lying in a pool of blood at their feet. "This has gone far enough. I won't be sent to a Turkish prison for this."

"We're leaving Istanbul tonight," Max insisted. "We'll hide him in the cistern. No one will find him until long after we're gone."

Yuri grabbed Max's and held him up against a counter. "I said no!" he yelled into Max's face. "Give me my money. I've done everything I've promised."

Max smacked Yuri's large hand away from his ragged, burnt collar and straightened his coat before he retrieved a handkerchief from his pocket. He dabbed at his bleeding cheek and a sharp pain caused him to grimace when the cloth rubbed up against the glass shards.

"What you promised was the Byzantine cross." Max sneered through his contorted face. "You haven't delivered on that promise, and until you do, you won't see one more dime." He winced in pain. "And if you don't get me the cross, I'll have you hunted until your dying day. I promise you." He stepped up to Yuri until their noses nearly touched and pressed the barrel of the now unloaded gun into the bigger man's chest. "And I keep my promises."

Yuri stood silent as his expression as a hint of fear crept into his eyes. At last, he relented.

"*Da.* Let's go."

Chapter Forty-Four

"You aren't jumping, are you?" Sarah asked Nicolai when she found him standing at the railing of the cargo ship as it cruised through the calm waters of the Marmaris Strait to the Aegean Sea.

Nicolai smiled. "I haven't decided yet." He held out a small white box. "The ship's cook brought me some lunch. Would you like part of my ham sandwich?"

She opened the lid and found a half eaten sandwich, an apple, and a pile of limp lettuce she assumed was a salad. "No, thank you."

"You're smart. It tastes awful." Nicolai tore off a piece of bread and threw it to the seagulls flying alongside the boat. "Although, the birds like it." He picked the apple out of the box and sat down on a barrel. "I see you found some new clothes," he said before biting into the apple.

Sarah tucked a strand of hair blown by the wind behind her ear. "Not exactly new, but clean." Someone left a pair of men's pants, a white cotton T-shirt, and an old army jacket on her bed during her meeting with the captain soon after they'd left the dock. They were a bit big for her, but after adjusting a few straps and tightening the belt, the clothes fit perfectly. "I'll need to pick up some shoes when we land, but I think everything else will work for the trip." She glanced around the empty deck, then opened the jacket. "And I've already sewn the cross into the lining."

Nicolai's gaze lingered over her. "How's your hip?"

Sarah ran her hand down her right side and winced. "I've got a horrible bruise, but that's all. I'll be fine."

"You landed hard when you kicked the monster off me. I'm surprised you didn't break something."

"I have softball to thank for that."

"Softball?" he asked.

"It's like baseball. When I was a girl, I was famous for stealing bases because of my slide."

"I'm glad you haven't lost the skill." He nodded toward the ship's bridge. "So, what did the captain say?"

Sarah glanced around the empty deck before she answered. "He's dropping us off at a port in three hours. Then it's eleven hours to Cappadocia. We can stock up on supplies there, then twelve more hours to Ararat."

"One day," Nicolai said, rubbing the back of his neck. "What are the chances your friends from the bazaar are following us?"

"Very good, I'm afraid. The cardinal knew the name of my contact at the CIA. He made it sound like they were working together, and if they are, it'll be easy for him to find out where we're going. When I called Rome, I told him I'd take the cross to the monestary at Mount Ararat unless he told me who the CIA was working with and what they want with the cross."

"Did he tell you anything?"

"We're supposed to talk tomorrow morning." She paused, thinking of Albert. "He'll be suspicious when I don't call in."

Nicolai smiled. "Should be an interesting trip then."

The twinkle in his eye— Sarah recognized this from her own reflection. *He loves the adventure as much as I do.*

She smiled as she watched the shoreline passing by. The white limestone cliffs of the Turkish coast towered over the turquoise sea. She sighed. "It sure is beautiful here."

Nicolai pointed to the top of a bluff. "See that? Way up on top of the cliff?"

Sarah squinted into the light.

Nicolai stepped behind her, resting his left hand on the railing and pointing with his right over her shoulder. "Right there, see the column?"

Warmth radiated from his body as he leaned into Sarah.

She followed Nicolai's line of sight and spotted a single Greek column capping the top of a large boulder. It stood alone like a sentinel, keeping watch over the sea.

"I—I see it." Nicolai's clean masculine scent was distracting.

"One of the crew just told me it's a temple to Athena, the goddess of heroic endeavor." He lowered his arm to the railing, keeping her inside his embrace. "Maybe you should say a little prayer to her," he whispered in her ear.

Her pulse quickened as his warm, sweet breath caressed the back of her neck. Heat flooded her cheeks.

Nicolai pushed himself away from the railing, breaking the electric current connecting them. He backed away, and Sarah pivoted around to face him. Their eyes locked, his searching her own, looking for something— Sarah didn't know what.

Her mouth went dry, and her pulse raced. She struggled for something to say, anything, to break the uncomfortable silence. They stood there looking at each other, connected by an invisible force until Nicolai cleared his throat.

"I should look at the map too. It sounds like I'll be doing some driving." He picked the lunch box up from the barrel. "If you'll excuse me." He strolled away, leaving Sarah standing alone and breathless.

The sensation of her body wrapped inside his arms stayed with Sarah long after Nicolai he stepped away. Deeper than friendship and more intense than she'd ever felt with another man, a new realization rolled over her as she watched him walk away.

Did he feel it too?

Chapter Forty-Five

Cappadocia, Turkey

A bump in the road rocked the car, shaking Sarah awake. She opened one eye and peered over the collar of her jacket. Stars filled the midnight sky and the air thick with morning dew, even inside the old jeep.

Sarah crouched down inside her jacket. It was too early. She didn't want to wake up and face the cold night air. She wanted to stay safe and warm inside her dreams where no one chased her or shot at her.

Nicolai had taken the wheel for the last few hours while Sarah got some sleep, and so far, the trip had been uneventful. The jeep he'd purchased at the port proved a tough, speedy vehicle—perfect for a trip over primitive roads.

Sarah studied Nicolai from behind the collar of her jacket. He hadn't shaved since the boat, and his beard gave him a rugged, swarthy look. *Handsome in the moonlight,* Sarah caught herself musing.

Heat rushed into her cheeks as she remembered the electricity they'd shared on the ship. Something shifted between them, and Nicolai knew it too. She was sure. The way he suddenly pulled back. The intensity in brown eyes right before he left her on the deck. She knew he was holding back. He wanted to say something—do something—but what? Nothing happened since then. He didn't make another move or allude to the moment in any way, and with each passing hour, Sarah wondered if she imagined the connection she thought they'd shared.

He reached over and touched Sarah's foot propped on the dash. "Sarah." He gently shook her leg. "Wake up. You should see this."

Sarah roused herself and stretched. "What's going on?"

"There." He pointed to something outside the jeep.

The white cliffs they drove upon splintered off into long finger-shaped outcroppings that reached out into a deep valley. They ended in a row of cone-shaped rock towers sixty-feet tall where erosion had worn away the softer sediment. The hundreds of pointed rock spires scattered around the valley were capped by boulders balanced on their peak.

"What is this place?" Sarah asked.

"I think it's Cappadocia. Our halfway point." He gestured out the window. "The person who sold me the map told me about it." He strained to look out the window. "There's a village down there."

"I see it." Light glowed in the windows of homes carved into the towers. Cave homes. A road cut through the center of the valley, with side streets splintering off into less populated areas before tapering into dead ends where they ran up against a cliff face.

Nicolai drove the jeep to an overlook and shut off the engine. "Let's get out. I need to stretch."

Sarah climbed out of the vehicle and stretched her arms wide, and then zipped up her jacket and stuffed her hands inside its pockets. Just as she'd done every time she'd put her hands in her pockets, she traced a finger along the edge of the cross still hidden in the lining.

"What time is it?" she asked Nicolai as she joined

him at the front bumper.

"Five," he told her, glancing at his watch. "I had a hard time focusing the last few miles."

"I could tell." She gave him a tired smile. "You were swerving all over the road. I was scared you'd drive us over the edge."

"You don't trust me?" he teased, but the word landed on Sarah with a thud.

Trust.

Marco's warning echoed through her thoughts. *Don't trust anyone.*

But Nicolai? He'd done nothing but help her. Even when he wanted to leave, he stayed with her. She had to admit she didn't really know him. He might be another Marco, using her for his own benefit. Didn't he say he'd lost everything?

Maybe he thinks I owe him something for coming with me. She studied him as he leaned back against the jeep and yawned. The moonlight softened his rugged look. *But he could have taken the cross and left several times already.*

And the moment on the ship. *I know he felt something when we stood on the deck together, just as I had.*

Sarah couldn't bear the voices in her head any longer. "Nicolai, can I ask you something?"

He toward to her. "What is it?"

"Why are you here?"

"We're taking the cross to Ararat." He shrugged. "Why do you ask me such a question?"

Sarah breathed deep before answering. "You couldn't wait to leave me when we got off the train, but now you are willing to cross this whole country to take this cross back to a monastery you've never heard of. Why?"

"Why?" Nicolai's voice was husky from the night air. "I've asked myself the same question."

"And?"

He sighed. "I guess it's because I believe in the cross, and I believe you are doing the right thing by taking it back to the ark." He paused, then added, "And I'm a military man. I don't leave my comrades behind."

Sarah searched his eyes for more. "Is that what I am? A comrade?"

Nicolai gazed out over the canyon. "Comrade, colleague, whatever you call it." A muscle flexed in his jaw.

"Those are the only reasons?" she pressed.

"What else would it be?"

"Maybe you want to take the cross for yourself. Maybe you think you can claim you saved it on your own."

"No." He chuckled. "That is not what's going on. I promise."

"What then?" she asked. "Why are you here?"

He rubbed his chin, then caught Sarah's gaze.

"When I turned fourteen," he began, "the Bolsheviks took me from my parents and sent me to a military school north of Moscow, where I became a soldier. They taught me responsibility and commitment, and even though I don't believe in communism, I believe in being a soldier." He took her hands in his. "I won't leave you to face this, this alone…whatever this thing is. I've seen what this cross can do, and I won't leave you to deal with this alone."

Nicolai sounded sincere. *Do I dare trust him?*

Sarah broke their connection this time, letting her hand drop to her side. "Thank you," she said, then climbed up to sit on the hood. She needed space until she understood what was going on between them, so she changed the subject. "How did you become a double for Britain?"

"Disillusionment." Nicolai rested against the jeep and folded his arms across his chest. "Maybe cynicism too. Whatever the reason, freedom sounded better than what we had in Russia. So, when the Brits asked me to join MI6, I took the offer as an opportunity to fight another kind of war." He glanced over his shoulder at her. "One where they don't take boys from their families."

"Are you in contact with your family?"

"No."

Sarah heard a note of sadness in his voice.

"They owned a bookstore. When the authorities searched it, they found banned books, so they took my parents away. That's why I requested a position in the Kremlin archives. I wanted to find out what happened to them."

"Did you find anything?"

"No. The recordkeeping was very poor during those years."

"What about your brother?"

"Killed in battle. I'm the only one left." He gave her a sleepy smile. "So, my comrades are my family."

"Yes," Sarah echoed. She believed him, even as her instincts told her his words were too convenient. Too perfect.

And nothing he said explained the electricity between them on the ship. Nor the way he watched her when he thought she wouldn't notice.

If he wants me, why won't he just say it? What is he keeping from me?

Before she could guess at the answer, Nicolai dangled the jeep's keys from his right hand and said, "We'd better get going. We've got a long way to go before we reach Ararat."

Chapter Forty-Six

"The place isn't open yet." Nicolai peered through the window of the village's only gas station. He walked to the pump. "But they've got gasoline."

"Someone should arrive soon." She counted the Turkish coins Nicolai had given her. "I saw a street vendor about a half mile back. I'll get some food for the trip while you wait."

Nicolai nodded as he leaned against the pump and put his foot on the jeep's back bumper. "Ask if they have any coffee," he called after her as she strolled down the dusty street.

A rooster crowed from a barnyard and an old man pushing a cart tipped his hat in greeting as Sarah strode to the market. It was a beautiful day and, for a moment, she forgot the cross and Max and Albert. She even banished Nicolai from her thoughts as she followed the old man down the street.

The market encircled the public well in the town square. Vendors selling everything from fruit to firewood waited for their first customer of the day. Sarah stopped at the first vedor's stall and loaded her bag up with bread, apples, and cheese before swinging the bags over her shoulder to carry them back to the station.

She'd only walked one block from the market when the low, steady rumble of a car's engine interrupted the peaceful morning. Parked on a side street, a 1930s black touring car idled in front of a hotel.

Why would an expensive car be way out here in this tiny village?

The door of the hotel swung open, and a hulking dark shape stepped outside. Sarah drew in a frightened breath. *The man in black*—Yuri, Max called him.

Sarah froze. *How? How could they have already gotten to Cappadocia?* She frowned as a new thought came to her.

Albert.

Max sauntered out next, dropping a cigarette on the stone steps and squashing the butt under his shoe. He still wore the scorched coat he'd worn at the bazaar, and his pulpy face glistened red in the early morning sunlight. He said something to Yuri as they walked to the car, then his gaze locked on Sarah standing motionless in the street. He froze, and they both stared at each other in disbelief before he reached in his coat and retrieved his gun.

Sarah clutched the bag of groceries tighter and ran. Apples spilled out of the top and bounced on the ground behind her as a bullet hit the street ahead of her and stirred up a puff of dust.

Nicolai was paying the attendant for gas when Sarah sprinted to the car.

"They're here!" Sarah gasped. She tossed the groceries into the back seat and jumped in the driver's seat while Nicolai got into the passenger seat.

"The cardinal and the man in black?" he asked as he glanced out the back window at the black car barreling down the street.

Sarah threw the jeep into gear and pressed the gas pedal to the floor as another bullet zipped over the top of the jeep. The heavier black car didn't move as well, but its engine was powerful. *I've got to get off this road!* Sarah shifted to high gear, and the jeep tore through the street.

"Are you hurt?" Nicolai's words, tinged with concern, caught Sarah by surprise.

"He missed," Sarah said between gulps of air. "I spotted them coming out of a hotel." The road curved around a forty-foot rock tower and continued weaving through the canyon toward the countryside.

Nicolai grasped the dashboard and glanced back at the black car. "They're having a hard time around the corners."

The big car handled the straight roads well, but when Sarah led them around a corner or over rough roads, the car slowed down to complete the maneuver.

"Where are you going?" Nicolai asked as Sarah wheeled the jeep off the main road and turned toward dozens of the cone-shaped towers filling a flat pasture.

"Their car can't outrun the jeep around those rock columns."

A shot rang out as the jeep climbed a rocky path. They rounded the base of another rock tower another bullet bit into its surface.

"Hang on!" Sarah jerked the wheel hard to the left as she raced around another rock tower. The jeep hit an incline and flew into the air, landing hard on the other side before racing off down the primitive road.

The black car roared behind them, its sides scraping along the jagged rock face as its tires ground the gravel to dust. Sarah peered into her rearview mirror and saw the front bumper growing larger as their pursuers closed in on the jeep. The big car might not navigate the quick turns like the jeep, but it sailed over the uneven terrain like a ship taking to the waves.

Sarah steered the jeep to the left, barely avoiding a large boulder as she twisted the wheel back and forth. She dodged boulders and plowed through scrub brush as she tried to outmaneuver the bigger car. When the road ended at four massive rock columns, she slammed on the brakes.

Trapped.

The roar of the black car's engine rumbled like thunder behind them.

"Hurry!" Nicolai said. "They're right behind us!"

Sarah glanced left, then right. The canyon's smooth walls soared fifty feet over the valley floor. Thirty-foot tall rock columns spaced six feet apart and capped by cone-shaped boulders balanced on top of each one blocked the way to their only escape.

Without missing a beat, Sarah aimed the jeep at a gap between the second and third columns and gunned the motor.

"What are you doing?" Nicolai yelled. "We'll never clear it!"

"I'm going through!" She focused all her attention on the space between the columns and shifted into first, and then released the brake. The jeep jumped forward and hit the incline at the base of the two columns, launching into the air and sailing through the gap like a thread through the eye of a needle.

"I can't believe you just did that!" Nicolai said, amazed.

"Neither can I," Sarah said as she glanced back through the gap. "That big car will never make it through to this side." She stomped on the gas, and the jeep sped off, leaving Max and Yuri blocked on the other side of the rock columns.

****

"Go! Go! Go!" Max yelled. "They're getting away!"

Yuri slowed the car as they approached the columns. He revved the engine and shifted into gear. The car moved ahead, gaining speed as it drew closer to the second and third columns. The bumper hit the base and bounced backward, too heavey to lift off the ground.

He rammed the columns again. Rocks the size of baseballs rained down upon the hood of the car, and the engine stalled.

"Hit it again! We have to get through."

Yuri twisted the key in the ignition, and the engine sputtered.

Max waved the gun at the jeep on the other side. "You're letting them get away!"

He tried the key again. As the engine rolled over, a loud crack echoed through the canyon. Yuri shifted into reverse and stomped on the gas pedal. The car lurched backward as the capstone broke loose above them and slid off its pedestal, crashing in the exact spot where the car had been only seconds before.

The jarring quake from the stone's impact rang through Max's body, but he shook off the sensation and stuck his head out the window to find the jeep's all-terrain tires digging into the earth as it climbed a steep hill. "We're losing them!"

"Shut up!" Yuri growled as he shifted into first gear, then second, and wheeled the car around. "I know what I'm doing."

Yuri sped up to third gear, and the car bounced over the uneven road, plowing like a bulldozer through the rocks littering the ground.

Max gripped Yuri by the coat sleeve. "I demand to know what you're doing!"

Yuri backhanded him, driving the shattered glass from the lantern deeper into his flesh. "Shut your fucking mouth," he ordered.

Max's hand shot up to cradle his cheek. "How dare you!"

"Shut up, or I'll hit you again," he seethed.

The road narrowed to a single dirt path dividing two forty-foot cliffs. Yuri hit the gas and followed the trail around several curves. The car scraped against the rock, leaving deep scratches in the black paint on both sides. Once through, Yuri caught sight of the jeep and hit the gas again.

"Yes! Yes!" Max jumped in his seat and waved his fist at the retreating jeep. "Go!"

****

Sarah spotted the mouth of a tunnel ahead. She eased off the gas as they neared the entrance, and the jeep slowed to a stop. She could see light coming from the exit at the other side. She eased the jeep through the opening, the tires bouncing over the interior's rocky floor as the sound of the engine reverberated all around them. The jeep plowed through the tunnel and exited into the bottom of a smooth, bowl-shaped depression double the length of a baseball diamond. Its sides rose thirty feet to a plateau at the top where Sarah spotted a dark spot in a rock wall.

The cave! We can hide in there.

Sarah heard the black car storm through the tunnel behind them, its metal body grinding through the small space.

Sarah glanced at Nicolai, and he nodded in silent solidarity. She maneuvered the jeep into position and gripped the wheel tight as the engine let out a piercing whine. She pressed down on the gas, and the jeep's tires dug into the rock, climbing the side of the canyon at an angle. As Sarah shifted into second, the tires gripped the rock, gaining speed as the jeep sped up to climb the incline of the canyon wall.

Sarah found a groove in the rock, and the jeep dropped into it. Inch by inch, they climbed the rock wall, the tires sliding, then catching, then sliding again. Sarah braced herself, hoping the jeep wouldn't roll over.

"Come on, come on, come on!" Sarah muttered, tightening her grip around the steering wheel. When the front wheels reached the crown, the jeep's body flew up and over the edge, landing front first on the flat surface of the plateau.

Then silence.

Nicolai wiped his brow with the back of his hand "Nice driving," he said before opening the door and getting out.

"Thanks!" Sarah said as she raced ahead to the mouth of the cave.

****

Max stared at the jeep as it began its ascent. "What are they doing? They'll never make it."

Yuri craned his neck to peer out the front window. "I don't know. I saw those jeeps in the war. They—"

"Shut up!" Max seethed. "You got us into this mess, and you're letting them get away. Again!"

Yuri bristled but ignored the comment. He surveyed the cliff, estimating the chance the old car could follow the jeep. He shook his head. "This car is too big. We'll never make it." He glanced back at the tunnel behind them. "We will find another way." He eased the car around and back toward the tunnel's mouth.

"What are you doing?" Max pounded his fist on the dash. "Go back! Go back!"

"Shut up!" Yuri commanded. "We've got to find another way."

The car ground its way back through the tunnel. When they emerged at the opposite end, Yuri rounded a corner and searched for another route to the top of the cliff. "There must be another way up there."

Yuri drove the car further down the road and veered onto another narrow dirt path leading up to the plateau. It was steep, but the engine had the power for it.

"The car's too big." Max shook his head. "We'll never make it."

"Quiet!" Yuri snapped, raising his arm to hit him again. Max recoiled from the threat and noticed a slight smile curling the ends of Yuri's mouth.

That insolent ox! He thinks he's in control.

Max remained silent as Yuri eased the car up the side of the cliff. When they reached the top, Max tensed, ready for a fall as it crested the edge. The front bumper rose high in the air and landed with a resounding crash. Yuri hit the gas, the engine roared, but the car stayed put—high-centered on a rock.

"You fool!" Max raised his fist, ready to beat the Russian, but Yuri grabbed his wrist.

"Do you want the cross or not?" He pointed out the window. "There it is."

Max's anger toward Yuri vanished at the sight of Sarah and Nicolai running into the mouth of a cave. He pulled a box of bullets from his coat pocket and reloaded his gun, then he flipped the chamber shut and said, "Let's go."

Chapter Forty-Seven

The roar from the black car's engine reverberated through the air. Sarah glanced over her shoulder in time to witness the massive front bumper rising over the cliff wall like a breaching whale thirty feet behind her.

"Come on!" She and Nicolai raced up a short stairway chiseled into the rock and entered the mouth of the cave as another bullet flew past their heads.

She led him into the dark interior, blindly groping her way through the tunnel. The deeper into the cave they went, the darker it became as they turned right, then left, then right again. Fifty yards in, they reached a small room. Light streamed in from a small oculus cut into the ceiling. It illuminated a wall to her left with a fresco of Jesus Christ surrounded by worshippers. She scanned the room and noticed a depression in the rock blackened with soot. A few primitive bowls lay near it and Sarah realized they'd stumbled into an early Christian home.

Voices echoed down the tunnel.

"We need to find an exit," Sarah said.

"This way!" Nicolai said low as he pulled Sarah into another tunnel. They turned a corner and ran down another twisting tunnel, tripping over an uneven rock floor. Overhead, light filtered in through narrow cuts in the rock and Sarah realized the deeper they went in this maze, the less chance they had of finding their way out.

"We've got to double back," she said.

Another shot rang out behind them and Sarah ducked. The bullet missed, hitting the wall a several feet behind her. She and Nicolai jogged down another corridor and through a small room before entering a large chamber.

Ribbons of light streamed in from four narrow slits cut high into the rock near a domed ceiling. The flickering beams fell across the room to land on eight twenty-foot pillars carved from the rock. Inside an alcove at one end, a cross-shaped recess crowned an altar.

"Come here." Nicolai patted a six-foot-tall flat, circular stone wheel standing in a trough against the wall next to the entrance. He tapped a wedge holding it in place with his foot.

A rolling door. A trap—already set.

Voices in the tunnel told them Max and Yuri were within a few feet from the room.

"Close it." Sarah whispered.

Nicolai shook his head and whispered, "We'll be trapped." He motioned for her to retreat back into the small room at the entrance and duck down in the shadow of a corner. "Wait for my signal," he murmured, and then he hid in the shadows on the other side.

Sarah held her breath and listened as Max and Yuri's voices grew louder.

"I saw them go this way." Sarah heard Yuri say, then Max responded. "You go first." Yuri entered the small room and passed Sarah and Nicolai hiding in the corners, then entered the chapel. Max followed behind the larger man.

As soon as Max stepped into the chapel, Nicolai nodded at Sarah, and she nodded back. He lunged forward, throwing his weight into the back of Max's knees and the cardinal fell into Yuri. They both tripped, lost their balance, and crashed on the ground.

Nicolai rolled sideways and called to Sarah, "Now!"

She leaned through the opening to the chapel and grabbed the wedge from under the stone wheel, and it rolled into the groove carved into the floor, gaining momentum as it rotated toward the opposite wall.

Nicolai stood up and threw himself through the doorway and into Sarah's embrace as Max rolled over and fired his gun at his back. The bullet zipped through the opening and hit the wall above Nicolai's head a second before the stone wheel slammed into the opposite and the trop door closed.

Max and Yuri were blocked behind the sealed door—trapped—and everything went silent.

"Are you ok?" Sarah whispered.

"Yes," Nicolai said between breaths. "That was close."

"We've got to go." But she didn't want to leave. She wanted to stay right where she was, in Nicolai's arms.

Chapter Forty-Eight

Max moved away from the chapel's entrance and cocked his gun at Yuri. "How many times will you let her get away before I kill you?"

"You're going to shoot me?" Yuri sneered. He pulled out his handkerchief and sat down on a bench. "Good luck getting out of here alive." His throat tightened, and a sharp wheezing sound squeaked out with each breath.

"I never should have hired you!" Max stomped across the room to the doorway and ran his hands around the outside of the stone wheel, searching for a way to release the boulder. He laid his hands on the edge of the rock and pushed, but the heavy stone refused to budge.

"Come here!" he ordered. "Help me shove this out of the way."

Yuri watched in silence as Max struggled with the stone. His movements were jerky and disorganized. The veneer of superiority was gone, replaced by the actions of a desperate, maniacal man. His blistered, ragged face glistened with puss and sweat, and his eyes held the same crazed look prisoners wore inside the gulag—a curious change which prompted a question Yuri hadn't thought to ask until now. "What is this cross?"

"Speak up!" Max ordered. "I don't understand your Russian gibberish."

"Why do you want this cross?"

"That is none of your business," Max snapped without looking up. "Get over here and help me."

Yuri crossed the room in six steps. He grabbed Max by the arm and spun him around, throwing him hard into the wall. The impact knocked the breath out of Max, and he gasped for air as Yuri pinned him to the wall with one hand. "You'll answer my question, or you'll never leave this room." Yuri leaned into his hand, increasing the pressure until Max's expression changed from anger to panic.

Max nodded, struggling for air, and Yuri released his hold letting Max collapse on the floor. He stayed there, breathing heavily and rubbing his chest where Yuri's hand had been.

When Max met Yuri's gaze, the Russian could see their relationship had changed. There was a new unspoken understanding between them that ended the game they'd been playing. Now brute force ruled, not money and prestige. Killing Sarah and her man and getting the cross was Yuri's game to win or lose now. He knew it, and most importantly, Max knew it too.

Max crawled to one of the benches and pulled himself onto it, hunched over, hands quivering. "Very well. I'll tell you everything while you work on the wheel."

Yuri nodded in agreement.

As Max massaged his throat and croaked out the story of the cross, Yuri worked to free the stone. The cardinal told him about his arrangement with the CIA, Sarah's part in his plan, and the cross's connection to the Romanov dynasty.

"And its powers are proven," he continued. "Rasputin used the cross to save the life of the tsarevitch."

"How?" Yuri panted as he struggled with the stone.

"The cross is a healing tool. Its power can heal the sick."

The Russian listened without comment. He gave up on the wheel and turned to kicking at the trough it rested in. He stomped on the groove until the rock ledge broke apart, and the wheel rolled free of the chapel's entrance. It balanced on its flat edge for a moment and then fell over and broke into several pieces on the dusty floor.

"You say this cross heals?" Yuri faced Max, who stared at the destruction Yuri had wreaked.

"Yes." Max met his gaze. "But only by those who know how to use it." He got up, strode across the room, and grabbed Yuri by the arm. "Help me get the cross, and I will heal you." His grip tightened. "I will repair your body, the wounds on your head, your lungs. Anything you need, the cross will provide." Max's eyes gleamed as he watched Yuri consider the possibilities. "It will cure any ailment. You could live a long healthy life. That's what you want, isn't it?" Max searched Yuri's expression. "To be free of your illnesses?"

Yuri snatched his arm away and walked into the shadow of a pillar. *Is it what I want?*

"I can make it happen for you." Max's voice followed Yuri, enticing him as he moved around the room.

"And the cross will heal my lungs?" Yuri murmured.

"Yes! Yes, it can do that. The cross can heal any part of the body. It can even bring people back from the brink of death. Rasputin proved it!"

Yuri fought back the rumbling cough building inside

his chest.

"Sickness, injury—the cross's power will erase all of it and make you a young man again."

Yuri stopped to cough, then spit into a corner. He pulled out his handkerchief and wiped it across his face as he thought of all the times he had relied on this same action to save him. Struggling to breathe, to move, to be free of the constant sickness threatening to steal each breath he took. Since the age of sixteen, he'd carried the burden of this cough. The beatings he'd taken in the ring, the smoke-filled bars, they'd made it worse, and he knew he would never get any better. This cough would kill him. Not a man. Not a bullet. Only the insufferable cough clogging up his lungs and choking the life out of him with every breath he took.

He turned back to Max and said, "*Da.* I will go."

Chapter Forty-Nine

Khor Verap Monastery near Mount Ararat
The black wolf bounded onto the hill's jagged summit and braced himself against the wind. Intense at this height, the gusts rippled through the wolf's fur and triggered memories from a past life. One spent in the human world, far from this place. A place where he was called Rasputin, the Mad Monk.

He sniffed the air. Scents from the river below carried a musky animal smell from the wild bears, lynx, and wolves living on the mountain.

Oh! To taste the flesh of an animal again!

Saliva dripped from his open mouth. He had not felt the pleasures only an earthly body could enjoy for a long time.

Too long!

A ridge on the hill flattened into a wide bridge. The wolf trotted across, sniffing before sitting back on his haunches and surveying the landscape below.

Scattered cottages made up a village along the bank of the river. Beyond it was farmland as far as the wolf's light-blue eyes could see. A dirt road ran alongside the waterway, skirting the base of a hill where a small monastery fortress was perched high atop a cliff. The road continued toward a mountain dominating the northern horizon.

Mount Ararat.

The steep volcanic cone soared boldly into the sky, its northeastern side marred by a three-mile-long gorge, a scar from a landslide that occurred long before Rasputin's spirit left his human body. Long before his ghost discovered its power to inhabit another.

He pointed his long bony nose to the sky and sniffed. *Gasoline.*

A jeep sped down the road toward the monastery, and Rasputin instinctively knew there were two passengers inside.

And the cross.

He blew out an indignant huff. *My cross.*

When the jeep disappeared behind the mountain, Rasputin wheeled around to survey the river. His mouth opened, and his tongue rolled out, panting as he tracked a pack of gray wolves trotting along one of the many trails crisscrossing the landscape. They searched for food, staying close to the river, following the scent of their prey.

Even from a distance, Rasputin's wolf eyes could see the health of the pack, their large size, their thick fur and large heads. They held their tails high, confident in their collective power and strength. Their leader trotted ahead of the pack, his head shifting from side to side as he searched for their next meal.

Rasputin smiled, exposing the sharp canine teeth that would soon tear into the leader's flesh. Saliva dripped from his pink tongue at the thought of the warm blood he knew would gush into his mouth when he delivered death upon the wolf, the crunch of bones between his teeth as he ripped his body apart in front of the other wolves. The pack would belong to him. An army of wolves under his control.

The urge to howl exploded inside Rasputin's new body. He tilted his head back and let out a long low growl grow into a high-pitched wail. Wild and haunting, the sound revealed a wolf's desire to kill—its need to kill— to satisfy its bloodlust. It triggered an animalistic emotion Rasputin couldn't contain. His base instinct fought with the little bit of humanity left after his death in the cold, dark water.

The wolf turned his gaze back at the monastery.

When the woman took the cross, she had set it free, along with his soul. He would hunt the cross wherever it went until it was his. Then, he would use the cross's power to become fully human again and seek his revenge on those who plotted against him—the conspirators who shot him and threw his body into the frozen river.

He convulsed as he sucked in more air. The memory of the pain resurfaced, but he could breathe in this new animal's body. He could alleviate the pain. And he could run and fight and take down prey. He could kill the woman and take the cross and gain its life force once more.

The cross is all I need to become a part of this world again, and no one, not even this woman, will stop me from my goal.

He stared down at the monastery where the woman crossed the courtyard. She had the cross with her, and he could feel its energy even from this distance. The power had grown stronger since his death.

For too long, he'd been trapped in a parallel universe. Suspended between life and death. The Byzantine Cross would break him free of his prison and shake loose the grip that confined him to this dark and lonely world, and people would again fear the Mad

235

Monk.

The black wolf stomped his paws in excitement, imagining his future. *The cross must be his!*

Rasputin's nickname had served him well during his life. And after his death. His dubious reputation as a mystic took on more significance when Rasputin became part of the spirit world. His powers grew stronger—more concentrated and adaptable but also more unpredictable. Instinctively, he knew his powers were based in the underworld, a more dangerous place. Death meant little to souls there who could never die again but neither did they live. They existed outside a state of being, empty and alone.

The wolf pack was in pursuit of its prey. Rasputin watched as they investigated a clearing, sniffing for information they needed to overtake whatever they were chasing. They were efficient and organized. Their leader stood off to the side, directing the activity with little yelps. He was indeed a strong leader. But Rasputin was smarter.

He lifted his head to howl into the cold mountain air. Far off in the distance, the wolf pack echoed back to him. They waited for him, sensing danger nearby.

The black wolf stood and stretched his knobby legs before picking his way down the rocky mountainside.

It was time.

Rasputin would soon hold the cross in his hands as a fully human, reincarnated man, and the power of the Byzantine Cross would be his.

Chapter Fifty

Late in the evening, the jeep rolled into Khor Verap, Mount Ararat's monastery complex, on its last drop of gasoline. Sarah scanned the dusty courtyard. "It looks more like a fortress than a monastery."

An arched gate with a cross carved into its keystone framed the famous Mount Ararat off in the distance. Sarah's heart skipped a beat when she saw it. *Just like the drawing in the book at the Vatican library!*

Inside the monastery's brick walls, a row of small buildings lined three sides of the defensive wall and surrounded a chapel topped by an eight-sided dome. It was a lonely, ancient place.

"It looks deserted. What if no one's here to take the cross?" Nicolai asked as he set the jeep's brake.

"The cardinal told me there is a monk living here who maintains the property." Sarah smiled at Nicolai. "Besides, we've come too far for it to end that way."

"Well, then." He grinned back at Sarah as he grabbed his jacket from the back seat. "Come on. Let's deliver the cross and finish this job." She opened the glove box and retrieved the cross where she'd kept it safe since cutting it free from her jacket. As she picked it up a spark from the wood lit up the dash. She touched the cross and felt a faint, nearly imperceptible, buzzing sensation. She examined the cross closely, but nothing had changed. Still a simple little black cross.

It's probably just my imagination. She shook off the feeling and got out of the jeep.

Nicolai had already dashed halfway across the courtyard when Sarah caught up with him. They climbed the steps to the church's portico and opened one of its ancient oak doors. Inside, smoke from burning frankincense drifted above their heads. The hazy atmosphere distorted ribbons of light—red, yellow, blue, and green—entering the chapel through four tall stained glass windows.

A monk stood with his back to them at an altar holding a long brass lighting stick in both hands as he finished lighting the candles on a tall candelabra. The light gave the dark chapel a warm heart.

He blew out the flame after lighting the last candle, then bent his head in prayer before turning to face Sarah and Nicolai.

He was an old man with a wiry, gray beard and a long black robe that hung loosely over his stooped shoulders. He shuffled toward them, using the stick to support his fragile body, and, in perfect English, said, "As it is foretold, so it has come to pass."

Sarah opened her mouth to introduce herself, but the monk raised a hand to stop her.

"No need to tell me," he said. "I already know who you are. I have been praying for you." He pointed a bony finger at her pocket. "May I see it?"

She brought the Byzantine Cross out of her pocket, but the monk didn't take it. Instead, he cupped his hands around her own and closed his eyes. After mumbling a prayer, he released her hand and bent forward to examine the cross. A sigh escaped him. "It has had a long and difficult journey," he said, glancing up at Sarah. "May

I?" She nodded, and he carefully picked the cross up and placed it on his open palm. "Time away from home has changed the cross's appearance."

Nicolai cleared his throat. "What can you tell us about the Byzantine Cross?"

His face serious, the monk pondered the question. "I know many things about this cross yet I understand very little." He placed it back in Sarah's hand. "Come. I will tell you what I know."

He limped to the nearest stained glass window, supporting himself on the lighting stick as he went. "For this story, we must travel thousands of years into the past. To an age we no longer comprehend and to a miracle that remains a mystery even to this day." He indicated an image at the top of the stained glass window. "The age of Noah's great flood."

"But what does the cross do?" Nicolai asked.

The monk smiled. "Patience. The story begins so very long ago." He gestured toward the window, where the topmost pane depicted a vibrant blue wave curling around the ark. Noah stood on its bow as a white dove clutching an olive leaf in its beak flew under a rainbow framing the scene.

"When the rain ceased and the waters receded," the monk began his story, "Noah found God's promised land a muddy wasteland." The monk moved on to the next picture captured in glass. "Unlivable, washed clean of seed and soil. Mud and salt water was the inheritance Noah and his family received from God when he delivered them from the storm." He pointed to the next windowpane where Noah's four sons knelt to pray upon the brown landscape. "They needed a miracle to bring life back to this desolate land. God answered their prayers by bringing forth fertile soil and fresh, clean water."

He gestured to the second window, where Noah and his sons were shown building shelters and plowing a field. "God provided Noah and his family with the knowledge, skill, and resources to rebuild the world. From mud and sticks, they constructed homes and farms, and eventually, their descendants built towns and cities and even empires!"

When he said the last word, Sarah remembered the Romani's trance and Princess Sophia's fist hitting her chest as she made the promise to build an empire for her descendants.

They crossed the church to a third window. Three religious pilgrims knelt at the base of a large stone, praying. A hole was cut through it's top and a small cross was embedded above the hole. Sarah recognized the boulder as an anchor stone.

The monk continued. "The legend of the ark's connection with God, and the miracles he bestowed upon Noah drew many believers to our region during the earliest years of Christianity. Over the centuries, these pilgrims carved out seven crosses from the ark's wood, each one representing one of the Seven Churches of Revelation."

"Seven?" Sarah glanced at Nicolai, then back to the monk. "You're saying there are six more crosses?"

The monk nodded, his beard bouncing gently against his chest. "Yes, seven crosses were cut from the ark's bow knee—a joint connecting both sides of the structure with the bow." He glanced at the first window. "Each cross was embedded into an anchor stone, one cross per stone, to mark a trail that began here, at Khor

Virap and led all the way up to the south side of the Ahora Gorge on the east side of the mountain where you can view the remains of the great ship."

"And as they prayed, their words passed through the crosses to God," Sarah said, remembering the story Max told her at the Vatican. "Over the centuries, each cross was infused with a miraculous power."

"Yes." The monk smiled. "For centuries, the faithful prayed to the crosses, and each time the crosses were penetrated by the Holy Spirit."

"Where are the other six?" Sarah asked. "Do they still exist?"

The monk motioned for them to follow him to the final window, where sunlight poured through a seven-pointed star at the top of the window. The light illuminated a bright orange circle and sent sunbeams through each of the seven crosses depicted around the circle's perimeter.

"When the region was overtaken by non-Christians," the monk continued, "the crosses were removed for safekeeping. Separated. Each one sent to one of the Seven Churches of the Revelation where our elders believed they would be protected." He glanced back at the window and added, "Despite their efforts, the crosses remained in great danger."

"What happened?" Nicolai asked.

The old man sighed. "Once they were separated, the crosses changed, tainted by the sins of the world. For some, their power became more intense; for others, the power weakened. Sometimes a cross would take on the malevolent spirit of the person who possessed it here on Earth, becoming the very antithesis of God."

"Evil?" Nicolai offered.

"Yes, the cross's sacred ability to perform miracles tainted by the spirit of its last possessor. When used for good, the cross accumulates goodness, and when used for evil, the cross brings forth even more evil." He mumbled a quick prayer of protection before he continued. "Each cross has lived a different life, and each carries the scars acquired along the way." He scrutinized the cross again.

"What about this cross?" Sarah's hand buzzed with energy as she presented the cross to the monk. "Do you know if the Byzantine Cross is evil?"

He took the cross from Sarah and shuffled to the last window. He held the cross up to the light and scrutinized it. "Yes. A black heart possessed this cross, and it has acquired a heinous, deadly evil."

"Rasputin," Nicolai whispered.

The monk nodded in agreement. "This cross, the Byzantine Cross, was first sent to Pergamum, a city known for compromising its faith," he said. "When the city fell to invaders in the seventh century, the church sent the cross to Constantinople, the capital of the Byzantium Empire. It remained safe there for nine hundred years."

"Until the Turks conquered the city and made it their capital?" Sarah asked.

"Yes, the priests gave the cross to the emperor's brother, Thomas, on the eve of the city's collapse, with the promise he would use the cross's power to build a new Byzantium."

"Russia?" Nicolai said.

"Yes. Thomas Palaiologos died before he could establish a new empire, but the cross was given to his daughter Zoe, the youngest princess of Byzantium. She took the Byzantine Cross with her to Russia when she married the newly crowned emperor, Ivan I. Renamed Sophia, the princess became Russia's first empress, always believing the cross's power of regeneration would create a new empire, a third Rome, in her husband's wild land."

Sarah's heart fluttered inside her chest at the mention of Sophia's name.

"And the Byzantine Cross has been in the possession of the Russian tsars ever since." Nicolai finished.

"Until now." The monk smiled at Sarah. "You have brought the cross home."

"But what about the other crosses?" she asked. "Have they been found?"

Wrinkles deepened in the corners of the monk's eyes as a smile lit up his face. "Come. There is one more thing I must show you."

Chapter Fifty-One

Rasputin's new wolf body worked well in this wild land. Lean and tough, it had abilities his human body could never claim.

He'd already covered several miles, tracking the wolfpack as they hunted for food. His heightened sense of smell zeroed in on their den hidden in the rocks. Now, he scratched and dug at the entrance until the pack emerged, enraged and ready to confront the black wolf with the penetrating blue eyes.

Rasputin picked out the leader immediately. The strong and compact alpha male, all muscle and bone. He stood still and calm until Rasputin snarled at him. The sound triggered the gray wolf. He laid back his ears and bared his sharp teeth.

Overconfident with his pack behind him, the gay wolf jumped into the fight without the usual overtures, but Rasputin was ready for the assault. They lunged at each other, clamping down on each other's bodies, biting into flesh and shaking their heads from side to side. The alpha let out a yelp of pain as Rasputin's teeth tore at the flesh until blood filled the Mad Monk's mouth and heightened his killer instinct.

Rasputin grabbed more fur and flesh in his jaws, working his way up the animal's body until he reached the wolf's neck. One last crushing bite, and Rasputin ripped open the gray wolf's throat, and the leader fell dead at his feet. The pack watched in vain as the lead female lifted her head and howled a terrible cry for her dead mate.

The pack turned on Rasputin. Nearly forty wolves growled and barked in agitation as they paced around him. The four strongest stepped forward—the largest three males of the pack and the alpha's female. She jumped at Rasputin first, but he stepped to the side, and she landed in a patch of snow. Another wolf on his left snapped at him as a third charged him from the front.

Rasputin crouched down and sprang at the first wolf, knocking him into the rocks, and then he spun around and faced the second wolf. This wolf went for Rasputin's long wolf nose, but the Mad Monk jerked his head away before the wolf could latch on. A third wolf bit into his rear, sinking his teeth deep into Rasputin's wolf flesh.

Wild with bloodlust, Rasputin ignored the pain and gave in to the thrill of the attack, biting and tearing at the flesh of any wolf who dared approach him. He forced three wolves to back away, and a fourth wolf lay motionless before the pack. Dead.

The three wolves regained their courage and confronted Rasputin once more, encircling him on all sides. But Rasputin didn't wait for the pack to make the first move. He leapt at the smallest wolf, the alpha female, and tore into her muzzle. Bones cracked under his powerful jaws, and she jerked away. As she did, Rasputin's sharp teeth ripped away the skin and bones of her snout, leaving the bottom half nothing but ragged flesh and exposed bone. She retreated into the crowd of pacing wolves, defeated, knowing the only thing left for her was a slow, painful death.

The last two wolves charged Rasputin and spun him

in a circle, but they failed to pin him down. One snapped at his shoulder, another at his tail. Rasputin bounded toward the one at his shoulder, knocking the wolf off its feet and sinking his teeth into its neck. Panicked, the wolf at his rear spun around in circles, dragging Rasputin along with him, but the Mad Monk held onto the wolf, and when the first bone shattered between Rasputin's teeth, he knew he'd won. The wolf let out a yelp and tried to shake him off, but Rasputin's jaws squeezed tighter. Finally, the wolf lay down, quieted, and submitted to Rasputin. But with a quick twist of his head, Rasputin ripped the wolf's throat apart. The dying animal made a gurgling sound before closing its eyes and releasing one last shuddering breath.

The wind whistled across the snowy landscape as the late alpha's mate lifted her head and let out a long, mournful howl.

Rasputin stared out at the pack over the wolf's body and snarled. The taste of the alpha's blood in his mouth provoked his own instincts, and he fought the urge to charge the pack. To crush each of their throats in his jaws and rip the flesh from their bones just like he'd done to their leader, but Rasputin needed them. To take down two riders on horseback, he'd need an army.

My wolf army.

Rasputin's wolf snapped at the wolf pack, and not a single animal challenged him. He stepped forward, and they cringed back. Then he snarled. First one, then two, then three and four wolves at a time submitted to him.

Rasputin paced before them, growling and snapping, his paws tracking the blood of their leaders across the ground as drool dripped from his panting mouth. No other wolf stepped out of line. Instead, they waited for their new leader to tell them what to do, but he sat back on his haunches. No more attacks would come unless someone broke rank.

Rasputin stood and trotted over to the biggest juvenile, putting the young wolf in his shadow. It whimpered as Rasputin sniffed its fur. He nipped at its ear, but there was no retaliation from the beaten wolf.

He moved through the crowd to the alpha female. Blood dripped from her mangled snout. She raised her head to look at Rasputin with desperation in her dying eyes. Agony radiated from her like a stench.

Rasputin growled a low, threatening noise meant as a warning for the rest of the pack, and a few wolves whined in response. A few others braved a quiet growl, but none made even the slightest move challenging him.

Rasputin had won the pack.

He barked, and the wolves formed a line. He climbed a boulder and stood over the pack as they passed by the body of their leader. His black wiry fur was matted with the blood of the fallen leaders, and his bright-blue eyes seared through each wolf's defeated gaze. There would be no more attempts on his life.

I am their alpha now.

Only the female stayed behind. She limped over to lie beside her mate. Blood dripped from the wound on her face to pool on the white snow. She licked his wounds and touched her nose to his to waken him, and then closed her eyes and waited to die.

Rasputin witnessed the loyal gesture. It'd been a long time since he'd seen death, and this time, he was the murderer.

He reveled in the thrill this new power gave him. *Giving life infuses a body with power, but death*—his tongue slipped out to lap up the blood still clinging to his lips—*death gives power to the killer.* Rasputin felt the power of the dead wolves surge through his body like an electrical current.

The female's breathing slowed, and Rasputin watched her chest rise and fall until it stopped altogether.

I killed her.

I caused her heart to stop.

I brought death to this bitch, and I will do the same to the woman who has my cross.

Chapter Fifty-Two

The monk gestured for Sarah and Nicolai to join him at the altar. "This monastery has been home to Noah's crosses for a very long time." He swept back a red velvet curtain behind the altar and revealed a gold ambry sitting in the center of a marble table. He opened its doors and removed a long gold box. When he opened the lid, she saw six crosses lying side by side on a pillow made of white silk. The monk took the Byzantine Cross from Sarah's hand and placed it with the others. "At last, they are together. God bless them all." He gave the sign of the cross over the seven crosses.

Something shifted in the atmosphere when he added the cross to the box. A low buzzing sound hummed softly in Sarah's ears, and she glanced at Nicolai, wondering if he heard it, too, but his gaze never strayed from the crosses.

The length and shape of the crosses matched perfectly, but each was slightly different in appearance. One had taken on a red tone, one green, and another gained a warm mahogany color. Two others had a blue tint, and the Byzantine Cross was the darkest of the group. Only one of the seven was perfect. Its surface showed no wear and tear at all.

Sarah pointed to it. "Why does this one look so new?"

"It was the first cross returned to the monastery," the

monk said. "It arrived in the eighth century and appeared similar in color to this one." He gestured to the green cross. "Each time another cross returned, the others gradually changed in color and texture, reversing the damage they suffered through the centuries." He pointed to the one Sarah asked about. "This one was the first to return and has almost returned to its original state."

"Are you saying they change back to when they were first cut from the ark?" Nicolai asked.

"Yes, the crosses can miraculously restore themselves to their original form when they are together. Now, because the last cross has been returned, the process will speed up for them all." He closed the box and held it out to Sarah. "But only after you return them all to the ark."

A strange vibration ran through her when she touched the box and she held up her hand to stop him. "But I brought them for you."

The monk shook his head. "No, not me. The ark. Their home."

"But why me?"

"You were chosen," he told her as he placed the box in Sarah's hands. She shook her head, but the monk continued. "Not by any person, but by destiny. You must take them all back to the ark."

The Romani grandmother said the same thing. A shiver ran up Sarah's spine.

She handed the box back, but he patted it and shook his head, refusing to take it. "The power of Noah's crosses cannot be cleansed any other way."

"But I'm not a climber. What if I can't get to the ark?"

"You have been chosen by God. You will do it."

"How will I know where to go?" she asked as another faint wave of tingling pulsations raced through her body. Starting in her hands and traveling up to her head, the sensation buzzed in her ears before moving down her body and settling in her chest.

What is happening? Sarah glanced at the box, then back to Nicolai. *Does he feel the tremors too?*

"I don't want to do this alone," she said.

A slow smile and a twinkle in his eye told Sarah everything she needed to know.

"Do you think I'd miss this?" Nicolai said before asking the monk, "Can you tell us exactly where the ark is on the mountain? Does the trail still exist?"

"There are three trails, but they haven't been maintained in decades."

"Are there maps?" Nicolai asked.

The monk stroked his chin. "Yes, in the library." He clapped his hands together and said, "You'll stay overnight, and we will go over them together. You can leave before dawn."

"We'll need supplies and gasoline for our jeep."

The monk shook his head. "I have no fuel. Only horses, but they will get you to the ark more easily than your vehicle can."

The strange pulsing sensation eased and Sarah thought about the task she now faced.

If it is up to me to take these crosses to the ark, I'll take them. I won't let them be used to harm anyone again. Sarah glanced at the depiction of the ark in the first window. *I'll take them to their home. Their final resting place.*

"Are you ready for another adventure?" Nicolai asked her, smiling.

Sarah smiled back and said, "Always."

Chapter Fifty-Three

Early the next morning, Sarah and Nicolai galloped across the plain on horseback to Mount Ararat. When they reached the Pilgrims' Trail, Sarah brushed away a strand of hair blowing in her eyes and surveyed the map they'd found in the monastery's library. "This is the most direct route to the ark, but the monk said it's a rougher trail than the other two."

"The horses can handle it," Nicolai said, patting his horse. They were stout horses, compact and muscular. Perfect for the difficult climb up the mountain.

She reached down and flipped back the cover of the saddlebag. A wooden box holding the crosses vibrated softly under her touch, safe and secure. "We better get going." She closed the bag and slapped the reins against her horse's neck.

Five hours later, they reached a granite boulder.

"The sixth anchor stone!" Sarah shouted through her scarf.

Just like the others they'd passed, the boulder stood upright and had a cross-shaped indention carved into the surface below the hole at its top. Sarah dismounted and retrieved the map from her pocket. She spread it at the base of the stone and said, "We're about a mile from the south side of the gorge. Once we get to the overlook, we should see the ark." She glanced up at Nicolai standing behind her. "Do you think the ark is really there?"

"Of course, the ark is there," Nicolai said. "The photograph I saw is only forty years old."

"But what if we can't find it? Or it's collapsed? What if it's buried under ten feet of snow?"

"It's too early in the fall for much snow." He smiled. "You worry too much."

Sarah stood up and folded the map. "I hope you're right," she said, putting the map back into her pocket.

"Unbelievable." Nicolai ran his hand down the front of the boulder. "Thousands of years have passed, and yet this stone still sits here, just as it did the day the ark ran aground."

Sarah removed her glove and ran her own hand along the face of the rock. She stood her toes to touch the hole at the top and a quiver ran up her arm. Like the other anchor stones they'd already passed, her touch awakened a vibration in the rock and spread throughout her body.

"Do you feel that?" she asked.

Nicolai reached up to touch the hole at the top of the stone. "What?"

"A tremor. The crosses are doing it, too." She held up the bag, and he laid his hand on the box holding the crosses.

Nicolai shook his head. "I don't feel anything."

"Maybe it's my imagination," Sarah said, but she knew it wasn't her imagination. It was the electric connection the crosses shared between themselves and the stone. It was the essence of the miracle of the crosses.

If I say a prayer, will it be answered like the pilgrims believed theirs would be?

The horses snorted and danced around, and Sarah glimpsed a movement from the corner of her eye. She whipped around and spotted a shaggy black wolf trotting their way with the same penetrating eyes she remembered from the Romani woman's trance.

Rasputin?

A pack of gray wolves, each one large enough to take down a horse, followed the black wolf. The horses stomped the ground and reared at their presence, whinnying in fear.

"Get the horses," Sarah yelled to Nicolai.

They swung up into their saddles, and the horses bolted, running ahead of the wolves through patches of snow and rocks. The black wolf led the pack, his light-blue eyes boring into Sarah's back all the way to the edge of a crevasse. He barked once, and Sarah glimpsed behind and saw the pack spread out into a long line behind the horses. The black wolf barked again, and the right flank moved ahead as the left held back.

Nicolai spurred his horse ahead of Sarah up the mountain to a group of boulders as the wolves drew closer. When they reached the top, Sarah's horse s reared up and spun around in circles when Sarah yanked the reins back before they tumbled into a crack in the mountain.

The black wolf fell back from the pack, barking orders as the wolves caught up to Sarah and Nicolai. The pack barked and snapped at each other, working themselves into a bloodthirsty frenzy. The black wolf bounded onto a boulder, always focused on Sarah, relying on the other wolves to hold Nicolai at bay.

The black wolf barked again, and the largest gray wolf lunged at Sarah's horse, sinking its jaws deep into its hindquarters. The horse screamed. Crazed with pain, it reared up, pawed the air, then came down on the wolf. The horse toppled over and Sarah and the backpack with the crosses landed next to them.

"Sarah!" Nicolai yelled.

As she struggled to stand, her horse got to its feet and ran away, with the gray wolf close behind. Four more wolves broke from the pack to join the chase.

Nicolai jumped off his horse, grabbed a pickaxe and his backpack from the saddle, and then slapped his horse's rump, sending it running after Sarah's horse with three more wolves chasing after the fleeing animal. Sarah grabbed her backpack as he grabbed her arm and pulled her to the edge of the crevasse.

The black wolf leapt onto a boulder as the rest of the wolf pack sprinted up the trail. Their backs were hunched over, their fur stood on end as they chased Sarah and Nicolai up the mountain.

"We've got to jump," Nicolai said when they reached the crevasse. He held the pickaxe high above his head, ran toward the edge of the crevasse, and launched himself into the air. When he landed on the other side, he drove the axe deep into the ice to stop him from falling over the edge.

He rolled over and got to his knees. "Come on! I'll catch you," Nicolai shouted over the barking.

The pack closed in around Sarah on three sides. If she didn't jump, they would overtake her in seconds and tear her body apart as if she were nothing but a toy.

Sarah glanced over the edge of the crevasse. The narrow crack went deep into the mountain. Jagged shards of rock and ice protruded out from its sides like teeth ready to chew her up inside terrible jaws.

"Jump!" Nicolai yelled from the other side. Behind her, the black wolf barked at the pack, and the wolves halted at his command. He snarled at them, and they growled back, then they turned to Sara, their heads low, snapping and growling as they moved closer to her.

Across the crevasse, Nicolai fell to his knees, arms outstretched, ready to catch her. Sarah took a deep breath and raced to the edge. She planted her feet in the snow and jumped across the gap.

The moment seemed to slow as she flew across the divide. Cold air lashed her face, and for one strange moment, she felt frozen in midair as she leaped across the empty space.

Two wolves followed her over the edge, one fell into the icy fissure and cried out in pain as its body bounced back and forth off the walls of the crevasse.

The second wolf jumped further and latched onto Sarah's foot. Its clenched jaws ground into the sides her boot at the same time her body hit the opposite side. She slid backward, pulled toward the abyss by the weight of the wolf. Her hands landed on a rock, and she grasped it with both hands to stop herself from being dragged over the edge. The rock came loose from the ice, and she slipped a few more inches, only stopping when her jacket caught on the edge of another rock.

As the wolf struggled to find its footing on the rocky crevasse, the lower half of Sarah's body twisted around. The desire to kill made the wolf fearless. Its survival instinct was gone, replaced by a raging madness that blinded the wolf to its own survival.

The earth crumbled under Sarah's body as she dug her foot into the ice to hoist herself up, but the wolf was too heavy. She slid back over the edge.

Just as she when she thought she couldn't hold on any longer, she heard Nicolai shout, "Sarah!"

Chapter Fifty-Four

"Where are they?" Max shouted in the old monk's face.

Tossed papers littered the monastery's library floor. Centuries of documents torn from books, ripped up, and tossed around like trash.

The monk's gray beard swung vigorously back and forth across his black robe. "No. They are taking the crosses back to the ark where they will be safe."

Max stopped. "Crosses? You have more than just the Byzantine Cross?"

"I will tell you no more!" the monk vowed.

"How many?" he demanded. "Do you have Noah's seven crosses?"

But the monk refused to say more. Max nodded over his head, and Yuri yanked the monk's arms back until his elbows nearly touched, his bones popping and cracking as they moved in ways they hadn't in years. The monk's face contorted in agony.

"Tell me, or I'll have him break both your arms." Max waved the gun in front of the monk's face. "Or do you need stronger encouragement?"

The monk grimaced in pain but remained resolute, so Max smashed the butt end of the pistol into the his jaw.

"Tell me!" He grabbed a handful of the old man's beard and pulled his face down to the map spread across the table. "What trail are they using?"

Blood dripped onto the map, but the monk remained silent.

Yuri glared at Max over the top of the old man's head. "I don't think he's going to tell us."

"He'll tell us." Max wiped spittle from his mouth with the back of his hand. "Even if I have to break his brittle back, he'll tell us which way they went." He pushed Yuri to the side and threw the monk to the ground, then he leaned over the table and examined the map. His finger followed the line marking the most direct trail to the gorge. "It shows the ark right here, but the car won't make it. The trail is too steep for too long."

He moved onto a second line. The trail wound around the mountain and climbed several switchbacks, reaching the gorge near the top. "This one is easier but longer."

The third line traced the road developed by the last Russian tsar forty years ago. Built as a road for cars, the project was abandoned when the Soviets took control, leaving three miles of unfinished road on the gorge's southwest side.

Max grabbed at the monk as he crawled across the floor toward a chair. He shoved the map into his face. "Which one is it?" His anger rose to a fever pitch. "Tell me!"

The monk stared back into the cardinal's crazed eyes, and he whispered, "No."

Max dropped the map and wrapped both hands around the monk's neck, shaking him violently and watching the blood drain from the old man's face before he threw him to the ground and kicked him in the stomach. His bones cracked under Max's boot as he stomped the monk's body again and again and again.

****

Yuri leaned back against the desk and studied Max as he beat the frail old man. He always found watching an untrained boxer fight interesting. No matter how informal, professional training always gave a fighter the edge. Untrained fighters like Max didn't know how to control their bodies. He favored his left leg, Yuri noted as he scrutinized him, relying on it only as a counterbalance to the right. It provided stability but left him vulnerable to attack on the left side.

With each blow, Max's face twisted into a sinister grimace, mangled from the lantern Sarah smashed into the side of his head.

Yuri smiled. *Raw meat. Worse even than mine.*

Max kept beating the monk, stomping him into a pile of broken bones. Even after his life ended, and the monk lay limp and unresponsive on the floor, Max continued the assault. But the old monk kept his secret, sacrificing his life to protect the crosses.

Finally, Max stopped and stood over the monk's shattered body, panting like an animal over its kill. Reveling in the power of taking another man's life, even just a little old man.

"He's done." Yuri announced.

But Max remained motionless, frozen by the spell death casts upon the living.

Yuri stood. "Come on," He said. "It's time to go,"

Max slipped the bloodied pistol back into his pocket and picked up the crumpled map. "We'll take the tsar's road," he decided.

"The car will never make it. It's too heavy to climb a mountain, and the road is too rocky. We had enough trouble in Cappadocia."

"Then we'll take their jeep."

They left the body of the monk and went outside to the cars. Yuri searched the jeep's glove box for a screwdriver and slipped the tool into the ignition. The engine sputtered several times, then nothing.

"No gas," he announced, "We'll have to siphon some from the car."

"Then do it!" Max shook with fury. "There's no time to waste. We can't let the crosses get to the ark."

Yuri went to the toolbox in the back of the jeep. He opened it and picked up a tire iron, tapping it against the palm of his hand. He glanced up at Max sitting in the passenger seat, reloading his gun, and imagined the tire iron smashing in his skull.

Too light.

Max kept the gun after Sarah got away in Istanbul, but he knew it wouldn't matter. *There are other ways to kill a man.*

Yuri tossed the tire iron back into the toolbox and searched until he found a large wrench.

Seeing the great and powerful cardinal groveling at his feet would be one of the best moments of his life. Yuri's lips curled back into an evil smile as he pounded the wrench against his hand.

Much better. Smashing in the skull of the arrogant prick is going to feel so good! He will know real pain for the first time in his life.

He laid the wrench on the jeep's roof and kept fumbling through the toolbox for a hose to siphon the gas.

When they reached the ark, Yuri intended to take the crosses for himself. *And the American bitch.* She would know how to use the crosses, and then he'd finally have the health and life he deserved.

Yuri grabbed the siphon and went to work filling the jeep's tank.

Chapter Fifty-Five

"Hold on!" Nicolai yelled down at Sarah as she slipped closer to the edge of the crevasse. "I'm coming for you!"

The gray wolf snarled through locked jaws as its fangs ground further into Sarah's boot. She struggled to hold on until her hand landed on a clump of dirt. she swung back her free foot and slammed the heel into the wolf's face. The animal whimpered but held on, refusing to let go until either she, or it, or both were dead.

Across the crevasse, the black wolf watched from a high boulder as the rest of the pack paced back and forth below him. They whined and barked, but the black wolf remained silent as he surveyed the scene playing out before him.

A spray of ice suddenly fell over Sarah's head and she glanced up. The brown soles of Nicolai's boots protruded out of the snow above her head and his outstretched hands latched onto her wrists. She let go of the rock and grabbed his wrists.

As he struggled to pull her up, Sarah landed another kick to the wolf's right eye. It whined through gritted teeth but didn't break its hold on her boot.

More ice shattered under Nicolai's boots. It hit Sarah in the face and her grip on his wrists slipped, but he caught her and tightened his hold. She could feel the strain in Nicolai's grip as he fought to drag her back up and over the edge, but her weight combined with the wolf's was too heavy for him.

Sarah kicked the wolf's face again, this time stomping her foot downward into its teeth. His mouth opened under the blow, and his weight suddenly dissipated as his clenched jaws release her boot. The gray wolf let out a loud whimper as he plummeted into the depths of the crevasse.

Relieved of the gray wolf's weight, Sarah dug the toe of her boots into the ice and pushed up. With Nicolai's help, she scrambled over the top of the cliff and into his arms.

"I couldn't hold on any longer," she said between gulps of air.

Nicolai wrapped his arms around her and she clung to him, listening to his heart beat rapidly inside his chest. One that matched her own.

"You're safe now," Nicolai smoothed her hair back from her face. "You're safe."

They stayed there wrapped in their embrace as the wolves howled mournfully for their dead companions. Only the black wolf remained silent. He sat on his rock and glared at Sarah and Nicolai as he ignored the cries of his pack.

"The wolf." Sarah sat up and glanced across the crevasse. "The black one, do you see him?"

"I see him," Nicolai glanced at the animal as he unwound himself from the rope he'd tied around his waist.

"He's different from the others." She'd seen those same brilliant blue eyes before. *In a dream? No, not a dream.*

"His eyes," she said. "They're the same ones I saw

during the Romani's trance." The old woman's raspy voice echoed through her head: *Rassputin! Rassputin!* She reached for her backpack, afraid the crosses had fallen into the crevasse with the wolf. She slipped off the backpack and opened the front flap. All seven crosses safe inside their box, still softly vibrating.

"We'd better get going." Nicolai broke into her thoughts. "We'll walk from here." He frowned at her mangled boot. "How's your foot?"

"Fine. Just a little tender. I don't think he broke any bones."

"We'd better check." He pulled off both gloves and gently picked up her foot. "The leather is punctured on both sides," he said, untying the laces. "And he chewed the heel up a bit."

"Will it hold the rest of the way?"

"I think so." He patted the toe of the boot. "I've seen worse." He carefully slid the boot off her foot and rolled her sock down over her foot. The bracing wind was icy, but the heat from his hands warmed her exposed skin.

"Does this hurt?" He traced a finger along the outside of her foot and over her arch.

"No." Heat flooded Sarah's face as he gently massaged her foot, and she knew she was blushing from the sensation of his caress.

"Next time you run into a pack of wolves, you should try throwing a stick instead of giving them your foot to chew on," he said without looking up.

"I'll remember that," she murmured.

He'd lost his hat, and his hair was caught by a breeze. In the sunlight, the color changed from a deep brown to a warm burnished gold. *Has it always done that?* Sarah resisted the urge to run her fingers through it.

"The wolves chased the horses straight up the mountain," he said. "So, we're a lot closer than if we'd stayed on the trail." He lifted his chin toward a jagged line of rock above them. "The gorge is just over the ridge." He rolled her foot around to test her ankle, taking care not to hurt her.

Sarah didn't reply.

"It doesn't look like anything is broken, and there's no blood." Nicolai slipped her sock back on, then her boot. "Do you think you can stand?"

"I think so."

"You need to stop playing so rough," he joked as he stood up.

She smiled. "Is there any other way to play?"

"I know a few," he said, holding his hand out.

She grasped his hand, but her head swam when she got to her feet and she grabbed his arm with both hands. *Is it adrenaline or something else?*

Nicolai cupped her chin, lifting it to gaze into her eyes. "Are you dizzy?"

"I, I..." she stammered as she gazed into his worried eyes. Memories of Cardinal Max, the man in black, and even the oppressive stare of the strange black wolf dissolved into the background. Only she and Nicolai remained.

Only they existed in this frozen world.

Together.

The kiss came so naturally. So gentle, so sweet. Their bodies melded together as she leaned into his embrace, transporting her to a warm, safe place that belonged to them alone. It felt so comfortable to Sarah, like coming home.

When they parted, Sarah was left lightheaded.

Nicolai hugged her close. "I was afraid you were going to fall." His voice was raspy with emotion. "I couldn't let that happen."

"Why did you wait so long to kiss me?" she asked him as she ran her hand down his bearded chin.

"I know how important this mission is, and I didn't want to get in your way." He lifted her chin to gaze into her eyes and smiled. His caramel-colored eyes radiating a warmth from deep within his soul. "But don't think it was easy. I really did almost drive off that cliff in Cappadocia when I was staring at you instead of the road."

They stayed there for a few moments, sharing another kiss—and another, and another—until Sarah forced herself to pull away. "We'd better get up the hill and finish this mission," she said between breaths.

Nicolai let out a mock groan. "Can't we just stay here and continue this?"

She kissed him on the cheek, a sweet little peck. "All good things come to those who wait," she teased as she stepped back.

"But I've already waited too long!" he groaned.

She threw him a mischievous grin as she picked up the backpack and slung a strap over her shoulder. "I'll be worth it."

Nicolai grabbed Sarah around the waist and drew her to him. He gave her one last lingering kiss, and said, "I knew you were worth waiting for ever since the night in the Romani camp."

"All the way back there? I don't believe you," she teased.

He smiled with a glint in his eye and squeezed her

tighter. "You'll know it as soon as we get off this mountain."

He kissed her one last time with a passion she matched in her own kiss.

When they broke apart, he stepped back and plucked the pickaxe from the snow. His eyes still blazed with the heat of their kisses. "When we get back to Istanbul, I'll take you to the best restaurant in the city."

"Is that all you've been waiting for? A dinner date?"

His lopsided grin told her all she needed to know.

Chapter Fifty-Six

"This is the last one," Nicolai shouted over the gusting wind. They'd reached the end of the Pilgrims' Trail and found the seventh and last anchor stone sitting on the southern ridge of the Ahora Gorge.

Sarah braced herself against the boulder. "It's so big." She shaded her eyes with her hand and gazed down into the three-mile-long trench. "How will we ever find the ark in there?" Staring down at the patchy cover of snow and ice, Sarah struggled to pick out any shape resembling the ark.

Nicolai stuck the pickaxe in the ground. "Let's look at the map."

Sarah handed it to him, and he unfolded it against the boulder. "This trail continues straight down to the ark." He traced the line across to a black rectangle. "We should search directly where we are right now." He glanced across the vast landscape of the gorge. Look for something resembling a black box over one hundred twenty yards long and seventy feet wide."

Sarah scanned the landscape back and forth until a dark object caught her attention. "The ark!" Sarah shouted, pointing to a long black rectangle two hundred yards below their feet. The structure curved on its sides and arched in the center, with one end embedded into the mountain, and the other a jagged end protruding over a cliff.

Nicolai followed her line of sight to the ark. "Amazing!" He put his arm around Sarah's shoulders and hugged her. "We made it!"

Not yet, thought Sarah. But they'd come this far, and she'd be damned if the Byzantine Cross, or any of Noah's crosses, didn't make it back to their home.

****

"Faster, you idiot!" Max ordered.

"Shut up!" Yuri grunted back at him. "Or I'll drive this jeep right off a cliff."

Max let out a huff and sat back. There was little he could do about Yuri now. He needed the brute to handle Sarah's man—Nicolai, she'd called him.

But this dumb ox's time is coming.

Max rubbed the outline of the gun in his pocket. Yuri knew he had the pistol, and that could pose a problem, but he didn't know he only had two bullets left—one for Sarah and one for him. And the big oaf didn't move quickly at this altitude. His breathing grew shallow as his wheezing increased. *Maybe I won't even need to shoot him.* He was nearly out of bullets, and he'd rather the Russian die on his own.

After finishing off Sarah's man, of course. When I have all seven crosses.

The idea of having them all excited Max. His breathing quickened when he thought about all the things he could do with the crosses. *The Byzantine Cross was powerful enough on its own. What powers the seven must hold when used together!*

He snuck a sideways glance at Yuri. *What a disgusting animal.* His bulbous nose and open, gaping mouth made him look unintelligent. Low brow. A peasant. He had let the cardinal down so many times over the last few days, it was a wonder Max hadn't already murdered him.

Max caught his reflection in the rearview mirror. *And my face wouldn't look like this.*

The red and inflamed infection on his cheek throbbed. The injury had turned into a pulpy, wet mass of lacerated skin and bits of glass. When the lantern broke against his faces, its panes had splintered, burying shards of handblown glass deep into his skin. Burning kerosene had spilled down his face too. From his hairline to his jaw, the flames singed his skin, hair, and coat. He was a mess, but everything would be fixed once he held Noah's crosses in his hands.

I will call the media and tell them I discovered Noah's ark.

Max caressed the gun's barrel through his coat.

On the steps of St. Peter's Basilica! Yes! Yes!

His palm wrapped around the gun's grip.

I'll show the world the wounds I received when I fought to save the Noah's Crosses from those who would destroy them!

His finger curled around the trigger.

And then, during an elaborate ceremony, I will prove the power of the crosses to heal and regenerate living tissue using my own body, just as Jesus Christ did at the resurrection!

Cold air blew into the jeep and irritated Max's open wound. The cardinal released the gun to shield his cheek from the pain as the jeep rocked back and forth over the uneven trail.

"How much longer?" he asked.

"Don't know," Yuri mumbled as he twisted the wheel left. "Depends on the road." Yuri cranked the wheel left and right as the jeep climbed the mountain.

Several feet ahead, a small boulder the same size as the jeep blocked the trail. Yuri pressed the gas, nudging the rock with the jeep's bumper. It didn't budge.

"Go! Go!" Max pounded the dashboard with a balled-up fist.

The engine groaned, and the rock rolled to the left, but it still blocked the trail. Yuri shifted into the lowest gear and stomped the gas pedal all the way to the floor. The tires spun, and the jeep pushed against the boulder a second time. This time, the massive rock tilted to the left and rolled downhill a few feet, crashing against another boulder.

Yuri shifted gears and drove on.

Max straightened his coat, noticing a splatter of blood on his lapel. *The monk's blood.*

A thrill ran through him when he glimpsed the dark stain. He never thought he could kill someone, but he had—twice. First, the jeweler, then the monk.

He opened and closed his fists, turning his hands over and flexing them again, savoring the memory of the monk's bones cracking under his fingers.

It was a powerful feeling to murder someone with your bare hands. Max decided he liked it much better than shooting someone, like it was with the jeweler. Taking a life using your own power was exhilarating. Like a drug, the act gave him an exciting, elevated sensation. *The ultimate power!*

Max turned away to hide a smile. *Soon the time will come for the Russian to die.*

He eased his hand inside his pocket to check the gun again.

A bullet to the back of his head and his life would

end in an instant. His heart raced at the thought of Yuri's big head exploding into a hundred meaty pieces.

And the blood! He craved watching it drain from the Russian's fat wheezing body as he lay dying in the snow.

Sarah would be next.

Maybe he'd let her beg for her life before he shot her. And not in the head, but the heart. Max wanted to watch Sarah's face as the light faded from her pretty blue eyes.

What a beautiful death that will be!

His tongue flicked out between his lips to taste the monk's blood splattered across his face.

Soon, I'll be a killer again.

Chapter Fifty-Seven

When Sarah and Nicolai reached the ark, they found the main part of the structure buried under layers of sediment. After a few minutes of searching, Sarah located a depression in the snow when she noticed a draft blow through a tuft of sagebrush. She studied the ground, waving her hand across the spot where the air whistled, and located an opening in the ground no bigger than a rabbit hole.

"We should start digging here," Sarah said.

Nicolai worked with the pickaxe, widening the hole as Sarah moved rocks out of the way. Soon, the opening revealed a dark tunnel into the ark. Sarah took a flashlight from Nicolai's backpack and aimed the light down the tunnel.

"I see wooden beams!" She rotated the light around the cramped space.

Within the space, a squared beam rested diagonally just below their feet. Sarah pulled her head out of the hole and swung her feet around to lower herself down.

A wall of wood planks ran alongside the beam, and a thin, patchy layer of ice covered everything. Sarah aimed the flashlight down the tunnel, searching for a way into the ship's heart, but the light faded well before reaching the end.

Nicolai's feet landed on the beam behind her, and Sarah moved further into the tunnel to make room.

"Look at this," he said, shining a light on a joint sticking out of a cross-section of the beam. "You can still see the chisel marks where the beam was cut to fit the joint."

"It's hard to believe this was cut thousands of years ago," Sarah mused.

"By Noah himself," Nicolai added in awe.

"I can't believe it's really here!" She took off her glove and trailed her hand along an exposed section of the wall as they continued down the tunnel into the depths of the ark. Sarah led, kicking loose sediment off the beam as she walked. She could hear the pebbles hitting the lower levels of the ark, swallowed up in the abyss.

"This tunnel doesn't seem to end," she said. "I wonder how far down it goes."

The dark recesses of the tunnel overpowered their flashlights until they stepped into the heart of the ark where shafts of light from outside streamed in through the broken stern.

A rise in the center of the ark created a slight slant from the middle of the ark downward toward both the bow and the stern. Broken beams and planks, rocks and boulders littered the deck, piling up at both ends. Likely due to shifting the structure experienced during an earthquake. Four rows of large cages divided by three narrow aisles filled part of the cavernous interior, and more cages hung suspended from beams overhead.

Nicolai pointed her flashlight at the pile of beams blocking the bow. "We'll have to crawl through the mess to get to the bow knee joint where the crosses were cut."

Sarah faced Nicolai and smiled. "The last stretch of our journey."

Nicolai gestured to the beams with an outstretched arm and bent over in a dramatic bow. "After you, madam," he said with a smile.

****

Yuri found the entrance first. A ring of rocks encircling an opening large enough for a person to squeeze through. The dirt had recently been disturbed and two sets of footprints, one the size of a woman's boots, covered the dusty ground.

The tsar's trail ended a half mile from the southern edge of the Ahora Gorge, leaving them to cover the last leg of the trail on foot to the last anchor stone. From there, tracks in the snow left by Sarah and Nicolai led them down into the gorge to the ark.

An annoying whistle accompanied each breath Yuri inhaled as he pushed the rocks away. He fished around in his pocket for the vapor soaked handkerchief and held it up to his face.

The climb the edge of the gorge did nothing to help Yuri's breathing issues, but once they stopped his struggle to breathe eased, and his confidence returned. He knew he could still kill when the right time presented itself.

Max stood up and glanced at Yuri. "That's enough." He gestured to the hole. "You go first."

Yuri dropped the handkerchief in his pocket and picked up the wrench he'd grabbed from the trunk. It was a primitive weapon compared to Max's gun. But smashing his skull in would be easy enough if he could get behind the man and take him by surprise. One hard whack to the skull, maybe a couple more to finish him off, and it would all be over.

Yuri glanced up at Max as he fit his large body

through the opening to the tunnel who stood. The cardinal stood over him, huffing and puffing through a frown, and Yuri imagined smashing his boot into his mangled face.

A fitting death for the arrogant prick. Face down in the dirt.

****

Max stepped through the tunnel and into the ark's massive inner chamber. "God bless us," Max whispered in awe as he made the sign of the cross. Like Jonah and his proverbial whale, they'd been swallowed whole inside the ancient tomb.

He grimaced as Yuri came up behind him, wheezing and sweaty. Even the sound of him annoyed Max now, and he relished the thought of seeing Yuri's disfigured head explode when he fired a bullet into its back.

There were only two bullets left in the chamber now. There'd been nowhere to buy more since leaving Istanbul, and he hadn't thought to restock while he was there.

Just two bullets. One for Sarah, one for Yuri.

It would have been so much easier if it had only been her. She'd already be dead by now, murdered at the Kremlin by Yuri.

Damn him!

"Which way?" Yuri asked as he held the stinking handkerchief up to his nose.

Max pointed his flashlight at the snowy footprints to the pile of beams leading to the ark's bow. "That way." He waited for Yuri to lead, but the bigger man prodded him forward with a poke in the back from the wrench he'd brought with him.

Who is he to push me around? The imbecile! The big

oaf thinks he will come out of this alive? Ha! Never! He will die in the dirt like the dog he is.

Voices echoed through the tangle of wood ahead of them, and Max held up his hand for Yuri to stop. Two people. Sarah and her man. But where?

Max climbed over a beam and into the pile of wood, and Yuri clambered after him. As they wound their way through the mess, the voices grew louder and more distinct until he saw a glimmer of light illuminating Sarah's face in the dark.

Trapped. An easy kill.

He aimed the gun's barrel at Sarah's head, then pulled back.

No. I need to draw them out. I can't risk losing the crosses.

A nod to Yuri, and they splintered off. Yuri went right and Max went left. They needed to get around Sarah and Nicolai to force them out of the bow and into the middle of the ark where he could get a clean shot at Sarah without endangering the crosses.

Chapter Fifty-Eight

The sides of the ark closed in around Sarah and Nicolai as they crawled through the beams and followed the curve of the ship to the bow knee joint.

"What if it's out of reach?" Sarah jumped over a hole in the deck. "I never thought about what we'd find once we were inside. The bow knee joint might be broken after all this time."

"It can't be after all we've gone through." Nicolai aimed his flashlight down through the hole at the ark's lower levels. "Let's hope the joint isn't down there."

Sarah moved her flashlight over the beams to the huge joint assemblage above her head. The light landed on seven cuts in the wood, shot through the holes, and seven crosses appeared as bright spots on the wall behind it.

"One, two, three, four, five, six, seven!" Sarah counted. "We found it!"

She grasped another beam and climbed up to the cuts but stopped when Nicolai tugged at her jacket. She glanced down. He held a finger to his mouth and pointed behind him through the beams.

"Someone's here," he whispered.

"Bring the crosses out, or I'll shoot you both!" Max's voice echoed off the petrified beams.

Where did he come from? A surge of white-hot anger roiled Sarah. *No! I will not let him have it.*

She took off her backpack, opened the box, and removed the first cross. As she fitted the artifact into the first hole, the bite of an electric shock startled her. A second spark of energy exploded in the cut and zipped around the edges of the cross. A pure bright light grew from the spark and levitated the cross in the center of the cut. Like a soldering iron, the electrical current sealed the cross to the wood and absorbed it back into the ark.

Sarah heard the click of a gun behind her. She grabbed the second cross and inserted it, and then the third and the fourth. Each time, a spark flashed like lightning as the cross merged with the wood and became part of the ark again. By the time Sarah pushed the fifth cross into place, the bow knee glowed brightly in the dark.

Nicolai backed away and covered his eyes as the light intensified, but as Sarah worked the sixth cross into the cut, she heard him gasping for air. She spun around and saw an arm covered by a black sleeve grab Nicolai by the collar and drag him back through the beams.

Sarah fitted the sixth cross into its spot and then swung the backpack over her shoulder and climbed through the beams after Nicolai. She followed the noise of a struggle to the center of the ark, ignoring the broken wood that cut and bruised her as she hurried back through the beams.

Max waited at the other side of the pile of beams when she crawled out, his gun aimed at her heart. "Agent Kraft," His white teeth flashed in the dark through an evil grin. "I didn't think I would travel this far to retrieve my cross, but here we are. Right in the belly of Noah's ark! Bravo!"

Sarah glanced left. Nicolai, having broken free of

Yuri's hold, faced the man in black. He threw a right hook, but the Russian stepped out of the way. Yuri raised a large wrench over his head and slammed down hard on the younger man's upper back. Nicolai's knees buckled, and he crumpled on the snow-covered ground as Yuri dropped the wrench. The old fighter threw himself on top of Nicolai, hitting him over and over again with a balled up fist.

"Let him go!" Sarah shrieked.

"Never mind him." Max's laugh echoed through the ark. "Your boyfriend won't be with us much longer."

"He doesn't have anything to do with this." She showed him her backpack. "It's this you want. Let him go."

"We're long past that point now." Max waved the gun in the air and clicked his tongue. "No, no, no. Neither one of you are going anywhere. This ark will be your tomb. You'll be sealed inside this monument just like you thought the crosses should be."

Out of the corner of her eye, she watched as Nicolai rammed his knee into Yuri's groin and pushed him off. Yuri shook off the assault, and they stood up to face each other. Blood dripped from Nicolai's mouth.

"Nicolai!" Sarah yelled.

Her voice momentarily distracted Yuri. Nicolai bent over and rammed his shoulder into the Russian's torso and a whoosh of air escaped the bigger man. They both fell to the deck, rolling over the edge of a hole and into the dark depths of the ark.

"Give me the crosses," Max demanded, still pointing the gun at Sarah.

Sarah felt the last cross, the Byzantine Cross, vibrating inside the backpack. The tremor grew stronger and the vibration rippled through her as she tightened her grip on the pack's straps. "The crosses don't belong to you. They belong here—in the ark!"

"No, child." A wicked, arrogant smile spread across his face. "The crosses shouldn't be hidden away inside this tomb. They are meant to be out in the world, guided by a holy man such as myself. Someone who will heal the world by ridding it of evil forever." He ambled toward her. "A new creation has come!" His chin jutted out with pride. " 'The old has gone, the new is here!' Second Corinthians 5:17."

"And you believe you are the 'new'?" Sarah challenged him. "That you will save the world?"

"Not the whole world. Only the believers." Max took another step. "I'll become their miracle worker. A new messiah. One who can heal the sick and raise the dead. I'll choose who to save and who to cast out."

His evil laugh echoed through the ark.

"Maybe I'll create a flood." His eyes flashed with unholy fervor. "Yes! Yes! I'll recreate what God did for Noah." He flicked the barrel of his gun at the backpack. "One cross will give me control over the people, but all seven will give me power over the entire Earth. There will be no stopping me when I have the crosses. Floods, earthquakes, fire! I'll be more powerful than any other man! I'll destroy the sinful and recreate society as God intended."

"God…or you?" Sarah challenged.

He shrugged. "The question is irrelevant. I'll be seen as God incarnate. Millions of people will proclaim me their savior—the Second Coming of Christ—and no one will question my authority."

A rock fell from the rafters above them. It rolled to

the edge of the Nicolai and Yuri had fallen into and dropped. Sarah stepped toward it, but the click of the gun's barrel stopped her.

"Worry not." Max lowered the gun and aimed at Sarah's heart. "You'll join him soon enough."

Vicious barking echoed around the room, growing louder until Sarah caught sight of the black wolf with his strange pale eyes snarling down at her. He jumped across the rafters above them, moving back and forth over their heads.

A chill raced up her spine as the sound of the Romani woman's voice echoed through her thoughts—*Rasssputin! Rasssputin! Rasssputin!* Buzzing from the cross inside the backpack intensified.

"Get out of here!" Max shouted at the wolf. He picked up a rock and threw it, but it fell short of the animal who swung around to snap at Max. He shouted again at the animal, but the wolf barely reacted. With the stealth of an assassin, the animal stalked them, jumping easily from beam to broken beam as it drew closer.

"Go on! Get out of here!" Max shouted again, throwing another rock. The wolf lunged at him but slipped and fell twenty feet from Sarah. Rock and ice tumbled over him from above as the animal scrambled to stand. A cage hanging from a rafter swung back and forth above the wolf until its hold on the beam broke and the cage fell, trapping the animal inside its bars. Sarah heard a yelp and then silence.

Max turned back to Sarah. "Now it's your turn. Hand over the crosses or—die."

Scratching sounds came from the cage, growing louder and more desperate until the wolf's snout popped out through a space at the bottom. The animal was trapped inside the cage. The wolf retreated back inside and clamped down on an iron bar, crunching the metal between his teeth and shredding his lips and tongue. His ferocious snarl, stifled by the blood filling his mouth, continued as he fought to free himself from his prison,

Sensing Max's distraction with the wolf, Sarah ran behind a pile of broken beams near the hole in the deck and crouched down.

A pop of gunfire exploded to her left, and Max let out a stream of curses as a cascade of rock and snow rained down upon Sarah. She bent over and covered the backpack with her body until the rocks settled. When she glanced up, Max was stalking toward her, his gun aimed at her head. She hugged the backpack closer.

"Give me the crosses," he demanded. "Now!"

Sarah stayed low, clutching the backpack to her chest as the crunch of Max's footsteps grew louder behind her. The wolf, still trapped inside his cage emitted a low growl as he dug furiously at the sediment under his feet.

As Max rounded the broken beams and closed in on Sarah. She jumped up and sprinted across the deck to stand behind another boulder next to a larger hole. Max followed but tripped over a rock. His finger slipped and the gun discharged. The bullet hit the deck above them, and more snow and ice rained down.

"Dammit!" he cursed as he regained his footing. "You thought you'd just leave the cross here? Never!" he exclaimed. "You'd be taking away the greatest power this world has ever known." He laughed again. "You are not the savior you think you are, Agent Kraft."

"And you think you're the one to hold the crosses' power?" Sarah asked him. "You are nothing! Nothing!"

"You bitch!" Max seethed. "You don't deserve Noah's crosses. Their power belongs to the church—to me!"

"You are not the church!" Sarah clutched the backpack close to her chest. "The crosses were cut from the ark, and they will stay with the ark."

Max closed the distance between them as he kept the gun's barrel leveled at Sarah's chest. When he was within reach of her, his arm shot out to snatch the backpack. "Give them to me. Now!"

"No!" Sarah snapped as she backed up toward the edge of the hole. "You'll never have them!"

"Then say a prayer." He smiled as he cocked the gun again. "You're about to meet God."

Chapter Fifty-Nine

Nicolai landed hard on a beam, and pain shot through the right side of his ribcage. He slid off and fell to the deck, landing next to Yuri. His flashlight flew from his hand. It hit the ground and spun across the deck near a thick curtain of icicles. Its beam of light bounced off the ice, casting shadows around the small space. Iron bars, pitted by erosion, surrounded them above and and on all four sides.

They'd landed inside a cage.

Nicolai's broken ribs throbbed, and a sharp pain ricocheted around inside his torso as he struggled to gain his footing.

Yuri took longer to stand. In the scant light of the flashlight, Nicolai watched the older man stumble across the cage and hold a handkerchief to his face as leaned against the bars. The smell of menthol drifted through the air. He gestured to the four corners of their enclosure as he tucked the handkerchief back inside his pocket. "A cage match for this fight," Yuri said in Russian. He punched a fist into his meaty palm. "Feels like home to me."

Nicolai readied his stance and fought the urge to protect his broken ribs. "You don't scare me, old man."

"I should scare you. I'm going to kill you."

They circled each other, moving around the cage, learning its boundaries as they moved. When Yuri slipped over a piece of ice, Nicolai leaned in with a series of jabs to Yuri's abdomen, but they bounced off his body with no lasting effect.

Nicolai shot a right hook at Yuri's jaw, but the bigger man caught his hand and squeezed until Nicolai thought his fingers would break.

"Is that all you can do?" Yuri laughed. "Your woman will give me more of a fight." He held onto the fist with one hand while he landed an uppercut to Nicolai's jaw with the other.

Nicolai's head flew backward. The room spun, and he saw stars floating around in the dark. He stumbled, tripping over a rock and falling into the bars of the cage. Pain exploded a second time inside his ribs.

"Get up!" Yuri demanded, ready for another round. "Let's finish this. I've got a date with your lady."

Nicolai took his time standing. He balled up his fist, waiting for the right moment to plant an uppercut into the man's diaphragm. As he uncurled his body, he put all his force into his arm and sank his fist deep into Yuri's stomach. A gasp escaped Yuri, and he staggered back a few steps but recovered quickly. Nicolai swung again, but Yuri caught the fist and spun him around, shoving Nicolai's face into the bars and dragging it across them like a ragdoll. He let go, and Nicolai dropped to the deck, his face bruised and bloody.

Yuri paced back and forth across the cage as he continued to bait Nicolai, talking about Sarah and what he planned to do to her. He told Nicolai what Marco had said about her and licked his lips as he spoke about savoring the fight Sarah would give him before he took her.

"I'll have fun with that bitch," he taunted. "I like

women who fight me."

Nicolai sputtered through the blood that flew from his mouth.

"I saw her kill the guard at the Kremlin," Yuri continued. "Hung him outside the window like laundry." He rubbed his crotch. "Oh, yes! She'll know how to satisfy a man like me."

Rage surged through Nicolai. He lunged at Yuri, throwing a right hook into the brute's jaw, but again, the move bounced off him without any effect. Nothing Nicolai did impacted the old boxer. Yuri was too big and too used to pain. Only the hat and the scarf underneath gave up the fight. The scarf unraveled from his head and drifted to the ground, exposing the bald head to the meager light. It lit up in like a beacon in the shadowy space.

Nicolai stepped forward and delivered a left hook to the side of Yuri's head, connecting where his left ear should be. Yuri only laughed and brushed the attempt away as if batting away a fly.

Just like the fight in the Grand Bazaar, Nicolai tried again and again to land the punch that would take Yuri out, but a lifetime in the ring gave the fighter the upper hand. He dodged, deflected, or countered each move Nicolai made with the efficiency of a professional boxer. The old man could predict Nicolai's every attempt as he fought the urge to grasp his broken ribs, only slowing occasionally to take a deep, wheezing breath.

"You're hurt," Yuri sneered during a pause in the fighting. He strode forward, backing Nicolai into a corner. "I can help." He flexed his big hands. "I'll do it nice and easy. You won't even see it coming. Just a quick little twist of the neck, and we can end this right now."

He'd taken on the look of an animal. Hunched over, head down and arms outstretched, he waited for Nicolai's next attack.

Light shining through the curtain of icicles caught Nicolai's attention, and he moved around the cage to stand between it and Yuri.

"You're an old man," he goaded Yuri. "You had your chance to catch Sarah three times, and each time, you failed. You'll never get her or the cross."

A right hook swept through the air toward Nicolai's head but missed when he jerked away at the last second. The move threw Yuri off balance and he stumbled forward.

Nicolai gathered the last of his strength and grabbed him around the waist before Yuri could recover from the swing. With all the effort he could muster, Nicolai threw Yuri headfirst into the wall of ice and knocked it free from the rafters. It tumbled down and broke into large chunks across the deck. Yuri fell among them.

"Get up! 'I like it when they put up a fight.' " Nicolai mimicked Yuri's own words as he picked up a large piece of ice. He reared back, ignoring the pain in his side as he took aim at Yuri's head. "Or maybe it's you who'd like this ended nice and quick."

Without warning, Yuri's arm shot out. It caught Nicolai around the legs and yanked him off his feet. He fell backward as another wave of pain blasted like dynamite inside him. Nicolai's head slammed into the iron bars and he slid to the deck. He lay there unable to move.

Yuri crawled over to him and rained blow after blow upon Nicolai's face until he could no longer see nor hear anything. His ears rang, and pain surged through his body. He knew it was over. He was done. The urge to fight slipped into the darkness awaited for him on the other side—where pain ended just before you died.

A moment before Nicolai's consciousness slipped away, the weight of Yuri's body abruptly disappeared when stood up.

Pain exploded inside Nicolai's chest when Yuri delivered a final kick to his broken ribs.

"Lie here and listen to her scream," Yuri sneered. Those were the last words Nicolai heard before everything went dark.

Chapter Sixty

"Give me the crosses," Max demanded as the gun's hammer clicked into place.

Sarah's eyes darted from Max to the gun and then back again. Open wounds on his face glistened in the light streaming down from a hole overhead. His fevered eyes were crazed. Manic—unpredictable and dangerous.

Stuck inside his cage, the wolf let out a mournful howl. He pawed at the ground and bit the bars as foam dripped from his jaws from the cuts. When the wolf caught sight of Sarah, his howl turned into a growl, snapping and snarling in his madness.

"Give me the backpack!" Max took a step toward Sarah.

"No!" She held the backpack out over the hole in the deck.

"You wouldn't dare!"

"Wouldn't I? Try me."

Sarah stared, unblinking, at Max, and he glared back at her.

He pulled the trigger, and the gun clicked, but nothing happened. No more bullets.

"Where's your miracle now?" Sarah laughed. "Go ahead, conjure up some more bullets."

"Bitch! Give me the crosses!"

"Go to hell!"

Sarah smiled and said, "You first."

Max gasped as she opened her palm and let the backpack dangle precariously from one finger over the empty space.

"Don't!" he shrieked. "Toss the backpack to me. I'll let you go. I promise."

Sarah shook her head. "Only one of us is leaving this mountain, and it's going to be me." Then she let the backpack slip from her fingers into the dark recesses of the ark.

"No!" Max screamed as the wolf let out a wail that echoed eerily around the hollowed-out ark.

"No! No! No!" Max dropped to his knees, letting the gun fall into the hole as he leaned over to peer into the empty space. When he glanced back at Sarah, anger raged across his face.

Max lunged at Sarah to wrap his hands around her neck, but Sarah lifted her leg and kicked him dead center in his chest. A loud whoosh of air burst from his mouth as he doubled over and clutched his chest. He stumbled to the edge of the hole, and Sarah kicked his backside. He lost his balance and fell over, down into the depths of the ark. His scream reverberated up from the depths of the ark like a banshee's wail until his body hit the bottom with a loud crack, and then—silence.

Sarah leaned over the hole as she took in big gulps of air. She could see nothing but black below. The backpack was gone for good and Max along with it.

A round of applause broke the silence and Sarah spun around.

Yuri, bare-headed and bleeding, stomped up behind her. Without his hat or the scarf, patches of black, frostbitten skin blended with the shadows, distorting the appearance of his head. Blood dripped from his nose and a cut above his eye, and his breath was punctuated by wheezing when and came in broken, shallow gasps.

He swiped an arm across his bloody face. "Mmmm…woman," he said through a low growl. "I love watching you kill." He rubbed his crotch as he drew near. "Come on! Let's see what your deadly magic can do to me."

"Where's Nicolai?" Sarah asked, backing away as he drew near.

"Don't worry about him. He's gone."

Gone? Agony gripped her chest at the thought, squeezing her heart until she thought she would faint.

"I killed him, just like your Italian boyfriend." He laughed at the confused look on her face. "That's right. I threw the cocky prick off the train right after he told me all about you."

"You killed Marco?"

Yuri nodded and licked his lips as he crept toward her. Sarah continued backing away, moving around the hole Max had fallen into.

"Oh, yes—it's going to feel so good," he said, massaging his groin. "And after I'm done, you can show me how the little cross works."

The black wolf barked from inside his cage. An angry, desperate sound, as pitiful as it was frightening.

Sarah glance at the wolf. *If it breaks free of the cage, who will it go after first?*

As if he read her mind, the wolf's mesmerizing stare fell on her, and he growled a hateful, menacing growl.

Sarah's foot tripped over a rock, and she stumbled backward. As she caught herself, she snatched a handful of dirt and threw it at Yuri, but he was too far away. The dirt flew through the air as a billowy cloud and dissipated into nothingness.

The wolf let out a long bone-chilling howl, catching Yuri's attention for the first time. He picked up a rock and hurled it at the wolf, muttering something in Russian as Sarah took another step backward. Her back hit a post connecting two sides of an animal pen. She looked up. The post was also a support for the upper level and held the ends of two rafters in place overhead.

Sarah climbed up the railing and hoisted herself onto one of the beams.

Yuri grabbed the bottom of the post in both hands and shook it back and forth. Dirt and rock cascaded over Sarah as she clung to the post as the joint loosened abover her head.

Sarah stood on the rafter. With her arms outstretched, she balanced her way across one beam to the next until she was out of Yuri's sight. She hurried to another rafter and crouched down in the shadows.

"Come down here, woman," Yuri ordered as he searched the web of beams above his head.

Sarah wasn't leaving the ark without Nicolai and she knew she'd have to kill Yuri before she could find him.

"Come out here into the light. Let me see your pretty face," he bellowed, creeping closer to her hiding spot. His monstrous left hand cupped the hole in his head where his ear had been, listening for sounds of her moving above him. "You'll like being with a real man like me. I'll make sure you feel it, not like your little boyfriends."

Sarah tracked him as he moved through the shadows. When he drew near her hiding spot, she picked up a rock. Yuri heard her move and glanced up in surprise just as she threw the rock at his face. A burst of

Russian curses escaped him as blood gushed from his mouth and ran down his chin.

Yuri wiped his mouth on his coat sleeve, smearing blood across his face, then he grabbed the post and shook it furiously. Small rocks and dust fell down around him, but Sarah hung on tightly and remained out of reach.

The wolf stopped digging for a moment, watching the action close with his eerie, pale eyes.

When the post came loose, Yuri kicked the center, and a loud crack resonated across the ark. He kicked a second time, and the post broke in half.

Sarah leapt onto another beam and held onto a post. She took note of the rhythm of his work. Push, pull, rest. Push, pull, rest. On the third rest, Sarah let go of the post and ran to the next one, and the next, and stopped at a beam behind Yuri. Silent and stealthy, Sarah moved closer. When she got within a couple of feet, she sat down on the beam and swung her legs over the side, holding onto the beam to brace herself against the sway of the post. As soon as Yuri's assault on the post paused, she swung her leg out and kicked him hard in the temple. The blow sent him reeling backward.

Yuri turned around and spotted Sarah. He let out a stream of Russian curses as he climbed a pile of rock to get to Sarah. She drew her legs away from him and moved to stand, but his hand wrapped around her ankle. He pulled her back, breaking the hold she had on the post. She lost her balance and tumbled down the rock, landing on the deck at Yuri's feet. He grabbed a fistful of her hair and dragged her to the center of the ark.

Off in the shadows, the wolf ground the bars of the cage between his teeth, ignoring the blood dripping from cuts inside his mouth. Two bars broke off, and his long thin nose popped through the open space and sniffed the air.

Yuri let go of Sarah's hair and stood over her. "Now you're mine, woman." He unbuttoned his coat.

With a snarl, the wolf's head burst through the cage. His madness overtook him, and foam flew from his mouth. His body flailed wildly as he squeezed himself through the hole in the bars. Twisting and turning, the wolf broke more bars with his frantic movements and he wriggled his way through the small opening with the madness of a rabid dog.

"I've been waiting for this a long time," Yuri said as he tossed his coat to the side. "I want you to fight me like you fought the guard at the Kremlin." His voice grew deep with lust. "But this time, I will win the fight." He unbuttoned the top buttons of his pants.

Yuri's shadow stretched over Sarah. She brought her knees to her chest and thrust her legs out like a spring. Her feet connected with his chest and threw him back into a beam. A loud crack rumbled through the rafters as the post broke apart under the force of Yuri's body.

Sarah scooted away as Yuri bent over and grabbed his abdomen. Above him, a portion of the upper deck collapsed and rock and ice crashed down, burying Yuri up to his waist.

Sarah smiled. *Caught in his own trap.*

A cloud of dust flew around Yuri and he coughed the same hacking, debilitating cough Sarah first heard at the train station in Rome. She jumped up and sprinted to the bottom half of the still-standing, load-bearing post and put all her weight into it, pushing as hard as she could until she heard the wood crack. She leaned in again, and the wooden post rocked back and forth. She stepped back and kicked it hard several times. It broke away from the deck and fell forward, pulling the deck above down with it. The wood beams and collapsed over Yuri, burying him up to his waist. Pinned down by debris, only his bloody, hairless head was visible above the pile.

Sarah backed away from the pile, listening as his raspy breath faded away. He was alive but dying the slow death he deserved.

Sarah rested against a post and breathed a sigh of relief.

Dead. Both of them.

A long, low growl brought her attention back to the present, and Sarah knew she faced another danger.

The wolf!

Chapter Sixty-One

The black wolf's growl changed. The barks, snarls, and whines transformed into what sounded like words. He crept toward her, stalking, head down, eyes locked onto hers. Matted fur, soaked in blood, stood up on his shoulders and his brows lowered over his mesmerizing, light-blue eyes.

A throbbing sensation like a heartbeat suddenly coursed through the ark. At first subtle, the tremors grew in intensity, moving across the ark as a wave. Rocks bounced and spun in its wake, and the smallest pebbles levitated among them. When the vibrations reached Sarah, they entered her body and her muscles to contracted painfully.

As the black wolf closed in, Sarah watched him change into something far darker and more fearsome than he had been before.

Bones broke and elongated inside the wolf's body and his long snout morphed into a thick, crooked nose protruding from sunken cheeks. He stood on his back paws as his hands extended into thin bony fingers. His dark fur fell away, revealing pale skin under a black robe that clung to his skeletal body like a wet rag. Only his luminous light-blue eyes, the same eyes Sarah saw in the trance, remained unchanged.

The black wolf is Rasputin, the Mad Monk! She slipped her hand inside her jacket pocket and wrapped her fingers around the Byzantine Cross. *He knows I saved it from being tossed into the hole with the backpack!*

Rasputin opened his mouth, and putrid green foam bubbled forth. Water followed the foam, and when he spoke, the words came out garbled and unintelligible. Sarah stepped backward, then turned around and ran toward the bow of the ship as the frequency of the ark's quaking vibrations increased until the largest rocks synched up with the others, all of them spinning and levitating in place.

Sarah sprinted toward the beams blocking the bow of the ship, but was thrown off balance when a loud crash reverberated behind her. She fell to one knee, rolled on her side, and ducked behind a post. When she stole a peek backward, she saw Rasputin's ghost step through the boulder as it rocked back and forth where it landed after falling through the deck above.

The ghost of Rasputin pointed behind her to the beams blocking her from the bow knee. He waved a finger at them, and wood scraped against wood as a beam moved inside the pile. The beam raised itself out of the heap and hung in midair, spinning around in a half circle. Rasputin flicked his finger, and it flew across the empty space and landed next to the ark's inner hull and broke into several pieces.

Before the remnants of the beam settled, Rasputin picked up another.

"Naughty girl," he spoke telepathically to Sarah. "You tried hiding the cross. From me, Rasputin. The Mad Monk!"

He flicked his finger again, and a third beam levitated up from the pile and flew to the side before going back for more.

"You do not understand the cross's power," his voice yelled inside Sarah's head. "It is *my* power!" He pulled out another beam and threw it out of his way. "Give me the cross!"

"I don't have it!" Sarah shouted.

"Lies!" Rasputin yelled back wordlessly. He pointed at Sarah's, and she felt a sharp electrical shock in her pocket pocket where the cross was hidden.

He knows I still have the Byzantine Cross!

Rasputin raised both arms above his head and clapped once. As he opened his arms wide, the pile of beams parted behind Sarah and cleared an aisle down its center all the way to the ark's bow. He rubbed his palms together, and the broken beams crumpled like paper against the sides of the ark. Sarah could see the light from the crosses glowing bright inside the bow knee joint.

"You will give me the crosses," Rasputin commanded as he floated toward her. "All of them!"

Sarah turned away from Rasputin ready to run, but as the vibrations increased inside the ark Sarah felt her body succumbing to its pulsing energy. The power throbbed through her and synched up with her heartbeat, sending painful waves of electricity through every cell of her body. She tried to run but her body was heavy and stiff, caught inside the trembling ark.

The bow knee blazed like fire twenty feet ahead, and she focused on the white light of the crosses emanating from it. Concentrating all her effort, she forced one leg forward and then another and another until she was running.

She felt the presence of Rasputin looming behind her. "They are mine!" he screamed inside her head.

The rising velocity of the pulsing energy slowed to a rhythmic throb, as if it were a heartbeat. It connected with everything in the ship—the broken beams, the planks lying scattered across the deck. It even jumped across the holes in the deck. All around her, everything moved in uniformity, overtaking her senses and buzzing in her ears.

Sarah pushed through the pulsing force that controlled her body and ran at full speed toward the bow knee. As she neared the bow knee, she removed the Byzantine Cross from of her pocket and took a running leap across the hole, grabbing the beam above the joint and hoisting herself onto a beam, then crawled to the seventh cut in the bow knee. She reached up to insert the Byzantine Cross into its cut when she felt Rasputin's bony finger grasp her ankle and jerk her back. Clinging to the beam with one arm, she thrust the Byzantine Cross into the last cut with the other right before she was dragged from the beam and fell to the deck. Dazed, she rolled over, dazed, and watched the Byzantine Cross merge, miraculously, with the wood.

A blinding light, so pure and bright, encased the seven crosses. Electricity zipped around the bow knee, sending sparks flashing across the wood as it fused the crosses to the seven crosses to the ark. When the light eventually dimmed, a jagged scar was permanently seared into the wood around the space, outlining where the seven crosses fused into the ark.

A terrible roar echoed through the ark and Sarah covered her ears as she glanced up at Rasputin who towered over her, head tilted back, and jaw open as water gushed forth. His body grew in size until it hit the underside of the deck above them. His blue eyes glowed as his mouth opened into a wide, black abyss. Sarah covered her ears as the ghostly apparition let out an unholy schriek louder than anything she'd heard before. The noise overtook the buzzing vibrations and shook the rafters all around them.

For the second time, Sarah watched in paralyzed silence as Rasputin's body morphed into a new horror. His skin took on the blue tones of a drowned man. Cavities formed on his face where creatures had feasted on him in his watery grave. They grew in size until his face, head, shoulders, and body were swallowed up in a blue-black mist, and nothing human remained.

Rotating like a black cyclone, it sucked everything near it into his orbit. Stones and broken pieces of the ark followed a path through the funnel, flying out of the top of the cyclone and shooting across the ark like bullets.

Rasputin's cyclone whirled around the room, picking up loose energy still sizzling inside the ark and flashing a strobe light around the electrified room. Sarah cowered in the corner of the bow as Rasputin's cyclone bounced around the ark erratically, gaining velocity until a loud boom split the air. Then, just as strangely as it had developed, Rasputin's black cyclone suddenly dissolved into a filmy black cloud and blew away.

Sarah glanced up at the crosses embedded in the ark. Their glow, now dimmed, was a soft, orange glow. Sarah reached up to touch them but pulled back from the heat still radiating off each one. The crosses were repairing the ark, stitching together the wood in a miraculous surgery. Electrical currents popped and sizzled as they penetrated every fiber of the ark, raising the posts and beams and reconnected the joints that held the ark together. Broken bits of wood and debris filled the fissures riddling the wood until the healing all came to a sudden halt as if someone had flipped off a switch. The last tremors stopped, and dust settled over everything like a death shroud.

Sarah examined the cages, the sides of the ark, the decks. The ark Noah built thousands of years ago looked new again.

As the tremors fizzled to nothingness, the atmospheric pressure dropped. With a final soft *pop*, the charged energy disappeared, and a cold, refreshing breeze blew through the ark, bringing the scent of alpine air to chase out the charged electrical scent that lingered.

Sarah let out the breath she'd been holding as she gazed up at the crosses. The wood appeared intact and smooth again. A jagged, broken line was burned into the wood, marking the spot where the cross-shaped cuts had been. She ran her hand over the crosses. Cool to the touch, each one still retained its own unique color.

Sarah smiled and patted the bow knee with her hand, but she pulled back when a soft pop exploded underneath her fingers. Several more pops sparked after the first, sending energy zipping around the crosses as if transferred through a copper wire. The current outlined all seven crosses, buzzing with energy as it enveloped the bow knee. When it connected with the ark's sides, Sarah felt the pressure in her ears increase.

Something new was happening. Something bigger than before. She stared back through the beams to the center of the ark, and alarm washed over her.

Nicolai!

Chapter Sixty-Two

The ark was awakening; repairing itself under the power of the crosses.

Sarah raced down the aisle between the crumpled beams to the hole in the deck where Nicolai had disappeared. The ark trembled around her. Wood undulated and twisted under Sarah's feet until she nearly lost her footing as she stumbled toward the center of the ark. Nicolai's battered face emerged through the open space in the deck when she reached it. Blood dripped from his face, and he grasped his right side.

"You're hurt!" she exclaimed as she knelt down next to him.

He ignored her concern and grunted through his pain as he heaved his bruised body onto the deck. "Let's go," he said through a grimace. Sarah helped him stand and they stumbled across the deck to the tunnel leading to the out of the ark.

Static electricity crackled in the air. A million lines of pure white light raced through the woodgrain of each plank as the ark reshaped itself. Beams and planks bent and stretched inside the wood as the broken ends reconnected. Noah's ark was becoming whole once more.

"Hurry!" she yelled above the clattering of the ark's transformation.

A boulder swayed precariously on the edge of a

beam in front of the tunnel's entrance. If it fell, the boulder would block their only exit out of the ark. A loud crack tore through the ark as the deck above gave way. The boulder tipped forward and rotated in a circle. It stopped and trembled in midair just before Sarah and Nicolai ducked under it and escaped into the tunnel. Sarah heard a terrible crash—and another and another as the boulder broke through the lower decks and crashed at the bottom of the ark.

The destructive electric current zipped along the walls of the tunnel, crackling and popping as it jumped across the gaps in the structure. The light flashed an uneven, confusing strobe that made it difficult to walk along the broken beams. Sarah covered her head as she moved up the tunnel to the ark's exit. Dust accumulated over thousands of years coated her throat and burned her eyes. Pebbles, dislodged from the walls and battered Sarah and Nicolai from all sides, but Sarah focused on the exit at the end of the tunnel.

She glanced over her shoulder at Nicolai and saw the tunnel collapsing inward behind them like a house made of sticks. Wood, hard and unyielding as steel only moments ago, flexed and twisted and rock and dirt crashed behind her like a wave crashing upon the shore.

Nicolai pushed past her and ran up the last few feet of the tunnel. He squatted under the exit hole and cupped his hands to lift her up. "Come on!" He gestured with his chin up toward the light streaming down from outside.

"No." Sarah squatted beside him and offered Nicolai her right knee to stand on, but Nicolai shook his head. "You first!"

"You're hurt!" she yelled back. Again, he shook his head.

"You need my help!" Sarah pointed to his ribs. She got into position again. "Go!"

Light from outside fell through the hole and lit up Nicolai's face. His brow creased with worry, his mouth clenched in pain, and his beautiful caramel-colored eyes... Sarah recognized the love he felt for her in their depths. And in that moment she realized she loved him too.

The thought exploded inside just as the electricity of the ark reached the end of the tunnel and exploded around her.

"Go!" she yelled. Nicolai glanced past Sarah to the wave of rock rolling forward through the tunnel. "Now!"

"Be ready for me," he said as he stepped onto Sarah's knee.

Adrenaline raced through Sarah as she stood and pushed Nicolai up. Then, she glanced down the tunnel at the wall of debris rushing forward.

"Give me your hands!" Nicolai yelled down to Sarah. She raised her arms above her, and Nicolai grasped her hands, yanking her up and out of the tunnel. Sarah felt the cold mountain air on her face as dirt and rock crashed beneath her feet inside the tunnel.

Sarah fell into Nicolai's embrace and he kissed her with a passion that conveyed the same intense feelings she held inside her own heart.

"I thought I was going to lose you," he said between breaths.

Before she could reply, a rumble brought their attention back to the entrance of the tunnel. The earth shook beneath them, and they bounced about the hard ground like toys.

Sarah lost her grip on Nicolai. He rolled away from

her as a new noise came from deep within the ark below them. A hollow, wooden rattle grew to a crescendo inside the tunnel. When it reached the top, everything stilled. A deep trough appeared on the land above the tunnel where the ark's interior collapsed. A moment later, a puff of dust blew out from the exit hole, and rock filled the empty space, closing the only entry point to the ark and sealing the giant, ancient vessel inside the mountain.

Sarah called to Nicolai, but before he could answer, the ground heaved above the ruins of the ark. The landscape lost its natural features, morphing into a smooth dome that grew into a giant hill with no rises or dips in the landscape. Sarah heard a soft sizzling sound become a hollow rattle before finally fading away.

"Nicolai!" Sarah shouted again.

"Over here!" he yelled from behind a large rock.

She jumped up and ran to Nicolai's side as cracks fanned out across a bloated dome twenty feet tall over the ark.

The mountain is breaking apart!

She grabbed Nicolai's hand, and they ran up the side of the gorge. When they reached the gorge's southern ridge, they stopped to stare at the dome as it rose and fell several more times.

"It looks like it's breathing," Sarah remarked between gulps of air.

A loud bang like a door slamming shut ripped through the air, and the ground stopped expanding and fell into a pile of dirt and rock. The mountain stilled, sealing the Byzantine Cross—along with the other six crosses—inside the ark.

Chapter Sixty-Three

Istanbul

The muezzin's haunting call to prayer woke Sarah. She rolled over, and sunshine caressed her face. A breeze blew through the open window and brought with it the fresh saltwater scent of the sea. It was morning in Istanbul.

Nicolai snored softly beside her. They'd been in the city for two days, and he'd slept through the pain for the first time last night. Sarah studied a bruise peeking out of a bandage under his left arm. The worst injury he'd received hadn't come from Yuri. The fall onto the beam was responsible for that wound. Other injuries, far worse than broken ribs, weren't as visible. Trauma to his kidneys and other organs would take longer to heal, but the doctor assured them he'd make a full recovery.

Sarah heard a phone ring in the next room, and it jarred her from her thoughts.

She hadn't contacted Albert in over a week. News of the missing Vatican cardinal should have reached him by now, and Sarah knew a dressing down would be waiting for her when she finally reported into him.

But I might as well get it over with.

Careful not to wake Nicolai, Sarah slipped out of bed and into a robe. She picked a phone up from the nightstand and carried it out to the balcony.

Two wicker chairs surrounded a table, and Sarah sat

down and dialed the operator. When a woman picked up, she gave her Albert's home number in Rome, and, after a series of clicks, her old mentor's deep voice answered with a sleepy "Hello?"

"It's Sarah."

She heard springs creak as he sat up in bed. "Sarah! Where have you been? Why didn't you call me after we last spoke?"

"I've been busy."

"Busy!" Irritation laced his worried tone. "What the hell were you doing?"

She paused and considered the question. Exploring Noah's Ark? Fighting the Vatican? How about saving the world? Maybe that would be the best answer. She ignored his question and instead said, "I'm coming in. I'll be there in a week."

"Where are you now?"

"Istanbul," she said as she fingered the sapphire necklace Nicolai had given her. "I have a few things to wrap up here before I fly home."

"To Rome?" he asked. "We're supposed to do the handoff here."

"Not necessary." She took a deep breath. "I lost the cross."

"You lost it?" he shouted into the phone before getting control of himself and lowering his voice. "Hang on, Sarah. I'm going to take this in the other room."

Sarah propped her bare feet on the chair opposite her and leaned back. She glanced over her shoulder at Nicolai as he attempted to sit upright on the bed. The muscles in his back flexed under the bandages wrapped around his torso. He eased himself up and walked to the bathroom, still nude from last night.

Albert picked up the phone again. "What do you mean, you lost the cross?"

"I didn't exactly lose it." She hesitated, searching for the right words to describe all that had happened. "It's more like I returned it."

"Returned?" The word stopped him for a moment. "Aren't you supposed to return it to me?"

Sarah chuckled at his sarcasm. "It's a long story. I promise I'll tell you the whole thing when I meet you in Rome."

"Why can't you tell me now?"

"It's *confidential*." He didn't say anything in response to her own sarcasm, so she added, "Don't worry, Albert. I know you were working with the cardinal and that he was the one who wanted the Byzantine Cross. Not the CIA."

"How did you find out?"

"He told me just before I killed him."

"What? Why?" Albert stumbled over his words. "Killing a Vatican cardinal is the same as assassinating a government official."

"I'm sorry, Albert, but when it's a choice between him or me... I chose me."

"You certainly didn't choose me," Albert complained. "How the hell will I explain this to the director? And the Vatican?" His voice rose an octave when he asked the second question.

"Maybe you should ask yourself how you missed seeing him as a killer."

"He told us he represented the Pope," Albert hurried to say. "We didn't know your life was at risk. I swear."

"You should have double-checked your sources."

"He was a cardinal, Sarah. We thought we could

trust him."

Trust. Would that word always make her think of Marco?

"Have you heard from Marco yet?" she asked.

"Marco? No. Why?"

Yuri popped into her thoughts, and she already knew the answer to her next question. "Did he ever show up in Rome after he disappeared on the train to Berlin?"

"No, we haven't heard from him."

"I think I might have some information about him, but let's talk about that when we meet."

Nicolai flashed her a pained smile as he stepped through the door. A towel was wrapped around his waist and he held two glasses of orange juice in his hands.

"I'll have to give the director a report," Albert said. "What should I say about the cross?"

"Tell them it's buried on a mountain in Turkey."

"And what about the cardinal?"

"Tell them he dedicated his life to the cross and is buried with it."

"What do you mean?"

"I'll tell you all about it when I see you."

"No one will believe you," he warned. "Hell, they'll probably canonize the cardinal for his sacrifice while you rot away in prison."

Nicolai handed her one of the glasses, then leaned back against the railing. After shaving for the first time in a week, his whiskerless face revealed dark bruises on both sides from his temples to his chin. It was the most visible sign the beating he withstood inside the cage, but the doctor confirmed no bones were broken.

"Listen, Albert," Sarah said with a smile toward Nicolai. "We can sort this all out when I see you. And I want to talk to you about the MI6 agent. I think you should consider him for the CIA. But right now, I need to go."

"Wait!" Albert pleaded with her. "I'll send a plane for you—"

"Fine. I'll call you when I'm ready. Goodbye." She hung up.

"Trouble?" Nicolai asked.

Sarah got up and walked over to kiss his cheek. He pulled her closer, but she held back. "Your ribs."

"Let me worry about that." His voice was deep and husky from sleep. "So, you're going to Rome?"

"Not until you're feeling better."

She ran a finger along a gash above his eye as he studied her face. "It won't be easy convincing your government you did the right thing." He nodded toward the phone. "I could hear him yelling."

Sunshine highlighted the straight line of his nose, his full lips, his warm brown eyes. "Let's not think about it now," she said as she kissed a bruise on his collarbone.

"Aren't you worried?"

"No." She kissed another bruise. "They can believe whatever they want."

"But you'll lose your chance with the CIA."

Do I want to go back? She thought about the question as she searched for another bruise. *Maybe Marco had been right about the CIA all along.*

Sarah slid her arms around Nicolai's neck and smiled.

"I think it's best if I trust my own instincts for now."

A word about the author…

Dena Weigel is an upcoming thriller writer who has studied art and culture in over thirty countries. Born in Western Kansas, she graduated with a Bachelor of Fine Arts before settling in the Pacific Northwest and building a career writing for businesses and non-profits around the world. She enjoys hiking with her husband and daughter, painting, and relaxing on her deck with a cup of coffee and a great book. Dena is currently working on the next Sarah Kraft novel. Visit her website at www.denaweigel.com.

www.ingramcontent.com/pod-product-compliance
Lightning Source LLC
Chambersburg PA
CBHW072106020726
47501CB00003B/731